THE BURDEN

JENNI WARD

MIRAWORTH
BOOKS

First published in 2021
by Miraworth Books
ABN 44 964 848 123

MIRAWORTH BOOKS
PO Box 3523, Mount Gambier, SA 5290, Australia

ISBN (e-book): 978-0-6488363-3-9
ISBN (paperback): 978-0-6488363-9-1

Cover design by Open World Book Designs

Jenni Ward dragon logo and dividers by Ross Zapata
Jenni Ward sorcerer logo by Ayhen Aikawa
Stock: Austria-Stock-06 by Malleni-Stock (DeviantArt)

 A catalogue record for this
work is available from the
National Library of Australia

When your head and heart disagree,

It can be a tough choice

If you want my advice,

Always listen to your heart

CHAPTER 1

The sword cut through the air. Too slow, as my opponent's sword ended its downward journey. She swung outward, and I moved back. She stepped forward. Swung the sword behind her body. The opportunity was there. My fist connected with her face. Her sword clattered to the ground as her hands covered her nose.

"Alexa!"

Bugger. I relaxed my stance as trails of blood ran through Leila's fingers. Her shoulder-length grey hair had some new red streaks in it.

"You okay?"

She glowered at me. I shrugged. I hadn't meant it. A few of the other elite warriors turned to look our way.

"Sorry?" I offered. Several strands of hair stuck to my skin; I wiped them away from my face. A few remained, but at least I got a couple behind my ears.

"Yeah, I'm sure you're really sorry."

Leila walked away from me to Mina. The conversation Mina had been in with her assistant trainer came to an abrupt stop. Those hands on hips as Mina looked my way rebuked what I did, but honestly, what did she expect? Training is to prepare us, right? Sometimes you do what's needed to have the upper hand.

My attention refocused on the ground. I moved my soft leather shoe over the blades of grass that hadn't got trampled in the exercise. The warmer weather had helped the grass to grow long in the field we were in. I preferred it short, so I had no resistance against my feet when I turned.

This field had become the second home for us. Every day we were out here. We trained but rarely had the chance to use the skills on our target enemy: dragons. As Mina strode towards me I knew I would hear the same lecture from her when she felt I didn't honour the elite oath I had taken.

Her loose grey hair rode on the breeze as she approached. "Alexa..." Mina began.

"Training can be a dangerous thing."

I shrugged and spun around with the sword raised high above my head. When I opened my eyes, I saw her standing before me with that look. The look. I seemed to be the only recipient of that look. My hand spun the sword full circle before I lowered it to the grass. I pressed the tip into the ground so I could lean against it before I attempted a smile.

"Alexa…"

"You want me to train, I'm training. How am I supposed to train if my opponent can't stand a little pain… a little blood occasionally?"

"Alexa…"

"And you know what, none of this would happen so often if you would let Zen come here as well. You know…"

"Alexa!" Mina's sharpness was because I'd mentioned something off-limits that wasn't open to discussion. "You know the rules of our people."

"I know, but Mina, with Zen I can refine my skills to a higher—"

"He shouldn't even be handling weapons. You are lucky that your skill with that sword prevents anyone from taking action against him. The other council elders would have stepped in years ago if your potential hadn't been so great. Gerda has made a case against you several times."

"He has potential as well," I mumbled. Mina might be old, but I knew she would hear what I said.

"Alexa, how many times must we remind you of your role and the societal rules? He is a male, and males do not protect our people, males do not go on hunts, males do as instructed by their betters. After all, you want to go on the hunt tomorrow, right? It's the graduation hunt for the new elite members and the elders are joining us."

"You know I do."

"Then stop leaving a trail of blood to be cleaned up."

"These sessions are to train us though, Mina. If all we do is behave like we're in a normal practise, then where is the skill development? How do we grow and learn new ways in the event of an attack? There is no fun in just going through predictable motions. I mean, the dragons aren't exactly going to stop and play by the training rules. "

Mina stepped forward and raised her finger towards me. Despite being a head shorter than me, she could intimidate with precision. "The fun for me is that Sabine won't need to be busy all day patching up the injuries inflicted by you."

"Ah, you know she likes the practise it gives her."

"Try to keep the blood to a minimum, Alexa." Mina turned and paused. "And be careful about sneaking out to practise with Zen. You're too young to understand the why, but never doubt that we elders have reasons for the rules of our people. It's time you stopped questioning and accepted them fully."

"But it doesn't seem fair. He is better with a sword than most of these women here."

"It doesn't matter. It has been, and is, a waste of a male's time and energy to learn the skill of the sword. The skills we refine have many purposes; none greater than the defence of our people from the dragons."

She walked away. I let Mina have the last word on it since I couldn't think of a snappy comeback and I didn't want to be reassigned out of the elite. It had never made sense to me why boys and girls had to be separate. Boys trained to cook, clean, raise children, and take care of the aged. Girls trained with swords and to fight, those who didn't meet the standards of the elders became healers.

Zen's family lived in the little house next to us. Back then, Leila wasn't an elder; she raised me and my older sister Helina like we were her own. As kids, Zen and I would sneak off to explore the forest around the village, and it had only been natural to take it to the next step. When Helina turned ten, the elders assigned her to the healers, and she moved in with Sabine to train. With a spare sword in the house, Zen and I made use of it with a new game.

When the elders found out though we got separated for several months, or so the elders thought. It hadn't been that hard to coordinate secret meetings with Zen. When the men needed stones to weigh the wash tubs down when empty, Zen would volunteer. The preferred stones were on the riverbank near where I liked to practise my skills. Getting the sword out had posed a problem, since it was almost as long as I was tall. I had soon discovered how much you could hide in your pants when they have a generous amount of fabric. Despite that, I still walked like an injured duck so I always left through the back door.

Some elders had cottoned on, but the number of girls competent with swords and hand combat had fallen. By the time I turned twelve, there were as many healers as warriors. That number changed when some paired off in the ceremony and became mothers. They returned to their duties as soon after the birth of the child as possible.

I paused. Motherhood weighed on my heart. Not that I yearned for the role, but Helina had passed the previous summer. Neither she nor the child survived. Another coupling ceremony loomed and her partner, Juan, would choose a new bride. In the village, that choice was one of only a handful that men could make and a female could reject their offer. At least I wouldn't need to worry about him asking me. The thought made me shiver; Juan had always been the distant type. I asked my sister why she had agreed and she replied she felt it only right to give the man that choice. Sisters, but there would have been no way I would have agreed to couple with a man because he asked.

I shook my head to rid the thought from my mind. Around me, the other warriors packed their bags and swords, ready to return home. When I glanced towards Mina, I saw her busy yelling at one of the younger girls who had put on her harness wrong. The little metal buckles took practise to master while wearing the harness. I hadn't bothered to take mine off.

My arms stretched skyward with the sword. I pressed the sword against my back and then to the side. The blade caught against the leather, and I slid it downward into the harness. The added weight of the sword meant I had to stop to tug on the front straps that pressed uncomfortably against my breasts. After a wiggle, it felt like I had no additional weight on my back.

I bent down and picked up the leather bag. After all that, I needed a drink before we set off home. The warm water inside the container didn't refresh me much. In fact, I spat most of it onto the grass as I put the container away in the bag.

"Be helpful if they ordered the men to invent a way to keep the water cool in these things," I muttered.

I followed behind the other elite warriors with

my bag in my hand. We trudged down the hill in a single line. At the bottom of the hill, a patch of trees separated us from the village. The shade cooled my skin after being in the open for most of the day.

The warrior before me stumbled on a fallen branch and caught herself by grabbing at the girl in front. Mina left the front of the line to check on them both. I walked around them and continued on until the houses of the village were visible.

Only those assigned as elite got the houses on the main street. The elders had the larger houses on the west side that surrounded The Hidden; a building which only elders could enter and the only building made completely of stone. The elite warriors got the houses to the east of the street, smaller but comfortable, with plenty of space for one person.

At the southern end of the street, a shallow river curved its own path to divide the village. A wooden bridge provided a way to cross the river so everyone could reach the well. Beyond the well, the healers' houses were behind it. To the west of the healers, the houses were for the single men who waited for the coupling ceremony. The single women lived to the east. There weren't many on either side, but the elders said independence made for stronger coupling arrangements.

My gaze drifted to the men's side. Zen would be with the other men as they finished the evening meal, ready to serve the women in the dining hall. I placed my hand over my stomach, but it failed to stop the rumble. Food sounded great.

CHAPTER 2

With the blanket wrapped around my shoulders, I held it closed with my hand. I stepped out of my house and goosebumps appeared on my arms. The nights had grown cold again, despite it being summer. My breath clouded before it vanished into the darkness. Concealed beneath a blanket, an unlit lantern hung heavy from my hand.

It sounded childish, but I liked the rush that coursed through my body when I intended to stretch the rules. Excited as I was, I didn't intend on getting caught by lighting the lantern. I didn't want to face the council accused of being alone with a man at night. I suspected if anyone else in the village caught Zen and me, it would force the elders to make an example of me. Zen might receive a punishment, if the elders spared the time to consider it.

My foot tapped against the ground as I pulled the blanket tighter around my shoulders. Tonight might not have been the wisest of nights to choose to head to our rock. A small part of me envied those in front of a wood fire.

"Alexa."

The lantern clattered to the ground. I froze. My gaze went from door to door of the nearby houses to see if it had drawn attention. I waited for a light to flood through an open door and for an elder to march out and grab me. Nothing happened. After a few heartbeats, I bent down and retrieved the lantern as my hands shook.

A smile covered Zen's face. His pale skin looked even whiter in the moonlight, especially with his long black hair tied loosely in the back. He shrugged before he nodded in the direction I knew we would go.

I stifled my desire to say anything as we moved off into the darkness of the forest. The moon provided enough scattered light through the leaves for us to navigate out of sight from the village. That didn't mean he was off the hook.

"That was stupid!" I hissed.

"I didn't expect you to react like that. You usually hear me coming," Zen said.

"You're usually on time as well. Here." I threw the lantern in his direction. He caught it before it hit the ground in his left hand. The cold air hadn't been patient as I felt the chill surround me as I tried to wrap the blanket tightly around myself again.

"Alexa, careful. You're running out of excuses why these get broken."

Zen placed the lantern on the ground and pulled a box from his pocket. He scraped the metal over the side of the box and a spark appeared. I watched as the light sent its glow over the grass surrounding the lantern. With the lantern lit, Zen shook the metal before he replaced it in his pocket. I paused a few steps ahead and allowed him to catch up. Not that I needed to. He continued to grow taller, whereas I hadn't grown at all in the past year, despite being one of the tallest women in the village.

"Then you'll have to come up with some creative ones for me to use. Speaking of excuses, what's yours for being late?"

"It's been an unusual day," Zen paused. "Plus, I had to wash extra bandages after someone got a bloody nose."

I rolled my eyes and turned away to walk to our spot. A little cleared space in the forest with a rock slab we had found when we were six. There we could train or talk - whatever we wanted.

"Well, to make up for the extra work you should know I defended you today," I said.

When I turned to look at him, he had his eyebrows raised.

"To whom?"

"Leila."

"Alexa." He dragged the word out.

"Oh, don't Alexa me. It's a ridiculous rule and the older I get, the more ridiculous it becomes."

"Yeah, but if you keep prodding a dragon, you'll get yourself bitten. Maybe even eaten."

"Nah, Leila isn't stupid enough to betray me to the council."

I kept my laugh light. When Zen's face didn't reflect the mood, I stopped.

His hand reached up and rubbed the back of his neck. "It probably doesn't matter, anyway."

"How so?"

My feet came to a standstill as we reached the slab. I stared at Zen and waited for him to elaborate. He ran his fingers through hair before he cleared his throat.

"We're not supposed to say anything," Zen said.

He walked past me and placed the lantern on the level side of the rock. His back remained to me.

I shrugged. "Then you shouldn't have said anything. Come on, what's the big secret the rest of us can't know?"

Zen's shoulders hunched forward.

"Come on, Zen. You wouldn't have said anything

if you didn't want to tell me."

He turned around and shoved his hands into the pockets of his pants. "This man came to the village today while all the warriors were up there training. They took a few of us aside; mostly those of us eligible for the next coupling."

"And?" I leaned forward.

"I don't know. The whole thing was strange. He talked to us, asked a lot of questions; then he went off with the council elders."

"The council elders? With a strange man?"

Zen shrugged. "I don't know. It's not the same man who I've seen appear before the couplings in the past." He finally looked my way. "You know how those men disappear each year? I'm thinking it's all tied to how we answered those questions. Part of me wonders if wherever they go is so much better than here; after all they never come back."

"Just remember the men that turn up, though. A useless lot who claim to remember nothing or how to do things. Then of course you tell them to do something and most can muddle through it. Some do a decent job, occasionally."

"But still, Alexa." Zen sat down on the rock and looked at the sky. "It makes you wonder."

I shook my head. "No, I don't. I do as I'm told."

He scoffed. "Like not being found in the company of a male? Not providing a weapon to a male? How about not sneaking out at night?"

I wrapped the blanket around his shoulders and sat down next to him. I pulled the rest of the blanket around myself and leaned my head against his shoulder. "That's different."

"How so?"

The bugs were too loud. They prevented me from thinking of a reasonable explanation.

"It just is different."

"Come on Alexa, are you telling me when you've been out on the hunts, you've never thought about it? You've never wondered what's beyond the marked trees? What might be outside this valley?"

"What's the point of wondering? This is where we live. It's not like we can change anything."

Zen's hand rested on my wrist, and he leaned his head against mine. "If you became an elder, then maybe one day you could."

I laughed. "Or they will divulge the truth about the Hidden and all the secrets of where things come from and I will hide under my bed for the rest of my life."

"I'm serious, Alexa. One day, one day, I would like to see what's outside this valley. Learn about things like those buckles."

My hand reached up, and Zen's hand fell to his side. The metal of the buckle felt cool against my hand as I touched one of the two on my harness strap. There was no need to have put it on after I changed from my training outfit, but lately, wherever I went, the sword did too.

"It's metal. Like the swords."

"But what is metal? Where do they get it? How do they make it into a sword strong enough it doesn't break? Or a buckle small enough to have a part that moves to fasten the leather? And leather, see there's another thing and all the fabric..."

I released the buckle and put my hands up. "Okay, okay, I get it. You want to know about everything."

"Is it wrong to want to know the answers to questions?"

"No, just wrong to ask the questions." The bugs were loud again. If I could see them, I would squish them. "Tell me about the man."

"You want to know an answer to a question?" Zen joked.

I clenched my teeth. "Yes, okay, point taken."

"Taken but not accepted, huh?"

Zen tapped his knee against mine, and I raised

my head to look at him. His smile could brighten any bad day I had. I sighed and stuck out my tongue.

"He wasn't old like the man last year. You remember how he had the white hair and beard? This man was maybe, I don't know, Leila's age. He had black hair, wore clothes that fit against his body rather than our oversized ones... The collar of his shirt —"

"What about the collar of his shirt?" I asked.

"High, like right up under his chin."

I looked towards the sky. "Something in common with the others. What's with the neck thing?"

"Who knows, I didn't get told. By the way, that's yet another question. You're on a roll at the moment."

"You think anyone will go with him?" I asked.

"They usually stay a week; I don't think I want to give him the chance to choose me."

He sounded serious. When I looked at his face, wrinkles lined his forehead. "What's that supposed to mean?"

"Maybe I just want to leave all this. Go find my own way." He turned and looked at me. "If I left, would you come too?"

Leave? Leave everything here? There was no smile on his lips, no twinkle in his eye. "I don't know."

"What's keeping you here, Alexa? Nothing, no

one. If I left my family behind, I'd like my best friend to come with me at least."

I reached out and touched his hand. "You're really concerned about him, aren't you?"

"In the back of my mind I knew a man would show up. I knew he would take men aside. I knew men would disappear when he did. Now he is here… I don't know Alexa. It's become so real."

"If I said I wouldn't go, would you still leave?"

Zen looked down at his hands. "That choice might not be mine. If I stayed and he chose me, I would leave anyway."

The blanket fell from my shoulders as I reached to draw my sword. I flipped it over in my hand. "He might not choose you."

"I know."

"And there might be nothing on the other side of the mountains. I mean, there could be… I don't know… a burning pit of fire and that you are within for all eternity."

"Alexa, that's not helpful."

"But it's the truth. You can't just go off on your own, or the stranger."

"You know he went with the council into the hall."

I paused. The hall only ever got used when the

council met for their meetings. It was a small room on the side of the Hidden, and only the elders could enter. The point that this man had arrived in the village while the warriors trained bothered me. In previous years, the man had always been visible. He would wander the streets of the village for a week before he would leave with the ones he chose. I had seen nothing of this man. The change made me uneasy. The tip of the sword dug into the ground.

"Long meeting?"

"Long enough." I heard the catch in his voice. "You keep that tongue of yours quiet on all this. I wasn't to tell anyone."

"You're really scared, aren't you?" I teased.

"I'd be a fool if I didn't have some hesitation."

"Well, if you're going away, I guess it wouldn't matter if I snuck you into the hunt tomorrow. Come on, we can't part without you coming out on one flag hunt."

"I think it would be obvious if I tagged along."

"Not necessarily. I'll think of something."

"Are you going to do all my assigned duties as well?"

Fair point. Zen stood up and crouched beside me as I pulled my sword from the soil.

"I don't want to see you hurt, Alexa. You're my

best friend."

"You just worry about yourself. I'm a brave elite warrior; I can take care of myself."

"You can get yourself into a lot of trouble without trying. Leila. Nose. Sound familiar?"

"Urgh, I saw an opportunity and took it."

"Do you think Leila ever regrets taking you in?"

I smiled. "I think she has moments when she questions what she was thinking. But come on, I'm adorable."

Zen's smile faded, and he reached out to touch the side of my face.

"Adorable but a little capai lurks in you too."

At the mention of the legendary creature of nightmares, I leaned forward. "One day, I'd like to see one of them for real."

He held my face for a moment longer. He opened his mouth as if to say something and promptly closed it again. The skin on my face chilled when he moved his hand back to the blanket.

"We should head back, or you won't get out of bed in time in the morning," he said.

Zen removed the blanket from his shoulders and wrapped it around me. He pulled it tight at the front and held it closed.

"Warm enough?" he asked.

I nodded. He picked up the lantern as I stood up.

"Alexa?"

"Yeah?"

"So many times we don't have a choice. If we went, the journey would be ours. Our choice. Promise me you'll think about it?"

"Sure, I'll think about it. Let's get home before we turn into ice."

CHAPTER 3

Sunlight. *Why is the sun so bright?* I rolled over and pulled the pillow close. My eyelids opened, and I turned to look at the window.

"Oh, no."

The blankets flew off my body as I stumbled out of bed. My toe connected with the wooden chair and I grabbed it as I hobbled towards my clothing rack. I tried to ignore the pain as I dressed in dark brown clothes we wore on hunts to better blend with the forest.

"I should have been up before sunrise. I've never been late for a hunt before."

The harness swung over my head. Of all mornings to not cooperate, the buckles chose today! They slipped under my fingers as I tried to thread the leather through them. Buckle. That brought back the conversation with Zen. The thought lingered as I grabbed my bag and hurried outside.

My feet pounded the dirt as I headed up the

track and then into the forest towards the clearing where we trained. Leila would enjoy the opportunity I had given her.

"Shouldn't have stayed out so late with Zen," I muttered.

I hiked until I came across the empty clearing. The hunt had begun, and they left me behind.

"No matter, I'll track them, somehow."

I cast my gaze over the ground to find signs of where they headed. A trampled path of grass headed towards the west. That wasn't a surprise. Leila preferred hunts in that direction as the tree markers were further out. I suspected she also liked the extra cover the trees provided to shield us from any dragons that might decide to pick a fight.

I paused. Silence. Not a pleasant silence. There were no chirps from bugs, no tweets from birds. My heart beat faster in my chest. I reached behind, my fingers wrapped around the hilt of the sword. I drew the blade, prepared for what might lurk.

I moved forward with precise steps and allowed time to pause and listen. My gaze darted from the ground, to bush, to tree, in an endless cycle. Broken twigs on a bush confirmed I was on the right track. I stepped over a fallen branch and ducked under another that hung low from a tree. My mouth felt dry.

A scream pierced the silence. A flutter of feathers

above and I glanced up to see a flock of birds flee from the canopy. Another scream accompanied the first. There was no more need to be cautious. I hurried towards the distressed cries for help.

Ahead, the trees thinned and I could see a clearing. We had been here in past hunts. A group of warriors stood circled in the open with their weapons drawn. A shadow darkened the grass and when I raised my gaze, I saw the creature that made it. A dragon.

We had seen dragons before, but rarely had the chance to fight. It swooped down towards the group with its claws angled down. Several warriors swung at the dragon. One drew blood as she sliced its foot. The dragon veered to the side and flew around. She had her weapon raised as it flew towards her.

Another dragon appeared, and the first changed direction. The warrior didn't see it coming behind her as it grabbed her within its claws. Her arms pinned to her side as the claws tightened around her body. A moment later, the dragon released its victim, and her lifeless body crashed to the ground.

The trees concealed me as I gazed out. Zen would caution me to stop, think, evaluate. In the sky I counted at least twenty dragons. They were above in all directions and moved as one to herd the warriors, who remained vulnerable in the open.

A warrior ran for the trees, her unprotected back grabbed by a dragon's claws. It flew high before it released her. Her scream mixed with those being attacked on the far side of the group. Her lifeless body joined the others that were scattered on the ground.

"No, not today. Not ever!"

I rushed from the trees with my sword high. A shadow appeared on the ground in front of me. I dropped to the ground and rolled over. My sword sliced at the belly of the dragon as it struggled to gain height as blood poured from its wound. Another dragon flew towards me. I stood my ground as it neared. I stared at its face. Its black scales shone in the sunlight, its red eyes glowed like fire.

It lunged forward at speed. I swung the sword and listened as it roared in pain as the foot dangled from its leg. It crashed into the other dragon I had injured and together they collided with the ground nearby.

I checked the sky. Still twenty. Either my count was wrong or more had joined the attack. I turned to see both the dragons' chests move as they lay on the ground. Each laboured breath pumped more blood from their wounds.

I moved closer to one dragon. It attempted to reach out to me with its front claw as my sword plunged into its neck. Blood sprayed on my face as I pushed it further down until the gargled roar ceased. I had to brace my foot against its body to pull the sword out before I turned towards the other one.

The claw had almost been completely severed and blood flowed fast from the wound. It raised its head and blinked. The red eyes dulled as its head flopped to the ground and its chest stilled.

"No need to waste more time on you then."

I turned around. The circle of warriors had thinned. Leila stood in the centre. She yelled something as another black dragon swooped in above the others. The dragons called to each other in low roars. The newest dragon looked larger than the others as it flew close to them.

"This isn't random," I muttered.

I ran forward. Ahead, a dragon fell onto its side and blocked my view of the group. I darted around its dead body. The hand of the warrior who killed it was visible on the sword that protruded from the dragon's neck. I didn't look too hard to see who it was. I couldn't help the dead.

Two more dragons dived and separated two warriors from the others. They flew behind them as the women ran. Each dragon seized a warrior in their claws. One warrior stuck her sword into the belly of the dragon. Blood flowed, but the dragon continued to fly higher. The other warrior's sword fell to the ground, and she followed moments later.

I continued to move forward. Leila turned my way and yelled something. I shook my head. With the noise of the dragons and the screams, I couldn't hear anything. Leila moved my way, and I quickened my run.

"Alexa!"

I heard that. An enormous shadow loomed near my feet. I glanced over my shoulder and felt my body crash to the ground.

My head ached. So did my body. Silence and darkness surrounded me. The ground below me felt so soft, just like my pillow. I snuggled my face against it.

Pillow? I opened my eyes to see a wooden ceiling. I pushed myself up and wished I hadn't.

"Not so fast, Alexa. Lay back down."

"No, I need... The dragons... The dragons are..."

I held my head with both hands and tried to focus. The room swayed back and forth. My hand moved to cover my mouth as I debated whether to be sick. I took a deep breath, and the room stopped moving. Sabine sat on the seat beside the bed; she looked much older than I remembered. Her hair looked a mess and blood stained her apron; on her sleeves as well. My gaze moved around the room; my room.

"What happened?"

"Shh, you need to rest first. They only brought you back a little while ago…"

"No, no, I need to—"

"To rest, the few of us here are trying to tend to the injured. The least you can do is stay put."

"I need to go help."

"Alexa," another familiar voice.

"Zen, you'll tell me what's going on, won't you?"

"You shouldn't be in here. You have duties to tend to," Sabine said.

"I'm caught up with my duties. Besides, I can make sure she stays where she is until you have a healer to spare."

Sabine looked from me to Zen and back to me. "It's not proper. I would object further, but I am needed elsewhere. You make sure she rests and don't you go encouraging talk, and the moment a healer comes you go back to helping the other men. Clear?"

"Yes, Sabine."

Zen nodded to Sabine; she collected her bag from the floor and left the room. She stepped back into the doorway. I suspected to check on Zen more than me.

Then she disappeared from view. Zen sat down in the chair Sabine abandoned and leaned forward.

"You really should lie down. You had me worried; you hit your head hard."

"I did? I don't remember." My hand reached up and touched the bandage wrapped tight around my head. I hoped there wouldn't be too much blood because otherwise combing my hair would be a nightmare for a few days.

"You did. Took me a bit to find you out there."

I leaned back on the pillow but refused to lie down. My mind tried to recall what had happened.

"I remember the dragons came. I was late."

"Late for a hunt?"

"I blame you. We stayed out too late last night; would have been back earlier if you hadn't been so late. Anyway, that's not important now. By the time I woke and got dressed, I had to catch up to them. By the time I reached them, the dragons were already attacking. Urgh, I can't remember what happened next. Tell me what I can't remember. Please."

"Sabine will give me extra duties."

"Blame me. Zen, please tell me."

"One of the elite came to the village saying you were all under attack. By the time we got there, the dragons had gone. Well, all those that survived the attack, at least. All we found were bodies of warriors and dragons on scattered over the ground."

"Am I hurt elsewhere?" I pulled up the blanket and saw I still had two legs. Blood covered most of my clothes, though. Sabine must have been in a hurry if she didn't bother to clean me up.

"No, but…"

"But?"

"I shouldn't say anymore Alexa. You really need to rest. I didn't carry you all the way here just for you to wake up and start—" Zen closed his eyes.

"What are you not telling me? I can see it's something important. Please, Zen."

Zen ran his fingers through his hair. He looked at the blanket before his gaze came back to me. "I had trouble finding you because of Leila. Her body shielded yours from the attack. Her injuries are much more severe than yours."

"Is she…?"

"She's still alive, but I don't think they have much hope."

"Why is it all so hazy in my mind? I can see scenes really clearly but it's all jumbled and nothing makes sense."

"You need to rest. There's nothing you can do at the moment. You are one of a few elite who survived.

The elders... Alexa, they're not sure how many will make it."

I tossed the blanket aside. Zen stood and held out his hand as I swung my legs off the bed.

"What are you doing? Sabine is going to kill me if she sees you out of that bed."

"I need to see. I can't just stay here and do nothing."

"You are better off resting. Come on Alexa, I don't want to be in Sabine's bad book."

"Think of this as a journey we're on together." I wiggled my bottom to the edge of the bed. "Give me a hand so I don't fall. I promise it will be a quick look and then I'll come back and rest."

Zen held out his hand and helped me to my feet.

CHAPTER 4

My heart weighed heavy in my chest as I looked around. The endless bodies lay covered with green cloth outside of the burial building. Green had always symbolised death in our village, a colour reserved for this most sombre of occasions. I'd seen people being laid out to be prepared before, but nothing like this. There were so many bodies that they blocked anyone from walking a straight line to the house.

The burial men had an enormous job on their hands. Their families would help him during the process to ensure they prepared all the bodies in time. No drums would beat as the bodies passed by through the village as people watched on out of respect. With so many bodies to burn, the single platform we had wouldn't be sufficient.

My gaze fell on the Hidden at the entrance of the village. Built on higher ground, it stood out amongst the little wooden homes that villagers had built themselves. The Hidden was built with stone and some kind of substance that could bind them together. When I was nine, I asked an elder why all the buildings couldn't be built that way. I received the response: Why didn't people try? My immediate task had then been to convince someone to build a house of stone. None would. The villagers continued to build the wooden houses.

There was nothing wrong with wooden houses, except if a lantern got knocked over, or lightning struck the roof. It didn't happen often, but the risk remained. Zen and I went into the forest a short time later. I remembered it was autumn as the leaves changed to yellow and crunched beneath our feet. We attempted to make a fort with stones and used mud as the stuff to hold it in place, but it crumbled for being too dry or the stone would slide off because the mud was too wet. We never discovered the secret behind the perfect substance.

My fingers tapped against my pants. I struggled to look away from the bodies on the ground. I had seen death many times, but this was the first time so many lay dead at once. Without the elders, our village would be without guidance. We were in a vulnerable position already if the dragons attacked the village. A decision needed to be made.

Stones crunched as Zen adjusted his feet beside me. He rested his hand on my shoulder.

"That's enough, Alexa. I need to get you back to bed to rest before Sabine sees."

"We need to end this, Zen. We can't let this happen again. Not one more villager should lose their life for no reason," I said.

I turned my head to see Zen shake his. It wasn't uncommon for us to disagree over something, especially when it was me pushing for it. Zen had always been there to reason things out and help me clear my head to form clear goals and plans. Today was not the day to argue. Anger simmered away deep inside. I wanted to make a difference; I needed to put it right.

"Come on, there's no point just running off. We're meant to talk this through. You need to have a plan, otherwise, you're giving yourself a death sentence and will help no one."

"Can't you see Zen? We don't have time to sit down and plan. How long do you think it will be before the dragons come back to finish off the rest of us now? How long before this entire village gets wiped off the landscape completely?"

His hand squeezed my shoulder. "If we don't plan on the outcome, then you help no one. You need to stop and think. You need to think about how many dragons there were. How did the dragons attack this time? Why were they so successful? The dragons have never killed like this before and we need to think about why that might be."

"We've never stopped them from attacking. I don't care how or why it's so different! They come and they always kill something or someone!"

Zen stepped around me. He stood in front of me as he held onto both my arms. "But they've never killed on such a large scale before. They've never had so many dragons in a coordinated attack. That's a change in behaviour and you know as well as I do it means something is going on. Something has happened that's made them change how they attack."

"I can't imagine that this is any type of accident. Look around Zen. Look at how many are dead. Their bodies are right there! Their blood is mixing with the ground!" My voice's pitch increased.

"Shhh, come on Alexa, we can't do anything about what's already happened."

"I can kill a dragon or two!"

"Alexa…"

"If it's nothing to you and nothing to me, then why does it matter what I do?"

"It matters because this village needs to be protected. You're one of the best warriors this village has. Leila isn't gone yet, she's still alive, Alexa. She has so much faith in you and she has trained you all your life. Are you really going to let her down when she needs you now?"

"She won't know about what I do because you

wouldn't dare tell her," I replied, and raised my arms to shake away his hands. *He doesn't understand. He wasn't there. Zen didn't see what I saw. He didn't see the blood. He didn't hear the screams.*

I wiped my face as the memory echoed in my mind and pulled away from him. My shoes pounded on the ground as I ran up the street. Behind me, I heard Zen's heavy footsteps as he closed the distance between us.

"Hey, Alexa. Wait up. Take a deep breath. Come on, you need to rest. I promise if you go back to your house, we can work out what happened. I'll help you do that. At the moment you're angry and upset." Zen paused. "You owe it to Leila."

Dirt cascaded around my feet as I stopped. *Curse you Zen.* I turned around to find him only a few steps behind me. My head ached from the rush of movement.

"You really like to push it, don't you?" I replied.

Zen shrugged; then smiled. Even with death casting darkness over the day, I smiled in return. It felt good, even if the smile wasn't entirely sincere. My shoulders relaxed and Zen stepped towards me until he caught my hand in his.

"If someone sees that you could get yourself in trouble."

"I'll tell them I have to hold it to make sure you

don't escape again," Zen replied.

"Probably the one time they'd take your word over mine."

"Come on, let's find somewhere comfy. You can wash up, eat, and cut up your pillow into a million pieces if it will make you feel better. Then when you're ready, I'll be here waiting to work it out with you."

"How did I get such a good friend?" I said.

We walked back down the main street of the village. Zen walked on the side where the bodies lay and I tried to focus on where we were going. A few people busied themselves with their assigned duties. Whenever I glanced at someone, they averted their gaze. I must have looked a sight with my blood-soaked clothing and bandaged head.

We made our way back to my house; a gift I received when I finished my training as a warrior and entered the elite. Zen took the sheets off the bed and shooed me inside. I leaned against the closed door. So much had changed in a single day.

My reflection stared back at me in the mirror. I never liked mirrors. Yesterday I didn't have shadows under my eyes, matted hair, cuts and bruises; I looked old for seventeen. I picked up a blanket and blocked out the girl. Bloody fingerprints marked the corners of the blanket, and I cursed; something else that would need to be washed.

At the table, I poured water from the jug into a bowl. The cloth got dropped in and once it soaked up the water, I squeezed out the excess. I wiped the cloth over each of my leather arm guards before peeling them off. My armour came off next; I hung it on the wooden stand and then leaned close to it. Blood ran between the crevices of the metal. Yet another thing I needed to clean. I turned away from it and washed away the dirt and dried blood on my hands. After I wiped them, I washed them again. Finally, I took off my leather pants. They protected well, but like everything else needed a thorough clean. My training dictated I should do it now.

Cupboard doors opened and closed. Zen must have given my neglected kitchen a purpose. I didn't need to cook from scratch; the men did that whenever the warriors were in the village. When we trained to catch what we needed, skin, and cook it when out on hunts. Nothing fancy. I knew Zen wouldn't be content with a piece of cooked meat. For him, a meal required much more thought.

I looked away from the pile of bloodied clothes and removed the last of my undergarments. I added them to the pile. The men would take them tomorrow. I cleaned the rest of my skin with the cloth and water, though the clothes had trapped most of the dirt and blood. My hair proved more difficult to clean. The dried blood stuck to the strands. At least the wound wasn't as bad as I thought; more of a cut. Eventually I tamed the hair to a point I felt almost normal.

Fresh clothes hung on my clothing rack at the end of my bed. I chose the casual clothes all warriors wore when not training. The loose fitting brown pants had wide legs that ended above my ankles and didn't irritate my skin where the scratches were. I chose a matching shirt, wrapped around myself, and secured in place with a knot. I should have followed the dress code for company and wrapped the additional belt around my waist, but I knew Zen wouldn't care either way. Besides, it was more comfortable without it.

I sat at the square table where Zen had set the plates. He turned with the cooking pot and removed the lid. I heard and felt the rumbling of my stomach; he certainly knew how to cook. I watched as Zen moved meat combined with vegetables from the local gardens onto my plate and then served himself as well. I waited until he sat down opposite to me before I picked up the fork.

The distraction of food quelled the need to talk. I wiped my finger over the last of the sauce from the meal that remained on the plate, leaving it as clean as it had been before. When I looked over at Zen, I saw him watching me. I wiped my finger with my other hand, and he smiled.

"You know I'll never tell. Glad you enjoyed it," he said.

I watched as Zen cleared the table. Sometimes I felt I should feel the need to help. Sometimes I saw some of those coupled helping each other, but the elite warriors had trained me to allow others to do their job. I broke the rules for my enjoyment but other habits were more difficult to break.

"You comfortable?"

I leaned back in the chair. "I don't think it matters where I sit."

Zen resumed his position across the table. I shifted on the chair. The wood felt harder than before.

"So, what do you remember? You know, besides what you already told me. If it helps though, you can go over that again."

"I was late and had to catch up. They had headed west for the hunt. I had to go through that part of the forest with those low branches the men were to cut soon. Everything went really quiet. Then screams and shadows of the dragons."

I shivered.

"Do you want me to build the fire more?" Zen asked.

My gaze shifted to the flame, and I shook my head. He got up anyway and retrieved a blanket from the box beside the front door. I leaned forward so he could wrap it around my shoulders.

"The last couple of hunts were south, weren't they?"

"Yeah, but Leila didn't organise them. She likes to go west." I leaned forward. "I don't think I've seen dragons fly in from that side of the mountains before. Usually they would come from the southern mountain area."

"So they came from a different direction then. I wonder why?" Zen sat back in his seat.

"I don't know. Do I look like a dragon?" I retorted.

Zen rolled his eyes. I should be more cooperative; I knew it, but my mouth was in charge.

"Keep talking like that and I'll put you to bed."

"I'm surprised Sabine hasn't sent someone to check on us."

"Unless she did while we were out."

"Let's not talk about that."

"Then try to focus a little, Alexa. If we can work this out, it will help prepare for another potential attack. After all, who else is going to lead the rest of the warriors that are still alive?"

"Hey, I never asked to be the 'chosen one' or whatever it is you're trying to allude to. Others think I have 'great potential'. I only did out there what every other warrior did. Yes, I can fight, I can plan if I absolutely have to, but it's not something I enjoy. It's not something I'm good at. I'm more of a girl who just follows whatever orders I get given. I don't know, maybe I've been lucky. The one thing I don't see myself doing is leading a bunch of others. Not by myself anyway."

"You don't give yourself enough credit, Alexa."

"I think it's the opposite, Zen. I think that I've always given myself too much credit. I've always believed I was invincible. I never thought the dragons would win. How many dragons have we seen get the upper-hand, especially with the elders? The elders Zen, this was the one hunt a year that the elders came on."

"So what does that tell you, Alexa?"

"That either they are extremely lucky in their choice of day to attack or they had information. That attack, there were so many of them. It's always been one or two, but not a pack."

"I don't know about them having information from anyone in the village. It's a ritual; the elders do it every year. The elders have always said dragons are creatures without emotional thoughts, without that ability to process like we do. Say one or two have seen that hunt in the past. If they communicate with each other, maybe that's how they knew."

"That's a scary prospect. They would be very intelligent creatures to work that out, then plan, coordinate, and then attack. What benefit would there be to decimate the village of the elders? What is it that the elders know, that we don't?"

Zen leaned forward. "That's probably the big question, Alexa? What do we know? The elders kept everything within their own closed circle. The council elders even more secrets."

"So there must be something else that's going on then. Something we're missing or don't know about? Who was the worst injured? Those that were dead when you all got there?"

Zen listed off names.

"I'm not going to remember that. I should have some paper over there in the kitchen drawer."

Zeb sighed. "I know where it is. I found it while trying to find where you moved the plates to."

Zen retrieved the paper and something to write with. He returned to the table and sat down in the seat. I hated to read things upside-down.

"You're too far away. Come sit here where I can see," I said.

"Any other orders?"

I smiled. "Please relocate your seat so that it's beside me. The advantage is I don't have to ask you to repeat each name ten times."

Zen moved his seat. I watched as he wrote the names. When he had finished, we spread out the five pages on the table. My gaze went from column to column, name to name, trying to find a pattern.

"Zen, can't you see it? Look, don't you notice?" I picked the pencil up and put a star beside certain names.

"They're elders, we know that... so what?"

"But it's not just the elders, is it? I mean, most of them are the elders, aren't they, but it's also our trainers they've picked off. All those in prominent positions in the village. Those people that might have knowledge the rest of us don't. Those that train the others. How many students do you see? How many of us that were trained and laying there dead right now?"

"There are some, but you're right. The majority of those killed were senior village members."

"We need to track these dragons. If we go through the old forest, there is a trail that continues past the tree marks."

"You think we can find them?"

"I think you have a good chance of finding them and between us we can kill them."

I blinked as my head ached again. I reached my hand up and held it against the side of my head that hurt a little more than the rest. Zen glanced over and frowned.

"We can discuss this more tomorrow. Come on, back to bed."

Zen led me to the bedroom and even stayed long enough to tuck the blankets in. He turned to leave while I snuggled into the blankets to get warm. At the door, he smiled and my eyelids closed.

CHAPTER 5

I'd avoided the task as long as I could, but I had to face the inevitable. I stood at the closed door to the bedroom where Leila would lie on a bed on the far side. As of this morning, Leila was the last of the trainers and it looked as if a couple of would survive their injuries. A handful of elders who felt they were too old for the hunt this year were in charge of the village.

Sabine tapped my arm as she passed by and left me alone in the hallway. She'd already told me Leila wouldn't make it. The wound to her back had turned black overnight after the skin failed to heal. Once that happened, only time separated the victim from death.

My hand raised in a fist to knock at the door. *Is that what you do? Knock and let them know you're here? She's not going anywhere.* To some it would sound harsh, but those dying were at the mercy of the people around them. I knocked and then opened the door.

In my mind, I expected something shocking,

though what I didn't know. Instead, I found a room with minimal furniture. On the bed, Leila's body didn't move as I walked nearer. My gaze drifted to her ashen face. A bandage stained with blood was wrapped around the middle of her body. The pillow and sheets beside her were stained red, and the pungent smell of death hung in the air.

My hands brushed at my hips. I looked down to reassure myself that no blood covered them. The soles of my shoes betrayed my presence as I stepped forward. *Perhaps I should have removed them?* I paused. Guilt rose inside me, but Leila didn't stir.

She looked so much older. They had tied her grey hair back. An image of her as she ran towards me with her sword held high flashed in my mind. I closed my eyes and took a deep breath. The sound of my scream echoed in my ears. When I opened my eyes to the room once again, I walked to the chair beside the bed and moved it. Leila never stirred, even as the wooden feet of the chair scraped on the floor. I sat down and reached towards her motionless hand. If her chest hadn't risen now and then, I wouldn't have been so keen. Her skin felt cold, but her head turned towards me and her eyes opened a little.

No warrior woman stared back at me; just an old lady. The strength and light I had always seen when I stared into her eyes had dimmed.

"You must be careful." Leila's fingers curled

around mine and tightened.

"You know me, Leila, I'm always careful," I said.

Leila's eyes closed. My shoulders slumped at my attempt to lighten the seriousness of the situation.

"Alexa, you need to know something, something very important about what has happened and why. The remaining council elders have suspicions about the attacks. Though none of us ever thought that it would happen but now that it has, someone needs to know. You must know that you need to be for extra careful because..." Leila took a sharp breath.

I glanced around. *Should I adjust the blanket? Move the pillow?* I felt her grip tighten on my hand for a moment. I moved closer to her.

"Leila?" I whispered. There was no reply. I squeezed her hand as I could feel that she was still gripping it and tried again. "Leila, can you hear me?"

Her lips parted, and I heard the sharp intake of air. One eye opened and looked up at me.

"The truth Alexa, the truth. You need to know the truth about the dragons. The dragons..."

Her fingers loosened from mine and I saw her body sink into the sheets. The one eye frozen in time stared up at me.

"Leila, Leila! Leila, what is it you need to tell me? What is the truth? Please, Leila, we need to know. I need to know. You can't leave me, not yet!"

I let go of her hand. I didn't want to feel the warmth of her hand that moments ago had been alive. Anger grew inside of me again. Anger at elders who felt the need to be so secretive. The act of keeping the men under such tight control instead of training them to fight alongside us. Now we didn't just need swordsmanship, we needed the strength of numbers.

If there was some truth about the dragons in the village, then I wanted to know. Anything that could help track and kill the monster that did this. I turned to see Sabine in the doorway.

"Alexa—"

I pushed past Sabine and headed outside. The afternoon sunshine wasn't welcome. I saw Zen beside the door where I left him earlier.

"You didn't need to wait. I have something to do."

My shoes stirred the dirt as I walked towards the Hidden. The one place that only the elders went. If there was a secret about the dragons, I would find it in there.

Zen caught up to me as I walked to the door. It faced away from the village to prevent us from seeing the elders as they came and went. My hand grabbed the handle and pulled. Doors had no bars in the village, but this one wouldn't open.

"What are you doing, Alexa?" Zen's hand reached out and grabbed mine.

I shook them off. "She's dead, Zen. Leila is dead."

My foot braced against the door and I gave the handle another pull.

"So you're breaking in to the Hidden?" Zen asked.

I released the handle and stepped back from the door.

"Leila tried to tell me something, but she didn't have enough time in order to do so. Whatever she was trying to tell me, had something to do with the dragons, but I have no idea what. She said there's a truth, it must be important if she wanted to break the rules by telling me."

"Do you really think they would've been stupid enough to leave something lying around where any village member could've come across it? Come on, Alexa—"

Zen reached out for my arm again.

"But the Hidden isn't somewhere any of us would have come across it. You know as well as I do only elders can enter this place. None of us are anywhere near the age to be admitted and, of course, you're the wrong gender, anyway."

"You don't have to remind me."

"Well, there's no one to stop us from going into it

now. We could have a look — I will if you will."

But Zen's hand didn't leave my arm. "Maybe you should wait until after dark? Wait until the others are asleep? There will be those that will continue to be loyal to the elders no matter what's happened. They won't be convinced by rash decisions a young woman has made in anger."

I didn't want to listen to the words. I didn't want to believe those words. Deep inside, I knew what Zen said made sense. The building contained something we weren't meant to know about, but if I got caught before finding whatever it was, then it could all backfire on me.

I nodded and allowed Zen to lead me back home.

"Not today. You need to grieve for Leila. Calm yourself down. Promise me you won't go back there today."

I folded my arms over my chest.

"I promise."

"I'll come check on you after I finish the washing. In you go."

Zen shooed me inside the door. I closed the door and leaned against it. It took a bit before I heard his shoes as they walked away. I moved to the window to be sure he had left, then went to my bedroom and put on my harness.

I exited through the back door and made my way into the trees. I followed the back of the houses up towards the Hidden. Towards the top of the street, I veered deeper into the forest. I had to walk a wide circle to ensure I wasn't seen as I approached the Hidden's entrance from the far side.

When the door was in sight, I sat down in the shadows and waited for the sun to set. During that time, I studied the door. The wood was thicker than what they used on ours and older. I studied every grain of the wood and every blemish of the wood from the elements. An indentation in the centre of the door emerged from the consistency of the wood. The sharp line concealed in the dark lines of the wood and I felt it was the key to get inside.

When darkness fell, I pushed myself from the ground and brushed myself down. My sword comforted me, as I didn't trust my senses. I walked to the door and ran my hand along the wood. On the second pass, I felt the crevice I had seen. It was thin but about four fingers long. I placed the tip of the sword into it and pressed. Something clicked, and the door creaked inward to reveal the dark interior.

With the door closed behind me, I looked around the room. I had imagined what it would be like in the Hidden. I had imagined fancy lanterns, a grand table, and paintings on the walls. As I looked around the room, I saw curtains. Lots of curtains against every wall.

When I lifted the first curtain, there were shelves of books. Each curtain hid the same thing. Books, useless books, hundreds of useless books that were not going to answer my questions. I chose a few books at random and opened them. The words made no sense, and I tossed them to the floor. I tried several other books on the opposite wall but they weren't written texts. Not like the stories we could read occasionally or the information books Zen wrote of things he observed.

I picked up a chair and threw it against one wall. The leg snapped and caught the curtain as it fell to the floor. The fabric tumbled from the high ceiling; a small cloud of dust rose from it as it hit the floor. I shoved the table and it scraped over the floor. I tried to lift it, to overturn it, but its weight prevented me. The chairs instead were my target as I threw and kicked them. I ripped down several more of the curtains. A handful of books landed on the floor in a pile.

I stood in the room and looked at what I had done. This was just a room with worthless books, and Leila wasn't coming back. I wiped my face and picked up my sword next to the door.

"There's only one way to solve all this. If the dragons die, then the secrets don't matter anymore."

I stepped outside and pulled the door shut.

CHAPTER 6

With nothing found in the Hidden, I rose before the sun the next morning. In some ways I felt disappointed in myself as I left women I trained the past year behind. Women I trusted with my life. I knew they were invaluable, but I also knew there had to be some bigger picture. No matter how much I wanted to stay, someone had to be the one to stop the dragons.

Maybe I could make a difference. My motivation being I couldn't let the dragons destroy what little remained of the village. And I still needed an answer to the question of why. Why our village? Why did they have to kill so many in that attack?

I packed the water container, the tea, and a change of clothes into my bag. The knife and fire box never left the bag, and I could feel them in the assigned pockets.

With the bag in my hand, I turned to leave the room and caught sight of my reflection. I had pulled my long dark hair into a braid since I couldn't bring myself to cut it off. The clothes were clean; the washerman had outdone himself to remove all traces of *that* day.

"Do I look like a warrior ready to hunt and kill, or a weak woman about to run away?"

My reflection didn't offer me an answer. I turned away, ready to sneak out the back of the door. Until I heard the front door open and close.

"No," I whispered.

There was a soft knock at the door. If I stayed quiet, he might go away.

"Alexa. Alexa, I know you're awake."

My shoulders slumped. I walked to the door and opened it.

"I figured as much. I paid an early morning visit to the Hidden and found the door opened," Zen said. He stood in full dress with his pack and bag.

"Did you go inside?"

"No, I figured I'd come find you first."

I felt relieved he hadn't entered. It hadn't been my finest moment. Definitely not something I wanted him to see.

"I'm going."

"I figured that too. If you're going off without a plan, then I guess we'll look at this as an adventure." He paused. "Best we go out the back as a few men have already started work."

I allowed Zen to lead the way south towards the mountain. I had seen the path beyond the marks many times. Zen didn't hesitate to move pass them whereas doubt crept inside me. I didn't know what the consequences were for going outside the boundary, as I'd never known anyone who dared.

"You coming?" Zen asked. He had paused on the trail several steps ahead of me. The sunlight had made it easier to move through the forest while we attempted to put as much distance between the village and us as possible.

"Yeah, I just can't help but wonder what the elders will say when they find out." I stepped past the markers and joined Zen.

"Of all the things we're doing, that's what is bothering you?"

"I know. So where to?"

Zen pointed off in one direction. "I reckon there is a stream over there somewhere. If we follow it, we'll have fresh water as we move towards the mountain."

"It still seems such a way off."

"I think we'll need to camp overnight at least once, maybe twice. Depends how much ground we cover."

"It seems this is a well-used trail. I didn't expect it to widen like it has."

"I noticed that as well. And see those grooves, I'm not sure what's made them, but I guess something to help move many things across a distance."

"You're already thinking too much about it."

Eventually, we left the trail and headed into the forest. It had expected it to be tougher going. The forest floor had few lifted roots or fallen branches to interrupt our walk. Zen used his tracking skills to find the stream. I envied his skills. It hadn't mattered how hard I practised, I never could track as well.

We finally came to a small clearing and I dropped my bag against a tree in the shadow. The sun still shone and my clothes were wet with sweat. The clearing didn't look that different from other ones we had passed through.

I sat down and listened to the sound of the water as it trickled downstream. Zen walked over to a fallen tree branch and crouched beside it. His fingers brushed over the bark.

"We need a break, Zen. I'm thirsty and hungry and worn out."

"I'm not sure this is the best place. There are deep scratches on this."

I let him focus on the branch while I retrieved an apple from my bag.

Patience wasn't a skill I was good at. "Come on Zen, tell me what you see and what it means."

When he didn't answer, I swallowed the bite of the apple and went over to him. He stared at the branch. I could see the marks clearly, and they were deep. We knew large creatures roamed the woods as we had killed a few in the past for food during the winter; some had tasted better than others. Even I knew those marks weren't from a gigantic bird of prey. They were deep and I'd seen the pattern of marks before.

"I've never seen this before, Alexa. There's something very different about these dragons. This branch would have posed no danger to them and yet one has ripped it from the tree, somehow stripped away the leaves and smaller branches, and then just abandoned it."

"If you ask me, it looks like they practised. I saw some pick up warriors and squeeze them until they died. Then they just let go of the body and moved onto the next one."

"It makes your argument about that attack being planned have more weight. We need to find a more secure spot to rest."

I groaned. "Just a little bit longer?"

"Not here. Come on Alexa, we'll take it slow and when I find something that will work I promise we'll stop for the day."

My legs ached as I stood back up and retrieved my bag. I kept to the tree line and joined Zen where we could see the stream to our right as we continued to walk. The apple hadn't satisfied my hunger but I didn't complain. Zen had drunk water but hadn't eaten, and he didn't complain.

We walked a short while later when Zen stopped and took off his bag and harness. I did the same and flopped to the ground.

"That's it for today, right?" I said.

"It's been one day and you're worn out already? Where's your warrior spirit?"

"Still at home in bed. It's not quite the same as the hunts. I mean, sure we're all in a hurry to collect the flags, but I don't think I've ever walked so far at such a pace before."

Zen removed his shoes and wriggled his toes. "If it makes you feel better, my feet are killing me."

"You need to eat as well." I leaned forward and ran my fingers through my hair.

"You offering?"

"Depends how hungry you are."

Zen smiled. "I'll go see if I can catch something and you can build the pit."

I wasn't sure where he found the energy, but he

headed off into the forest again. My legs tingled, but I forced myself to get up and gather enough wood. I piled it up in the clearest section where we had stopped. My gaze fell on my bag.

"I should have grabbed that first," I muttered.

I crawled back to my bag and rummaged around for the box before I returned to light the fire. Three strikes of the metal and still no spark. I wiped my hand on my pants and tried again.

"I don't know how you survive without me."

Zen's arms appeared on either side of me, and he took the box from my hands. One strike and the spark flew from the box and onto the dried leaves on the wood.

"You just got lucky. I warmed it up for you."

I reached out to take back the box, aware of his closeness.

"You haven't asked if I brought back anything to eat."

I turned as he rested his chin on my shoulder. My fingers found the box, but he didn't release it.

"I doubt you'd be back so quick if you hadn't already caught or found something."

"I seem to have caught you."

I felt myself fall to the ground with Zen beside me. Laughter filled the air as he attempted to pin me down. I raised my knee in time to push against his waist. He fell onto his back, and I seized the opportunity. I straddled him and pinned his arms to the ground.

"It would appear the hunter is now the prey," I said. "Surrender?"

"Never."

I felt his arms twist under my grip. My body leaned forward to try to keep him still. With one push, he flipped me over and now had the advantage. I tried to wriggle my arms free, like I had before, but his grip held. He leaned down so his face was closer to mine.

"Surrender?"

"Not yet." I tried again to move and failed.

"I think you need to surrender."

His eyes looked so green at that moment. I could see the shades as they blended outwards. Zen's smile faltered a bit. We'd wrestled many times but...

"Alexa?" he whispered.

His gaze remained on me. I felt a warm rush through my body. Aware of how strong his arms were, how his knees pressed against my hips... I swallowed as he moved closer. His lips were so close to mine.

"Okay, I surrender, but only because I'm hungry."

Zen looked away and I felt his grip loosen. When he turned his face back, his smile had returned.

"Come on then."

Zen had caught a snake. I let him take care of skinning it ready to roast over the fire. They weren't my favourite meal, but it sat better in my stomach than just fruit or nothing at all.

We set our sleeping mats near each other. The night air felt colder here than in the village and we would need to put out the fire to lessen the chances of a dragon sensing our location. I tossed and turned on the mat, his green eyes disrupting any attempt I made to sleep.

When I rolled over, I saw his eyes were closed. His hair had loosened from its tie as strands covered parts of his face. I reached out to move them away, but stopped. There was something about the way he had looked at me before. Something more intense than it just being a game.

If he had stayed for the coupling ceremony, I doubted any woman would have turned him down. He was smart, creative, could cook better than most of the men, and he was handsome too. I hadn't seen him look at any woman in the village. He hadn't mentioned who he had planned to ask either, and they required him to ask someone.

Zen eyelids fluttered open, and I looked away.

My cheeks burned as I pulled the blanket closer to my chin. Maybe I had been quick enough to look away. Maybe he would think I was asleep if I remained still enough.

"Goodnight Alexa," Zen said.

I smiled. "Goodnight Zen."

CHAPTER 7

I rose early the next morning. If I had to talk about anything, I had to make sure I was prepared in my mind of how to respond. My mind wouldn't stop turning the events of the previous night over. I wondered if I should have said something different. Had I given him any indication that I wanted more than best friends? Would he have kissed me if I hadn't said anything? I paused with my hands in the water at that thought.

I knew I couldn't say I hadn't. At one point, Zen had been nothing but my best friend. We'd done everything together. We were closer than I was to anyone else in the village beside Leila, but that was different.

I thought of Leila on the bed, all alone, with no one to give her more than a sympathetic look. I didn't want to end up alone like that. But then, why would anyone want to be tied to someone like me? I was an elite warrior in the village. Maybe one day, I would even become an elder. A lot of power that would leave me little time to spend with anyone else, and that didn't seem fair either.

I swished my hand over the water's surface. That didn't stop me from wondering though. Wondering if all the villages existed like this with such rules and ways. Perhaps it was just me. I knew I felt like Zen deserved someone more feminine than me, someone who would treat him well.

Giving the water a final flick, I stood up and returned to where I'd left Zen. His rolled-up blanket and mat lay where he had. I took a deep breath; he was probably doing his business, no need to panic.

My eyes looked up to the sky overhead. The sky still had a tint of orange to it, but it was fading fast. The mountain seemed to continue higher and higher. We really needed to find a way around it. If we were forced to reach the peak before progressing further south, then the dragons would probably be gone.

"So, I was thinking about something," Zen said from somewhere behind me.

I turned away from the disappearing mountain and focused on Zen. My cheeks burned and I welcomed the coldness the mountain air provided to combat the feeling.

"About what?" *Please don't mention last night. Please. Please.*

"I think we might need to split up. I mean, I know

that wasn't our intention when we first left the village, but we need to find a way around this mountain. We've been climbing already for two days. If it takes us this long each time, we'll be frail and old before we even find the dragons."

Perhaps he had read my mind, or maybe we were too familiar with one another's thinking. "I've been concerned about the constant climbing. Leila once told me that the air gets thinner the further you climb up into a fog. I'm not sure we're in a position to tackle that with what we have."

"Agreed."

"So how do you think we should do this?"

"Not like you to ask for suggestions," Zen commented. He picked up his pack from the ground, slung it over one shoulder and attached it.

I should probably get mine as well.

"Well, you said you'd been thinking, I assume you have one ready."

He smiled and nodded. "I think you should stay here, it's fairly concealed. You've got a good defensive position over there if you are attacked by dragons, but if you stay hidden by the trees, you should be safe."

"And where do you plan on going?"

"I want to check out the fork in the path ahead.

One I'm certain continues to head up the mountain. It looks like that's also the more travelled of the two paths. I want to see where the other one leads. I'll follow it far enough to see and then I'll come back. If I leave now, I kind of hope to be back before sundown."

"You want me to sit around here and do nothing?"

"I want you to let me do what I'm good at. This could cut days, weeks even, from our journey," Zen said. I diverted my gaze to the ground. "Come on, you can practise and plan, and do all that stuff they have trained you to do."

"You promise you'll be back by sundown?"

He nodded. "Of course, I only need to know if that path leads around the mountain, and if there's a chance it's an easier route. I'll keep an eye on the sun, promise."

I knew he was right. Tracking wasn't something I was as good at, and it made little sense for me to go as well if we had to turn back. Then again, if it was a clear path, then it would make sense. Training made making non-strategic decisions difficult.

"You take care while I'm gone," Zen said and took a few steps towards the worn dirt path that wove in and out of the trees we'd used for cover. He paused and turned to look back at me. "Alexa?"

"Yeah?"

"About…"

"Later Zen, they'll be time to talk about that all later."

He nodded. I watched as his muscular figure blended into the darkness of the trees. I kicked at the dirt. Time: I had been up for ages and now I had all this time on my hands. My sword lay on the ground underneath my pillow. I should probably practise a bit. I hadn't done much of the exercises I'd done with Leila daily since her death. Still, as I looked at it on the ground, I didn't feel motivated to go and grab it.

Moving off, I started in search of some plants he told me about. I only had basic training in plants and medicines. It wasn't something considered necessary — it's why they trained those that didn't make the elite warrior training. I knew about a couple of plants, like the one with the yellow flower that grew amongst the grasses. If you boiled it in water with some of the purple flowers that grow on the vines in the trees, it would mix to make a drink that could take away some of the pain if you'd been hurt. The flowers had proper names, but I couldn't remember them. At the time, it seemed much more important to remember what they looked like.

I found a few of the purple ones hanging from the tree near to the little stream I'd been at before. They were tangled amongst the higher branches, which were just out of my reach. Warrior girl I might have been, but even blessed with height they were out of reach. Annoyingly, there were no lower branches that were within reach that I could use to pull myself up the tree. I needed to either find something to stand on, or go back and get the sword and try to slice them from amongst the leaves. The sword probably had the highest possibility of success, but I felt lazy.

Turning to look at the river, I couldn't see anything I could move. Maybe the fallen tree trunk if Zen had been there, as well as three other strong people. Then again, if Zen had been there, I could have just hopped on his shoulders and reached for the flowers that way. We'd done that a lot as kids to sneak some of the duai fruit. Duai fruit only appeared on the trees in the elders' garden near to Sabine's house.

Like everything else, it was off limits to all villagers, but once a year at the coupling ceremony they would allow people to have one each. The red flesh was the most delicious thing I'd ever tasted, sweet with a tiny bit of flavour that lingered in your mouth long after you finished it. I should have thought to help myself to some to bring with us.

A stick about half my height lay further up the mountain near one of the boulders. My eyes looked up to the bright blue sky above. That part of the stream was out in the open, but the stick was prefect.

I waited and listened for a bit. I could hear the wind disturbing the leaves on the trees, the air that pushed down from the mountain and snuck through gaps in the rocks in places that dotted the sides, but there was no sound of the air being pushed aside by wings, no roars of instructions, though they rarely made noise prior to an attack.

I edged out of the shadows and into the light. My shadow appeared at my side and made me look a lot taller. I could have used that height right at that moment. Still, I looked up above for a moment. Something in my gut made me want to flee back to the safety of the tree cover. But that stick lay only a handful of steps away. One last glance to the sky and I ran for the stick. I snatched it up from the ground and breathed with relief. My heart thudded in my chest as I smiled at my worry.

Shaking my head, I walked back towards the trees. A whoosh and I hit the ground; my hands covered my head as a darkness passed over me for a moment. I turned my head enough to see a smallish dragon, still three times my size, sailing back up into the sky in an arch. It hadn't finished with me yet.

I scrambled to my feet with the stick still gripped in my hand. It was the only weapon I had as I heard the roar overhead. My toes slid against the dirt, and I braced myself against it with my hands. Another roar and I could hear the approaching glide. I had to get to the trees. My feet slipped in the dirt again, sending me back to the ground. The stick narrowly missed my eye. I saw the shadow growing as it drew near. I waited. Gripped the stick. Waited. The shadow engulfed me. I rolled over and stabbed the stick. I caught the dragon on its chest. It veered off its course and headed away from me, taking the embedded stick with it.

I pushed myself up from the ground and crawled toward the trees. They were close. So close. A roar above me differed from before. I looked skyward to see a larger dragon had joined the smaller one. It reached its claw out and extracted the stick. The smaller one flew out of my view as the larger one hovered in the sky. Its gaze appeared to find me and it twisted its body around, ready to attack.

I continued crawling towards the trees. As the grass thickened beneath my hands, I pushed myself up and stayed on my feet. I ran for the cover of the trees and felt the rush of air behind me as I headed for my pack. I needed the sword.

Behind me, I could hear the dragon's wings beating against the tree line. It roared again. I turned to see the outline as I got closer to the camp. I slid towards my pack and grabbed the sword. The trees above provided me with some cover, but I wasn't about to take any more chances. I stayed as still as I could. The dragon had ceased intimidating me with sound. I could hear the wind again. A bright light above me and I looked up. Flames licked at the leaves. As each one fell from its hold on the tree, it floated onto those below, igniting them as well. I could just make out the dragon above the vanishing canopy. I needed to move before I got trapped by the flames.

My eyes darted from the path I'd just travelled to the one Zen had taken. I turned south and headed into the thicker canopy as a branch crashed to the forest floor. It ignited the grass nearby, and I turned to focus on the path. I wanted to deviate off the path. *Did dragons understand what paths were? Did they know humans used them to find their way? To connect to other places?*

At the same time, I didn't want to leave the path and go into the unknown. Dragons were a known threat, but I had no idea if other creatures just as dangerous lurked in the forests of the mountains. It made sense to me there would be more, as my feet once again slipped on the dirt as the incline increased. My boots seemed to find every loose stone that lay on the path. I used the sword as an anchor to pull myself up. *How had Zen made it up this way?*

CHAPTER 8

I raised my head to see that the incline got worse. The trees were thinning too. I had no choice. If I continued up the path I would be dragon food. I turned to the side and skidded over the loose stones that lead back into the trees. The sword stabbed at the ground. My boots found some traction after I clambered over a fallen tree trunk.

The ground levelled off slightly as long as I concentrated on moving straight ahead. The sides showed the extremes of the mountain. Above me, I could hear the dragon calling out. Up ahead, a bright flash caused me to pause. The dragon seemed to know my plan. I turned back as another flame engulfed the canopy behind me. I had three choices: head up the mountain, down the mountain, or burn to a crisp.

My gaze moved downwards. I could see the slope changing, but then it stopped where I had an unobstructed view of mountains in the distance. I'd come far enough around that the layout of the mountain changed. There were cliffs on this side; probably why the path made me formed where it was.

I looked up. If I went that way, I was going closer to the dragons. The trees were few and far between only a short distance away. Heat from the flames that spread with a contagious agenda drew closer. I had to decide.

With my sword back in the harness, I climbed up onto the rock in front of me. My hands struggled to find the handholds and footholds. I gripped one hold and felt something crawl over my hand. A large brown spider had crawled out onto my hand and paused on my wrist. I resisted the urge to shake the horrid thing off and looked upwards to see the tail of a dragon disappear from view.

My foot found a jutted out rock. I reached my other hand up until I found another handhold and pulled myself up. The spider twitched on my wrist. I let out a breath and pulled my other leg up. It found a hold and I looked for a new handhold. Only one that I could see and it would be a stretch. I gave my wrist a shake but the spider obstinately wouldn't oblige.

"I'm going to fry you myself when I have a spare hand," I muttered to the beast.

I pulled my hand from the hold and reached upward. Now the spider moved. It scurried down my arm, getting closer to my face.

"Wrong way you stupid creature. Don't you dare come near my face. Back off, you little horror!"

It had reached my shoulder. I turned to blow the thing away but only succeeded in provoking it to turn and watch me with its multiple black eyes. I could see the hairs that covered its body. Its body was flat and compact, but with legs that defied logic because of their length. The spider turned towards the rocks, and I was freed from its gaze.

My foot slipped. My body's weight pulled me down and slammed against the rough rocks. My cheek hit something sharp and I watched as the spider granted me some relief and scurried back to the safety of the rock and away from me. I breathed in relief. *Still, one day I'm going to burn you, spider, or chop you up as dragon food; either is acceptable.*

With my foot still without a hold, I brushed it against the rocks and tried to find anything that would work to help me continue. My fingers ached from holding onto the weight, my other knee longed for relief. I just couldn't find anything to use.

I turned my attention above. There might be a chance I could pull myself up if the hold was close enough. I scanned the section above me but saw nothing. A shadow moved across the rocks. I still had company to deal with.

I rested my body against the cliff for a moment. To the side, I saw the spider hadn't totally abandoned me. It sat a way off, watching me with its unhelpful beady eyes. I glared in its direction.

The staring match ended as a rope fell in front of my face. Glancing towards the sky, I saw Zen's head appear not far above. A platform must be up there, but I sure couldn't see it from my position. I moved my nearest hand to the rope and pulled it towards me and clamped on my other free hand. Immediately I felt myself rise upwards. I tried to keep as still as I could, but the dragon called again.

Zen wasn't to be seen when I glanced up. I could see the edge of where he separated from the illusion of a solid cliff. A dragon circled overhead. My only shelter was a small bush I was currently passing that grew in the tiniest of crevices.

"Hurry up!" I yelled above.

The edge drew closer and I freed one hand to grab it. The rope steadied and stilled. I saw Zen's head as he peered down at me and offered a hand. I took it gratefully, and he pulled me over the edge. The reunion would have to wait as the dragon dove towards us, another dragon not far behind it in the sky.

Zen pulled me to my feet and towards the side of the cliff. We crouched down behind a boulder as the dragon swooped past us. My hair flew in front of my face. I reached behind for my sword and found the hilt.

"Not the time, Alexa."

"What do you mean? That thing is out for blood. I'm not going to sit here and wait for it to work out how to reach us."

"You can't think they can..."

"They followed me. They knew I was on that path, they knew I'd get trapped. If that fire continues to burn, there is a chance it could reach us here and there's no way I'm getting stuck in a fire."

Standing up, I drew the sword and edged out from behind the boulder. I kept myself looking as small as possible as the dragon glided to the side to head back our way. The other dragon joined it this time and they flew towards me in tandem. I stepped away from the cliff face, so I stood somewhere in the middle of the plateau. I pressed the toes of my boots into the ground as I took my stand; the sword raised, ready to strike out when they passed by. One of them would not go home today. It could pay the price for taking Leila from me. I squinted as they moved out of sight behind the mountain. They used the fire to reveal my location, to draw me out. I felt fairly confident they wouldn't attack with fire.

I adjusted my feet. Bent my knees a little more

and leaned forward. My ears listened for the sound of the approach. I waited. A roar sounded as the dragon's head came into view. It flew closer to me and swung when in reach. I sliced its clawed foot as it attempted to grab me. Blood dripped onto my face as it called out and flew over the trees I emerged from. The second dragon changed course. It flew out wide before flying out of sight. I pivoted on my foot ready to strike. It had come on quicker than expected, and its leg knocked me to the ground. My sword lay on the grass. I rolled over and gripped it tightly. Looking up, I saw the two dragons flying away south.

"They're going, Zen," I called out.

Pushing myself from the ground, I saw my red streaked arms. Inspecting the blade, I saw a corresponding stain. Blood settled on one side and I crouched back down to wipe as much as I could on the clumps of spiky green grass on the ground. I turned the blade over; it wasn't a perfect job but it would have to do. I sheathed it and wiped my hands on my pants.

"We need to go this way, there's a narrow path along the edge of the cliff that leads to a cave."

"Cave?" An image of the evil creature flashed through my mind.

"I promise I'll keep an eye out for spiders. You can fight a dragon and yet a spider sends you into a quivering mess."

He walked away and I followed in his footsteps. "I'll have you know I managed to tolerate one of those horrid things on my hand as I climbed up there."

"Ah, so that's who you yelled at."

"I didn't yell."

"Loud enough for me to hear you. I saw the dragons circling as I was heading back to you. Watch your step here."

I concentrated on where my boots went as the plateau narrowed to a pathway only wide enough for a slim person. I tried to imagine some of the elders edging along there. Each time the vision ended with the rocks collapsing and them hurtling down towards the trees. I pressed my back against the cliff, allowing my hands to follow the rocks and stay as close to Zen as I could. Anytime a pebble or two skipped off the ledge, I hesitated a little inside, but I continued.

"In here."

Vines covered the entrance to the cave. Zen held a couple to the side from the inside as I entered. At least my feet had plenty of room to step without disaster in here. He let the vines fall back into place. I turned to see the dark abyss in front of me.

"You can't seriously think we should go that way."

"We don't have much of a choice now."

Beside me, he crouched down and opened his pack. Pack, everything I had brought with me was in the pack that the dragon had so kindly destroyed. I didn't even have a change of clothes. Zen pulled out a rock and picked up a torch I could just see near the entrance.

"One I prepared earlier," he said, and struck the rock against the cave wall. A few sparks glowed as they fell onto the dry naja. It didn't take long for the spark to overwhelm the naja, and the cave brightened.

"You didn't make it through here though, did you?"

"Almost, there are these vent type things. They have like a pool of water on the ground and if you look into them it shows you the view from outside. I don't really understand it, but it saved you from being dragon food."

"That would never have happened. Come on. Let's see where this goes then. Standing still is making me nervous."

CHAPTER 9

It felt like hours since I'd seen sky, daylight, and breathed fresh air. I wanted to sit down and give up for a while, but I didn't want to stay in the never-ending darkness. The vent Zen mentioned earlier was interesting - the first time I saw it. They appeared consistently along the path. The path itself had remained steady; occasionally it would veer up or down, but never too much.

Zen walked ahead with the torch in his hand. We'd passed the point he'd explored a while back, and now we headed into the unknown. My feet ached for a rest, my eyelids blinked slower than earlier in the day, and the naja had almost burnt away. Because of the dim light, I couldn't see enough of the tunnels to reassure me that no eight-legged creatures were poised, ready to pounce in my direction.

"I think the opening is ahead."

"I hope it is," I muttered.

I felt a softness brush against my face. My feet

froze mid-stride. Goosebumps appeared on any bare skin. I waited. Nothing. I exhaled the breath I held. As I rubbed my arms, I felt the grittiness of the dried blood, dirt, and sweat. My nose didn't miss out on the hyper-awareness and my nose twitched. I turned my head and sniffed my arm. The dank smell I had attributed to the cave I realised was me. My hand fell to my side; I needed a wash.

"Alexa?"

"I'm coming."

I hurried to catch up to Zen. Twice my shoes caught on the uneven ground. I reached Zen only for the naja to burn out.

"Now what?" I grumbled.

I heard the stick clatter against the rock floor. My gaze looked around. We weren't in the eternal darkness I expected. The walls of the cave emitted a soft light. Curious, I stepped towards the nearest wall and ran my finger over the rough surface. Not flowers. I rubbed my fingers together and they glowed like the walls.

"Alexa!" Zen called.

"it's alright, just some kind of glowing crystal."

"Don't even think about licking those fingers."

"Hey, I have some decorum." I rid myself of the glow on my pants. Not my best idea.

"Come on, I can see more light ahead."

That's when I realised he had moved further down the tunnel. Zen stood silhouetted by pale light around a long curve in the tunnel. I stopped to sigh before I breathed in the fresh air that lingered around us.

"It's not what I expected," Zen said.

"Well, I can't see a thing around you, so move forward if it's safe."

I nudged him in the lower back, and he moved forward. My mind expected a steep drop like I had climbed to escape the flames, but as my sight adjusted, I saw a pleasant view. A forest spread out before us. Beyond the forest I saw mountain ranges that reached into the misty clouds. At least where we were, the land lay flat. That would be an agreeable change.

"Wasn't expecting that either," I said.

"It's certainly welcome though," Zen replied. "Let's make the most of it. The sun is a fair way over and we need to find some water and shelter before it's gone."

"Lead the way, tracker."

Zen stepped into the grass. The blades reached his knees as he moved forward; I saw the knuckles of his hand turn white as he gripped the hilt of his sword. I took one last look at the sky. I expected to see a dragon. More specifically, I expected to see the one that attacked earlier, but the blue sky remained uninterrupted. My finger twitched. It wasn't natural for the sky to have nothing at all; I couldn't even see a bird.

My tongue flicked over my bottom lip; I tasted dirt. I needed to find somewhere to clean up. Another pass of sky and I still saw nothing. Perhaps the journey through the tunnel had made me paranoid. I still wasn't sure how long we spent there; how long my senses had become accustomed to the sounds of the cave.

"Are you coming?" Zen said.

I bit my bottom lip and turned to look in his direction. He had crossed the small grassed area and waited at the edge of the forest. My hand waved him off as my head nodded. I managed a smile as I crossed the grass, despite the bottom of my feet objecting with each step. It had been a long day.

"What's the plan then?" I asked when I reached Zen.

"I can hear water coming from somewhere over there." He pointed into the heart of the forest. "I'm hoping it's not far because I'm hungry and tired."

"Well, you get to do the cooking, so let's hope the water isn't too far away."

It didn't take long before I could hear water as

well. It took a lot of restraint to not run ahead and dive in fully dressed — that would have amused Leila. As disciplined she had made me while fighting or hunting, there were times you just had to do what was necessary.

The water turned out to be a river. It snaked around the trees I could see and headed off somewhere else I didn't care to know about yet. The water, the water I cared about. I tore my gaze from the temptation after Zen nudged me and we moved away from the water.

Once Zen found a place that satisfied him, I heard a soft thud as his pack fell to the ground near his feet. I let Zen fuss about as he searched his pack and studied the clearing we were in. He had good taste. The trees were far enough away to minimise the chance of a fire, but close enough to provide protection from the wind. I noted some of the denser parts of the forest beyond the immediate trees; I would have use for the privacy they provided later.

"I'll go and find some wood for a fire, you should…" Zen began.

"I know, I know." I waved him off and he vanished into the shadows of the forest.

The dark sky above and little moonlight deepened the shadows. I rubbed my arms; up this high, it wasn't a surprise that the air felt so cool. I turned in the stream's direction. It beckoned me through the trees. The odds were I'd end up sick, but my choices were limited.

Once I located the water, I moved downstream to make sure the trees continued their barrier of both protection from the sky and privacy, though from whom I wasn't sure. I chose a spot and took off my harness that held the sword. I drew it from the leather, dipped my hand in the water and wiped it across the blade to make the stains disappear. I repeated it until the sword looked clean and rested it upright against a nearby boulder to dry.

When I stood up, I saw the forest had darkened. The grass swayed and the cool breeze I had welcomed when we exited the cave now felt cold. I rubbed my arms as I looked out into the forest as I turned around. Despite all the hunts over the years, I had rarely had the chance to bathe out in the open like this. Usually we were restricted to a designated area and strict routine. They had taught warriors at least to swim as part of the training. I recalled the pleasure the instructor had telling us when we were eight, that only nine had drowned while learning in the past fifty years. If it had been intended to motivate, then it had done the trick, but I still wondered who those girls had been. This, of course, wasn't the same. Swimming had always been done with special suits or full-on outfits and I always had spares. I could either wash with the bloodied clothes on or not.

I put my heel on the toes of the other shoe and pulled my foot free, then repeated with the other one. When I reached down and removed the socks, I saw they hadn't escaped being marked by the day. My eyes went back to the forest. A scratching sound. *Some kind of animal?* I glanced at the sword. Waited. Nothing ran at me so I turned back to the water. At the edge I could see the stony bottom. It probably wouldn't make a difference if I bathed with the clothes on; they needed to be washed anyway. Loosening my hair, I let it tumble down my back. My feet edged into the cold water. I clenched my teeth knowing I would get used to it, maybe.

I stepped into the river. The current moved around me, and I reached the middle of the river without incident. My feet barely touched the bottom, but that didn't matter. I allowed the water to close in around me, to wash away the dragon's blood, and hopefully the sensation on my hand where that spider had perched itself.

The last of the light faded as I floated on the surface of the water. Despite the chill, I could have stayed there forever, but we had a journey to complete. We had to stop the dragons. I rolled over and gazed towards the bank; something cream rested on the grass. It hadn't been there before. My legs sank into the water as I righted myself. I swam towards the bank and saw a fabric shirt awaited me.

"Sneaky," I muttered. He'd been silent enough that I hadn't heard him at all, but that's why his tracking skills were so good. "Time to return I guess."

With effort, I left the stream. Water ran down my legs and dripped off my arms as I stood feeling five times heavier than before. I checked my surroundings with a quick once over to ensure I didn't have an audience. Though even if I did, they'd be unlikely to admit to it.

I shook my head. I was overthinking it. I stripped off the wet clothes and let them fall one piece at a time to the ground. Goosebumps covered my entire body before I even picked up the shirt. The fabric fell down to cover my body to my knees. *When had Zen gotten so tall?* I hugged the shirt to my body to elicit some warmth. It didn't provide much.

My toes nudged the pile of wet clothing. A sigh escaped my lips as I crouched down and rung out each piece of clothing. I did some pieces twice but it didn't seem to make that much difference. Defeated, I picked up the drenched pile and, with it held as far from my body as possible, I turned to walk back to Zen.

I smelt the burnt wood before I saw the flame. Zen had built a small fire pit where the fire flickered in the centre. Beside the pit I saw Zen had made a stand out of branches for me to hang my clothes on. I headed to the stand and allowed the soaked fabric to fall to the ground.

"Did you try to get rid of the excess water?" Zen asked.

He walked over and crouched beside the pile. He picked up my shirt. I cringed at the waterfall at before he twisted it. Water spilled from the fabric and pooled near his feet.

"I swear I did that." He glanced up at me and I shrugged. "You have experience with it that I don't."

I stepped away to let him finish doing the rest. Laundry had been one task the males started when they were ten; apparently before at age the risk of clothes changing colour or size was higher. As I watched him work, I appreciated the speed and skill. Even when he did my undergarments, he showed no embarrassment, in stark contrast to the warmth I felt flood my cheeks. My laundryman had always been a middle-aged man — all the warriors got those with the most experience.

With the last of my clothes now draped on the stand, Zen returned to the fire. He crouched down and turned the stick, which had a succulent rabbit on it cooking. My mouth watered at the thought of having rabbit. It had been a while since we had fresh meat in the village. The dragon attacks meant the warriors had spent more time training and less on hunting, so only the smaller game the men had caught near the village had been available. If they'd permitted the men to help with the hunting, the stores wouldn't be half empty.

"I caught this little guy while you were out," Zen said.

"I noticed."

His shoulder nudged mine. "Remember the first time we had rabbit?"

I laughed. "That afternoon we snuck away from doing the preparations for the Summer Welcome Festival."

"You had been so determined to avoid Leila putting you in that dress."

"Well, why should a warrior be forced to wear something that is a tripping hazard?"

Zen smiled. "You only tripped once, and you were six at the time."

"It left a lasting impression."

His shoulders shook as he turned the rabbit. He attempted to cover the smile with his hand, but I'd seen children do a better job. I remembered the hours I spent getting ready for that festival. The elders had been keen to ensure all the girls wore the traditional blue dresses that flowed out and had white flowers embroidered over every hem. The beauty of the dress had entranced me until I had to walk in it. At that moment I learnt beautiful things required practise to wear and the elders should have prepared us. Still, I had looked graceful until my skirt caught on a twig. That twig pulled the fabric tight as I lifted my foot before I crashed to the ground. The one and only time I wore a dress.

Something nudged at my hand. The memory faded away as I looked down to see the makeshift bark plate piled with steaming meat ready to be devoured. I accepted the plate and picked up a piece of meat. I held it to my nose and breathed in the aroma. My mouth salivated in preparation.

My meat froze a fraction from my lips. Leaves rustled in the darkness again. My gaze glanced over the bushes nearby but I saw nothing except silhouetted trees and bushes. I waited for the noise again. Nothing. Zen's raised head looked in the same direction I thought the noise had come from. Unlike me, he had managed to take a bite of the food. His attention remained on the bushes as he chewed.

My teeth bit into the meat and I savoured the taste. I heard it again. My gaze focused back on the bushes across the fire. It could have been an animal, but nothing small, the noise didn't indicate that. I wondered what types of animals were in the forests here besides rabbits. I assumed they were similar to home, but we discovered new animals several times a year.

"Wasn't just me, was it?" I whispered.

From the corner of my eye I saw Zen shake his head.

CHAPTER 10

"There are probably some night creatures living in the forest, but the fire would deter most. I'm certain that there's a person out there."

"You probably encouraged whatever, or whoever, it is with the smell of your cooking," I rebuked.

The next sound wasn't a rustle. I heard the distinct crack of a twig break and grass as it brushed against fabric. I swallowed the mouthful of rabbit and placed the plate on the ground. My hand reached out until my fingers curled around the hilt of my sword.

Zen got to his feet, his food discarded near mine. He took tentative steps towards the bushes. I should have followed, but instead approached the rack in hope my pants were dry enough to put on. My hand brushed over them; just my luck, they were still damp in places. Still, if I had to fight, I would be more confident with them on. I continued to watch Zen edge closer to the trees, as I cringed as I pulled on the pants.

Uncomfortable, but at least covered, I stepped around the fire. I glanced back at the warm flames and wondered if we should extinguish it, but didn't stop to act. Zen had paused. He gazed out into the darkness. My ears pricked at the whistled tune that confirmed a person, and not an animal, approached.

Zen's shoulders lowered and I nudged him in the side. It wasn't the time to let our guard down. It might be a person, but they're often far more dangerous than any animal. The whistled tune continued and goosebumps appeared along my arms. I tried to work out what the tune was. It sounded familiar, and yet... nothing came to mind.

"Greetings, young ones," a tall man said as he emerged from the darkness.

The man's white face reminded me of the tales of spirits the elders would tell us when we were kids. Tales to teach us lessons and others I thought were to scare us. The black clothing the man wore enhanced the whiteness of his face. His loose black pants and shirt were not dissimilar to Zen's. He had the collar of his long black jacket turned up and it fit snug against his neck. The man's long dark hair with hints of grey fell from beneath the hood on his head to frame face.

"Greetings stranger," Zen replied.

My fingers squeezed the hilt. I eyed the stranger as my heart thumped in my chest. He paused near the fire and rolled his sleeves up his arms. I noted the ease with which the jacket folded; I hadn't seen such thick but malleable fabric before. He stretched his hands towards the fire and focused on the flickering warmth.

"Such a lovely night, a bit cold but nothing a bit of warm fire can't soothe." His voice had a rough edge to it.

I stepped forward to put myself between Zen and the man. The fire formed a small barrier between us, but something about him made me keep the sword poised, ready to fight.

"There is no need for that, lady. I mean you no harm. I am nothing but a man who travels from place to place. I seldom meet others on my way, but your fire was a welcome sight."

I turned the sword in my hand. Leila had taught us about the power of words and the way they could persuade. She had often spoken about those that might try to endear themselves; those that appeared as a friend with light conversation. Leila considered those were the people who would deceive.

Zen's hand reached out and touched the blade. I felt the downward pressure he placed on it and tried to counter it without success. I adjusted my stance and lowered the sword. My teeth clenched as I refused to give the stranger the opportunity to move unseen.

"Ah, that is better. I have never been fond of having a sword pointed at me. Swords, my lady, can do a great deal of damage in trained hands," the man said.

"I'd be happy to give you first-hand experience," I offered.

"Alexa," Zen hissed.

"What?" I protested.

Zen clearly didn't share the same concerns as me. Had I been alone, I would have tried to slice the stranger into little pieces by now. That was another lesson Leila imparted — the dangers of men. Still, nothing assured me more of my safety than my sword.

"It's fine, young man. She is young and has much to learn; I see you don't have a sword as well." The stranger remarked.

I paused as I walked back towards where my food still lay on the ground. My luck it would be cold by now and I hated eating meat cold. It always made bile rise in my throat.

"I don't need to have one with Alexa around." Zen returned to where he had been before and kicked at his own sword on the ground. "I do have one though."

I smiled. *Okay, he gets a point for that comment.* When I looked at the stranger, his attention had turned to me. I waved the sword in my hand before spinning it around. The sword paused. I gripped the handle and pushed the tip into the ground. I sat down next to it. *Deal it with.*

"The lady's name is Alexa. What about you, young man?"

"Zen."

"Zen and Alexa, I am Ojerren." He sat down on the ground.

Zen returned to where he had been sitting and immediately started to finish off his meat. My fingers brushed against the cold rabbit beside me. My stomach turned the wrong way and I pushed it back towards Zen. I wish he'd left the rabbit on the fire, even if it had burnt to a crisp — at least it would have been hot.

"Ojerren, would you care for some rabbit?" Zen asked.

"I would Zen, I would. Yes, that would suit me well."

Zen took more meat from the rabbit and placed it with my leftovers. He stood up and made his way around the fire. I watched Ojerren; if he made the slightest movement towards Zen, he would be a dead man. Ojerren accepted the offered food and Zen returned and sat down. No drama, only the sharing of a meal, as if Ojerren had been from our village.

Ojerren ate in silence. My fingers tapped against my legs as I sat with them crossed. When they felt numb, I pulled them up to my chin and my bare feet shuffled back and forth on the grass. *Shoes; I should put them back on as well.* Ojerren's attention remained on the rabbit during his first serving through to his third. By the time he tossed the bark onto the fire, I had slipped my feet into the shoes. The clothes were still too damp to wear and the pants continued to stick to my skin in places. I left the other clothes to dry but would put up with the pants.

"So what brings you both out here to the Tiarana Mountains?" Ojerren said as he stretched his own legs towards the fire.

I looked over at Zen and narrowed my eyes at him in warning: *Don't you dare.* He glanced at me before throwing his empty bark into the fire. The flames consumed the bark and reduced it to ash.

"We're journeying south to find a possible new location for our village," Zen said.

"You plan on moving an entire village? I'm intrigued." Ojerren leaned forward.

"Not so much the village itself, just the people that remain."

"You make it sound as if some have recently

departed."

"They have, they're dead. The dragons, you see, have decided to cull the population of our village. For the safety of those that remain, we seek somewhere to move them too." True, even if I stretched it a little.

"So you have no intention of finding the dragons then and exacting some kind of revenge?" Ojerren asked.

I looked away from him and at the fire. Killing him still seemed like the sensible thing to do.

"It's true. We would like to know why the attacks have become more frequent. In the past they have been destructive. The odd person killed, but nothing like the most recent attack," Zen explained.

"I have a long history with dragons myself, having lived in the southern regions of this land as a child." Ojerren leaned forward and plucked a blade of grass. He spun it around in his fingers before he balled it up and flicked it towards the fire.

"Are you saying you've lived near where the dragons do?" I heard the hope in Zen's voice and felt he betrayed our mission with that one sentence.

"Yes, they lived in the mountains that overlooked our village. As a child, I would look up to the sky and watch on fascinated as they flew overhead with such power and grace. Life at that time was peaceful with those dragons at least. You see, there was a time when that was how dragons and humans lived. Everyone lived at peace without fear or worry, but with mutual respect. They would help humans if needed and vice versa."

"Must have been a very long time ago," I muttered.

"I am a little older than I look, Alexa," Ojerren said. He turned his face to the side. As he did, the hood surrounding his face fell away and revealed his smooth hair. He looked older than Leila, but not as old as Kaera, the oldest of the village and the former head of the elders. "You see, like any group of creatures, there are always those that follow the rules and those that choose not to. Why, I'm sure in your very village there are those who wouldn't break a sacred rule, but also those who would dare."

My legs lowered to the ground. I rested my hands on the ground and leaned backwards to look unconcerned by the statement. Inside I pushed down the guilt that rose. *Am I one of those rule-breakers?* Ojerren's mouth twitched before his attention went back to the fire.

"When I was probably your age, Zen, give or take, things began to change. Believe it or not, I was a strapping young man at that time, eager to make my mark on the world. But people changed, dragons changed. The peace that existed was swallowed up almost overnight. People no longer trusted the dragons, even though no one I asked could tell me why. Then the dragons stopped trusting the humans."

"Are you seriously trying to say humans are to blame for what the dragons are doing? That somehow it's all because they stopped trusting them? If that's not blaming the weaker of the two sides then I don't know what is," I stated.

"Not a human fault, no, not directly I would say. You see, when I finally left my village, I went to many places. In one I met a man much older than myself and he told me a story. A story about dragons I'd never heard before. It made me question what I thought and how I felt. Perhaps though, it failed to provide me the answer I wanted to my questions.

"As neither of you have interrupted, I will tell you the story the man told me. Many years ago, a woman fell in love with a dragon and the dragon with her. They had grown up as sort of neighbours and she had this gift of being able to talk to this dragon with her mind. She understood him, and he her. A rare gift, but even a gift can go wrong. Something happened that destroyed the bond the two had for one another. When the dust settled, all that remained of the love was the burden. The burden would affect each dragon that came into contact with the first. In time, the burden spread beyond that clan of dragons to others across the land."

"Burden?" Zen asked.

I turned to see he'd leaned forward. Something in the story captured his interest. Ojerren reminded me of a skilled storyteller and nothing more.

"That's what the dragons would come to call it: the burden. No one quite knows what it is or how it spreads, but what they do know is the consequences it had for the dragons. They are not the same once the burden touches them. It spreads so fast that many don't understand the changes they feel inside before it is too late."

"So you're saying dragons can't get rid of the burden and that might be why their behaviour changed over the years?" I asked and rolled my eyes for good measure. It seemed to me that Ojerren liked to make excuses for the dragons. In my mind, there was nothing accidental about their attacks. That last one was too strategic. Those dragons knew exactly what they were doing, and killing appeared to be the goal.

"Over the years I've heard whispers. Some say that maybe the burden can be removed by the one who placed it on them. That woman, however, has been dead for a long time. Until the dragons can work out a way to rid themselves of the burden, they will suffer for it and so will the humans."

"You're talking in circles, Ojerren. You spin a pretty tale but it tells nothing, it's too vague to be true," I said.

"Alexa!" Zen rebuffed.

"What? Aren't you listening? It's like some human came long and cursed a dragon with a sickness to punish dragons for all time. Please humans, forgive us for killing you all because, really, we didn't mean it. We just couldn't help ourselves because of the burden we bear. Piffle."

Zen shook his head. Two lines appeared on the ridge of his nose — the words had annoyed him. I tried to hold my tongue.

"How long ago do you think this happened? A hundred years? Two hundred? More than that?" Zen asked, and the man looked over the fiery divide at him.

"I don't know, Zen; it existed when I was a boy. People don't like to talk much about the past, especially the old people. They think the younger ones don't need to know and that, by saying nothing they are protected. I believe they're wrong to do that, by knowing the past you can shape your future. How much of it is truth and how much is fiction is anyone's guess, but I have no reason to doubt the validity of what I am told. Those men had nothing to gain. I am content in believing what I do."

"Now, you need to forgive me children, I have been walking for several days without a fire to warm me. I do hope that neither of you will not mind if I stay the night with you?"

Neither of Zen nor I had a chance to object to the man's proposal. He curled in a ball, bunching part of the hood underneath his head. His eyes closed and his breathing steadied. I envied how easy it had been for him to sleep; I yearned for that, and yet with Ojerren there, I felt on edge.

CHAPTER 11

"That was interesting, don't you think?" Zen asked.

I turned my head to him with my eyebrows raised. *Seriously, would he even attempt to go there?*

"You think so? I didn't think it sounded that interesting. You know what it sounds to me? Like someone who is making excuses for the dragons' behaviour."

"But what if there was something more to it, Alexa? You said the dragons never used to attack us in such a brutal, coordinated manner. That last attack was the first one that ever wiped out people in high numbers. For once, the dragon behaviour couldn't be excused for a need to carry off with our livestock. It makes sense that there would be something more to all this."

"Sure, the attack was horrific — I was there, remember? If you think I'm going to believe the word of some man we've met for the first time, you're mistaken. I'm not going to just be able to forgive the dragons and go back home and pretend everything is alright. The elders have always been there for us. Why would they lie about anything? The dragons attack and we fight."

Zen leaned back and propped himself up with his hands. His gaze remained on the flames.

"But Alexa, if there was something that was going on, then don't you think it's important to know that? It could change everything we know."

"Zen, why would I want to help the dragons?" I gritted my teeth. "Consider what exactly have the dragons ever done that was good for us or our village? Huh? Nothing? Not a single thing. All they have done is make our lives harder with more work and less time to enjoy living. And now, with over half the village dead, there is nothing else to blame except the dragons. Don't be so foolish to believe his silver tongue that tells pretty stories filled with excuses."

"But they might not be excuses, Alexa, can't you see that? We have lived a sheltered life in that valley. We don't get to meet people from outside the valley. We don't get to hear about their lives, their beliefs... Maybe the elders are retelling what they were told. What if no one had ever questioned it before? What if the story of the dragons somehow got twisted as each elder retold that story over the years? If the dragons aren't able to control their behaviour because of this burden, then we should work to solve that. There is nothing to gain by punishing them for something beyond their control."

"Actions have consequences, Zen. Besides, if you believe this man's story, only the woman that gave this burden to the first dragon can lift it. If she's been dead so long, then this discussion is over before it begins. Who are we to interfere with what somebody else did? I mean, if she gave the dragons some type of burden, how do we know they didn't deserve it? No, I think dragons have this burden because of their greed and bloodthirsty nature. It seems to me that any creature that would kill without mercy wouldn't be too concerned about accepting responsibility."

"Not everyone looks to shift blame, Alexa. Sometimes there are legitimate reasons why things happen."

"I don't believe that. Everyone is responsible for their own actions, no matter what it was. Look at it this way Zen, why would some dragon even be near a woman? And why would she fall in love with such a creature? I think if there is any truth to the tale, which I highly doubt, it was the dragon who cursed himself with the burden."

Zen's attention left the fire and turned to me. He didn't say anything, but tilted his head to the side. I shook my head and turned my gaze to the stars. I knew what his gesture meant and I was not going to budge. We didn't disagree on things often, but when we did, we usually shrugged it off. When I glanced back over at him, his jaw was set and that line on the bridge of his nose remained. I had the feeling that this might be harder for us to move past. Best friend or not, I had a duty to the elders to end all this. They took the time to train me, to make me into who I am; for that, they deserved to be repaid. It felt like a slap in the face to all that work with Zen trying to rationalise the enemy's behaviour.

"Don't look at me like that," I said.

"Alexa —"

"I need to check on my clothes," I said.

"Again?"

I ignored Zen and walked over to the stand. I wanted to kick myself. Why had I announced it? I didn't need permission. My hand ran over the fabric, though I could see they were still damp. Not a single piece had dried enough to wear. I rearranged a few of my undergarments so the larger clothing items concealed them.

From the corner of my eye, I watched Ojerren on the ground. Sound asleep and unfazed by the conversation that had occurred. I felt anger towards him. Who imposes their views on someone they just met?

I hoped Zen would see me busy at the stand. My hands idled on the shirt closest as I stared out into the darkness of the forest. I trusted Zen with my life, but it concerned me he would believe anything a stranger would tell him. Go against what we had always been told. I may not have always agreed with what the elders said, but I always listened.

"Maybe we should follow this man's example and get some rest? We've had a long day ourselves," Zen said.

I nodded. I should have turned around, curled up by the fire, and gone to sleep. Instead, I moved away towards the bushes. My feet didn't stop until the sound of the flames quietened, and I knew I had gone far enough. I desired my own company for a while. To clear the thoughts tainted by Ojerren's words. Zen would likely think I had gone off to do my business, which wasn't a bad idea.

In the solitude of the forest, I wanted to see Leila. So many questions I wished I'd asked. So many answers I would never have an answer to. I had been so certain of what I needed to do just days ago, but Ojerren's words messed with my thoughts, not just Zen's. I wanted to kick myself for the weakness. Tears welled, but I pushed them back. There would be plenty of time for tears after I accomplished the task.

I completed what I needed and turned to go back to the camp. I hoped Ojerren would leave us in the morning, and any doubts we might have would go with him. I wasn't convinced of that, Zen thought too deeply to push it aside and forget.

The warm glow flickered and beckoned me to return quicker. When I got back, I saw Zen curled up on the ground where I left him seated, a blanket over his body. Beside him I saw the thicker of the blankets there for me.

I smiled and felt some of the anger inside subside. Despite the disagreement, he had still been thoughtful. It didn't mean I wasn't still annoyed with him for what he said, but I knew he'd never say anything to hurt me, or out of spite. He liked to give his opinion, even if it was completely wrong.

As I passed the stand, I checked my clothes one more time in hope they would be dry enough to wear. The pants weren't too bad, so I pulled them on. I could feel the damp hems of the legs against my skin, but if I kept my feet close to the fire, I hoped the heat from the fire would finish the job while I slept.

I moved around Zen, careful not to disturb him, and crouched beside the blanket before I sat. I watched the flames dance for a while. Fire had always been associated with dragons. I couldn't remember a time from my past when I hadn't heard the tales of evil, destructive dragons.

In some ways I think it had been easier for the elders to stick to certain subjects. I asked Leila many times about my parents. She assured me they weren't dead, there were out there on a journey to another village. Leila promised me they would return, but I had given up on that. For me at least, they died a long time ago, whether real or imagined.

I curled up on the ground and used my arm as a pillow. My other hand grabbed at the blanket and threw it over my body haphazardly. There were more comfortable positions to lie in, but from there I could see both Zen and Ojerren. Despite a desire to stay awake, my eyelids felt heavy. The tiredness I felt earlier returned with a vengeance, and a yawn escaped.

"Good night, Alexa." He hadn't moved, but I knew Zen's voice.

"Good night, Zen," I whispered back.

CHAPTER 12

I wasn't sure how much sleep I had. My gaze had remained focused on Ojerren until my eyelids dictated it was time for me to sleep. Now I could see the trees lightened by the sunlight.

I remained still and watched Zen. He must have woken some time before me, as he had dismantled the fire pit already. Ojerren remained in the same position. The way he curled up in front of the fire reminded me of the stories the elders told of pets who loved the warmth from the fire, even after they had burned out.

I should move but I felt warm wrapped in the blanket. Zen turned around and looked my way before he came over and knelt beside me.

"Uneventful night. Our new friend over there hasn't moved at all since I got up," Zen said. "We can head off when you're ready. Your clothes are all dry. I'll grab them for you."

Grab wasn't how I would describe the way he

retrieved my clothes. Zen knelt down beside the stand and folded each piece. He managed to balance the pile of clothes on his knees until the stand stood empty. I watched as he brought them over to me.

"Thanks."

I sat up and took the pile from him. My shoulders shivered as the cold air hit where the blanket had fallen away. Zen smiled before he turned and began to fold his blanket.

After one last glance at Ojerren, I pushed the blanket aside, knowing Zen would pack it for me while I was gone. I picked up my harness and sword and left the camp. I remained in earshot as I relieved myself and took the moment of privacy to remove the clothes and redress without Zen's shirt. Normally I'd just scrunch discarded clothes onto a pile and let the houseman take care of them, but that felt wrong to do. It had a few dirt marks on it and I brushed them against my pants to try and dislodge them, but they stubbornly remained. Defeated in the art of cleaning clothes, I folded it the best I could. My hand brushed over the front of the shirt with the handmade wooden buttons at the front. The softness of the fabric had felt nice against my body. My own shirts had been woven with different fibres to make them thicker and more durable, and that meant they compromised on comfort. I raised my head and looked back towards the camp; nothing to be alarmed about.

Despite no calls for help, I had spent enough time away from Zen. I slung the harness over my head and adjusted the straps at the front until the pouch that contained the sword fit snug between my shoulder blades. I had to adjust one buckle to tighten it before I picked up the clothes and walked back.

A few birds in the canopy chirped as I made my way towards the camp. I noticed the bushes were full of leaves, but wondered where the flowers were. Back home, the bushes had started to flower already, and these looked the same as the ones on the edge of the village. I paused and pulled a leaf free from one bush. The softness of the leaf reminded me of a feather. I turned it over twice more before it floated to the ground.

When I entered the camp, I saw my prediction had been correct. Zen had folded and packed my things, ready to continue. My gaze fell on Ojerren. He brushed his sleeves with his hands to rid himself of a few leaves that had stuck to the fabric overnight. I wanted to chat with Zen, but with Ojerren there, I felt I couldn't do that. I couldn't trust a stranger even with general conversation.

"I can't help but notice that your supplies are running low," Ojerren commented.

I twitched at the reminder. We wouldn't be short

of food if the dragon hadn't attacked. My finger itched to touch the hilt of the sword. Zen looked toward me as he tied the top of his bag closed.

"We are low," Zen said.

"There is a town not far from here. It is actually where I had been headed to when I came across you last night. Let me repay your kindness of the meal you shared by offering to escort you there. You will find everything you need in order to continue the journey you are on."

Beside me, Zen nodded in agreement. I sighed at the little choice I seemed to have in the matter. To follow a strange man into a strange place was contrary to what Leila spent years teaching me.

I glared at the ground and hoped Zen would get a sense of my unhappiness with the situation. Perhaps it worked as I saw his feet come into view.

Zen leaned in close. "I know you're not happy about this Alexa, but we do need supplies. I think we can at least trust that he's taking us to a village and at that point we can separate. Even if you don't trust what his motives are, or anything else, we need to replace those lost supplies before we move on."

He appealed to my common sense because he knew I couldn't argue against it. I let out a soft growl. He must have heard it, as when I looked up he had a smile on his face. Damn it, he knew he'd won that one.

Sometimes that little glint he got in his eye could be a tad aggravating. Go I would, but I had made my objection.

Once Ojerren readied himself, we followed him out of the camp. My hand remained ready to draw my sword if Ojerren even thought about doing something nefarious. Zen walked beside Ojerren as he chatted about himself as a boy and the village he grew up in. I noticed how Zen listened, asked questions; he did what I should have.

I didn't mind Zen being ahead. It meant I had an unrestricted view of them both and what lay ahead. Periodically I looked up to check on the sun's position. We headed in a south-west direction for most of the walk, which suited where we planned to go. I hoped we would arrive at the village before night fell. As selfish and unwarrior-like as it sounded, I wanted something comfortable to sleep on.

"I think we should stop and rest for a bit," Ojerren said.

Both Ojerren and Zen turned to look at me.

"What? I'm fine. I don't need a rest," I said.

"Alexa, you might not need one, but I do. I'm not as young as you and believe it or not I get tired and hungry." Ojerren sat himself down on a fallen tree trunk nearby and stretched his legs.

Zen approached me and took off his pack.

"You sure you're okay? You look a little pink in the face."

I felt a little warm but we had crossed a lot of land. The sun was almost directly overhead. That meant we'd walked for at least four hours with little more than the occasional drink of water.

"I'm fine. Don't fuss," I said.

Zen had the pack on the ground and pulled out a pear. He offered it to me and I gratefully accepted.

"Remember, it's my job to fuss," Zen said.

I took a bite of the pear. The sweetness refreshed my mouth for a moment. I swallowed it. It seemed to take a long time to go down my throat. My mouth also felt dry.

"Alexa?"

I waved Zen off and found a space to sit down. The air felt warm. That probably accounted for the headache. Hot weather and a long walk weren't a brilliant combination. I took another bit of the pear and relived the same experience. By the time I took the last bite of the pear, I didn't feel hungry. I felt ill.

"Are we ready to continue?" Ojerren asked.

I wanted to punch him for his cheerful attitude. The air felt warm as I breathed it in. A hand appeared in front of my face, and I glanced up to see Zen. *Did I look that bad? That weak?*

"I'm fine, Zen."

"Alexa —"

"I'm fine."

To prove my point, I stood up and started to walk. I saw the creases on Ojerren's forehead as I approached, but lucky for him he said nothing. The sudden movement hadn't done me a favour. I felt sick and my body ached like when Leila made me complete the running course twice. I closed my eyes and took careful steps. My breathing. I just needed to focus on something. Ojerren's back seemed like a good idea to begin with, but after a while I had imagined slashing my sword across him to the point he was in shreds.

Ahead, Ojerren continued to chatter about random topics. He pointed out different plants, trees, and bushes as we passed them by. He knew a lot about them and included descriptions of their characteristics and uses. Zen seemed to pay particular attention to this. My interest in plants and animals only extended to whether it could be eaten or could kill me. Nothing else mattered. I paid a little more attention when Ojerren talked about a village where they only ate plants. I didn't think I could convince myself not to eat meat again, though it was rare for us this season anyway.

Despite my reservations, the trees thinned in the

afternoon, and a dirt road came into view. My feet ached, but at least being on the road required less effort than traipsing over grass and fallen logs. From there it didn't take long before I saw the familiar sight of chimney smoke as it rose above the trees. *Has it only been a couple of days since we left?* It felt like much longer.

I thought about what we needed. Besides food and water supplies, we would need to source a fresh change of clothes and a bag for me. I thought of the jar that had been in my bag, the contents of that would be another thing on my list, even though I wasn't fully certain what the elders' mix of herbs contained.

At the entrance of the village, Ojerren paused. I stood there and watched as he reached his hand out to Zen, who looked as puzzled as I felt.

"In these parts the handshake is a way of parting on good terms," Ojerren said.

Zen turned to look at me, and I shrugged.

"Thank you for bringing us here," Zen said. He took Ojerren's hand.

"I am sure we shall meet again."

Ojerren only nodded at me. Either handshakes weren't for women, or he knew better than to try. I watched as he moved off. His confident walk and lack of need to check his surroundings indicated he had been here before, most likely on a regular basis. Not only that, but this town put him at ease. He turned a corner and I lost sight of him.

Unlike Ojerren, who had walked away without so much as a second glance from anyone, Zen and I were the centre of attention. We walked into the village and several women turned to their children to usher them inside of homes and closed the door. Twice I'd seen the people peer out of the window to watch us as we walked further towards the village centre.

It seemed that strangers were treated this way. At least that's what I told myself. I felt under-prepared for the stares. They permitted only a select number of elders to leave the village, and they always returned with needed supplies. Those were the occasions that men would appear as well without recollection of where they were from. Those men had skills that were needed as sometimes no amount of training seemed to pass the talent on for certain jobs.

Sweat covered my hands. My skin crawled at the extra attention. I resisted the urge to draw my sword since no immediate threat presented itself, but I would've felt more comfortable with it in my hands.

I passed another woman who straightened herself and watched as we passed her by. She wiped her hands on her apron and then rested them on top of her large belly. Her hand paused, as if it would protect the unborn child from me. I couldn't understand that, how those expecting a baby carried on. My sister had behaved similarly before she died. Sometimes a woman died, and the baby lived, but the trade of lives didn't seem equal to me.

I noticed women tended to children as we passed them by. I saw another woman with the washing basket on her hips, another cooking on an outdoor stove. Some men were doing the same, but I noticed they were also working in the fields. It seemed apparent why I drew attention with the sword so prominently on my back. Things here were not the same as our village.

Zen's elbow connected with my ribs. I needed to have a word with him about getting my attention. He nodded towards a well that stood next to a shed. A large tree partially concealed it from view from where we stood. It seemed to be the place Ojerren had recommended we go to earlier in the day.

"I see it," I said. "Anything to get away from all the attention."

"Come on Alexa, you like attention."

"I like attention when people are admiring my sword skills, this type of attention just makes me uncomfortable."

"Things are definitely different to what we're used to."

CHAPTER 13

We approached the shed. The darkness within it made me cautious, and I stepped ahead of Zen. I needn't have worried. A large woman emerged from the darkness and wiped her hands on the stained apron she wore. She then took out a cloth from a pouch on the front and then gave her hands another wipe. When she looked up, she didn't exactly smile, but nothing about her demeanour gave me a reason to be defensive. She kept her distance as she stuffed the cloth back into the pouch. We paused on the road; distance would still be a smart decision.

"What brings you to our village?" she asked.

I decided to take the lead before Zen said something I wouldn't be happy about. "We are just travellers in need of supplies."

She nodded back up the road. "Is interesting company you've been keeping with that old man. Some say that he comes from the south. Is that where you're both from as well?"

I shook my head. "No, no, no we're from the northern regions."

"Then why head south? There is nothing this way except dragons that rule the skies and people that run for their lives."

"It's no different where we are from," I commented. That had been unnecessary. I would kick myself later for it, but for the moment I had cornered myself. "Our village was also attacked and so we are heading south to see if we can find any answers as to why the dragons would be attacking with such ferocity."

The woman laughed. "What? You two young'uns think you can go and solve the big mystery of why the dragons are attacking?"

"I don't see why we should be dismissed. I've been trained all my life to fight. It's my opinion we have to tackle the dragons head-on rather than wait in our village to be killed," I commented.

"You know what you both should do? 'Cause you look tired, you look in need of some time to relax. I suggest you go across the road into that big ol' building and you tell 'em that ol' Stevie sent you. You ask for a forget-me-not."

I took a few steps towards the well but continued to watch Stevie as she chuckled to herself. She lost interest in us and returned to the darkness of the shed. I could feel the stone of the well against my legs as I reached out for the handle.

"Let me do it," Zen said.

He had the handle in his hand before I did and wound it down. I heard the bucket hit the water below. I couldn't see the bucket as I leaned over the edge of the well, but the rope passed my sight as I waited for Zen to bring it to the surface.

"What do you think she means by all that talk?" Zen asked as he grabbed the bucket.

"Why do you think I would know more than you? I've never heard of such a thing," I said. "Do you know what she's talking about?"

Something about that slight smile on his face made me wonder if he knew, or at least had a good idea, what she had been referring to.

"Not really," he replied.

"Well, since we don't know these people, let alone their intentions, I don't think it's wise we listen to what 'ol' Stevie' says," I hissed back as he tightened the lid on the water canister. "Besides, it was bad enough you hung on every word that Ojerren said the past day. I don't think I care to go into some strange place and... I don't know... consume something that will have goodness knows what effect on us."

"We can't keep pushing south without supplies and this late in the day we're unlikely to get very far."

"I need to end all this Zen. If we stop here for no good reason, then what does that make us?"

"What does it make us? It makes us human, Alexa. Come on, after the last couple of days, who would it hurt? Let's spend one night enjoying ourselves, refreshing ourselves. You never know, we might actually enjoy it before we have to face whatever it is that we are going to face out there. And don't be so hard on Ojerren, I liked him."

"You know Zen, that's the problem. You trusted in him too easily. You never trust people so easily. Why him?"

"I don't know. There was something about him. Something that, I guess it came across as being truthful. I could believe what he said."

I pointed my finger at him. "See, that's the difference between us. I didn't believe a word that came out of his mouth. As far as I'm concerned, he was making excuses and using his words to be dishonest. Leila often says… said how clever men will use their tongue to get into the good favour of others."

With the water container filled, I turned and looked to the building the woman had pointed out. The elders had dictated so much of our lives. I knew we should keep going, but a part of me knew this was an opportunity to make my own decision, experience something new. *Is it normal to want to break the rules for no other reason than because?*

"Come on," Zen said.

Together we walked across the dirt road and approached the large building opposite from the shed. The size of the building was comparable to the Hidden, but I'd never heard such noises coming from there. The chatter of people drifted through the half-doors that hung to enter. Music played as well, not just the drums like I had become accustomed to, but different sounds, some metallic sounding and others... my curiosity had been piqued to find out more.

We ascended the four wooden steps onto the little veranda. Zen reached ahead and pushed open the door for me and I walked through into the building. It took a moment for my eyes to adjust to the dimness inside. I saw people at tables who talked in hushed voices to those beside them. Others loudly drowned out the music that played from the corner. On the tables I saw drinks of all colours: blue, purple, yellow, a green one that made my stomach turn a little as my mind associated it with something else.

I felt out of my comfort zone. There were too many people to watch for danger. The noise level didn't help either. Zen stepped up to the counter at the back of the room we had entered and leaned on the wooden surface.

A man on the other side of the counter raised his head and nodded at Zen.

"A couple of strangers have found their way to my humble establishment," the gruff voice commented. He wiped a glass with a cloth before he placed it on the counter. "Well, what would you like?"

Zen turned back to look at me, and I shrugged.

"Stevie said that we should ask for forget-me-not."

The man behind the counter chuckled. "Yeah, that sounds like Stevie. She's got good taste for a woman. It's a nice little drink that's bright blue. Will the young lady have one too?"

I nodded. The man reached under the long, polished wooden counter. My hand gripped the bottom of my shirt, and I hoped his hand wouldn't hold a weapon when it appeared again. I relaxed when I saw two small glasses in his hand. He looked up and smiled at us as he placed the glasses in front of us. Turning around, he surveyed the array of bottles and jars that sat on glass shelves. He reached for a tall bottle that was half-filed with a blue liquid. I watched as the liquid sloshed in the bottle as he spun back to us. With a pull, the cork was free of the bottle. He filled each glass and held out his free hand.

Zen reached into his pocket, pulling out two small gold chips. He looked at me and I shrugged. I had no idea what the drinks would cost. We had never had much use for the gold the elders paid us yearly, but clearly they knew it had value outside of the village. The man pointed to the smaller of the two, and Zen handed it over. After inspecting the gold, he placed the bottle onto the counter and pushed it towards us with a nod, then made his way to another customer.

"I guess we get the whole lot," Zen said.

I picked up the glass and looked at the liquid. If it hadn't been blue, it would have looked like a glass of water. I raised the glass to my nose and sniffed. It was an unfamiliar smell and I tried to decipher. It didn't smell sweet, but a bit like some spices the elders would bring back to the village on their supply journeys. I had seen the different spices in jars, lined up on racks, ready to be used. Many times I'd wanted to know what they tasted like since they were so vivid in colour and smell, but the elders preferred to keep those and the cooks received the other spices.

"I guess it's now or never," I said.

I gulped the liquid down. A little sweet but it didn't taste horrible. In fact, the taste lingered as I put the glass back on the counter.

"Well?" Zen asked.

"It's good. In fact, I think I'll have another."

The silence differed from what I had become accustomed to. Bugs chirped as my eyes focused on the stars that blanketed the sky above us. It wasn't often I had the chance to stare at the sky. The stars twinkled and I noticed they weren't even the same colour.

"Makes you think, doesn't it?"

"Huh?" I turned to Zen. He lay beside me on the roof of the building. I couldn't remember how we'd even gotten on the roof. Much of the past few hours were blurry.

"The stars, they've been up there so long, seen so much. They were there before us, they'll see us grow up, and then they'll continue on after we're gone."

"Sounds sad for them," I muttered. There seemed no point in watching people from afar as their lives went on day in and out. In fact, it sounded rather boring.

"No, think about how much they've seen Alexa. They probably saw what happened with the dragons. They probably know the answer to how to rid them of the burden. They would have seen us born, they'll see us in the years to come..."

"Zen, I don't even think that much about the years to come."

"I have. I can see exactly how I want my future to be. The men having more of a role in the village now that many of the elders are gone, I mean, look here — there are men who do more than just the cooking, cleaning, and raising children."

"There are, but everyone has a role to play, Zen. It's how the village stays in balance."

"It's never stopped you inviting me along to training."

"But that's different. I can't help but wonder if there was a reason behind it. There had to be."

"Forget the elders for a moment. What about you, Alexa? What do you want to do?"

I exhaled and watched the little cloud that appeared above my face as it blended with the night. "I don't know. Maybe be an elder one day."

"Elders remain solitary. Leila taking you under her wing was out of the ordinary."

I shrugged. "I've never imagined myself with kids and all that."

"Never imagined yourself spending a life with someone else?"

A warmth spread across my face. *Thank the day for the night.*

"I don't know."

"I can see you with someone, being a mother and

yet still being an elite."

I felt something brush against my hand. I saw Zen's hand had moved closer to my own where it rested on the wooden planks. My fingers rose from the roof. *What am I supposed to do?*

"Alexa, don't you think that maybe..."

When I turned my head, I saw Zen looking at me. I had thought about it, but he deserved someone who could give him the life he imagined. I wasn't convinced I could make him happy, maybe for a while, but you never knew what the future might bring.

"I don't know," I said.

"Is there someone else you'd rather be with?"

A laugh broke the tension. "No, no, it's not like that, Zen. You're my best friend and I guess... I guess I'm afraid that maybe it wouldn't be the same, that..."

"How will we know unless you give it a chance? I've loved you for years Alexa. There will only be you for me."

"I'm an elite, Zen. I don't have that choice."

He rolled onto his side and reached out with his hand towards me. His fingers ran down the side of my face and into my hair. He moved his body closer to mine, and the distance between us failed to exist. I looked up at his face, the line of his jaw, the fullness of his lips. My heart beat faster, bringing back thoughts of the forest and seeing him shirtless.

"Maybe everything that has happened was for a reason. We're not in the village anymore."

CHAPTER 14

The sun seemed too bright, too happy, and too early. I blinked a few times as my eyes struggled to adjust to the cheeriness of the day. My eyelids tried to return me to darkness several times, so I forced myself to sit up. The blanket fell to my lap and I stretched out my arms, rolled my head, and circled my shoulders. I had slept well, maybe too well. It had been a while since I'd spent the night actually asleep and not listening for danger. I had meant to keep watch for a bit though.

The trees hadn't changed from the previous night, other than the way the light now lit them up. Jiggling my legs, I tried to shift the last of the sleep. I turned to see Zen asleep beside me, his mouth open slightly. My mouth twitched at the view. It wasn't the most flattering of states to see someone in.

It seemed hard to recall any details of the previous night. I remembered collecting the fresh water when we arrived in the town. Then we had gone to that large building, the inn. Stars twinkled in my memory and I remembered them and... my fingers touched my lips. *Was that real or am I still half asleep and being haunted by a dream?* The memory felt real at least.

With the landscape now in focus, I rubbed my forehead to alleviate the dull ache. A glass of blue liquid flashed to mind — forget-me-not. That had been what Stevie had suggested we ask for at the old building. The name of the drink was accurate enough.

"What time is it?" Zen asked and then yawned. His outstretched hands came into my peripheral view.

I looked back at him. "Mid-morning at least, judging by the sun's height."

"We slept that long?"

"I'm not sure," I replied.

"Everything's a bit of a blur, isn't it?"

"I think it was the drink."

He nodded. "I think you're right. Best that we avoid that until we've dealt with the dragon issue."

The dragons. It wasn't an issue. He might be concerned about that burden, but I felt just as happy cutting them down. A dead dragon can kill no one.

"What's that?" Zen asked.

I spun around as he reached across, close to where my head had been before. He pushed my sword aside and picked up a piece of paper. He sat up and I crawled to his side to get a look at the contents as he unfolded it.

"If you want to know about the dragons, then go south-west along the mountain trail next to the dancing tree. Follow it until you pass through two tunnels that will appear to be caves. After the second cave, go through the waterfall and you will find something of interest. This journey will take you no more than a couple of days."

"So someone has left us a cryptic note that we're meant to just follow?" I said.

"Seems so. I mean, they could have slit our throats in the night, I certainly heard nothing at all." Zen turned the note over and held up the blank side.

"Me neither, and that worries me a little."

"What do we have to lose?"

"Our lives. The lives of the villagers back home…"

"But what if there are answers there? Something that could help the dragons?" Zen looked at me as I stared at him, stony-faced. "What if there is information about how to destroy them?"

I rolled my eyes. *Damn it, he had a point.*

"Okay, why not, it's only a day or so, right? And it's sort of in the direction we're heading anyway, but if there is nothing there, then no more detours. I have dragons to hunt down and kill and I want to do it before winter arrives."

"Deal."

Zen packed up our belongings while I read and reread the letter. It was nice of them to include the little diagram as well, but a direction on it would have helped. I assumed it was drawn so that it faced south west. I turned it up the other way and doubt crept into that assumption.

"Thought they taught you how to read maps," Zen said as he snatched the map from my grip.

I looked at him and saw he had already turned it up the way I had it to begin with. "They did, but they also taught the importance of creating clear maps so anyone can understand it without second guessing it."

"It's clear, we go that way."

"You assume."

Zen smiled. "I confess! I am assuming it was drawn by a man who thought it would be blindingly obvious to draw the map the way that made most sense."

"And what if a blade sliced off part of the note in the night when I had? It wouldn't be so obvious then, would it? That's why you put the heading on the map." I pointed my finger at him.

His hands went up in mock defence. "Okay, okay, they're a shit map maker. Noted that should I ever draw one, I will put the heading on there."

"Good, you're learning well."

Zen stepped forward and hit my shoulder as I passed. I would seek my revenge for that later, but right now it seemed as if we would have a lot of walking ahead of us. I hated walking. We did so much of it in training to be prepared to run for long distances and still be able to wield a sword to cut down a dragon, or a man. I had thought that funny when I was younger, how Leila and the other elders would sometimes group men and dragons into the same group as if they were as bad as each other.

Looking back now, Leila probably suspected something between me and Zen. With so few males in the village, they were both needed and shunned at the same time. The elders had many rules applied to men that didn't apply to women. One rule Leila would often repeat was that men couldn't be trusted. She never said that about dragons — those we were free to kill without question. But men, men could use words and words can lie.

I had laughed it off each time Leila had brought it up. I trusted Zen to tell the truth. He wouldn't lie to me, or at least, he'd never given me a reason to think he was lying. If he disagreed with me, he told me, there was never a reason to make up a lie, because lies were for people who had something to hide and we knew everything about each other. Even as we weaved around bushes and clambered over fallen trees with singe marks on them, we were a team.

"I think that's our tree up ahead," I said.

A tree with a trunk that branched out in two directions stood ahead of us. Each branch that grew on the tree seemed destined to make its own winding path towards the sky. Its canopy towered high, thick with dark green leaves with white stripes.

When we finally reached it, I paused to look up from the base. Not one of the branches I saw grew straight. It did indeed resemble a dancer, with the branches stretched out as arms and the leaves acting as a shawl, fan, or some other fancy thing to make people stop and watch them for a while.

"What do you think makes it grow like that? Apart from its deformity, it appears to be the same trees as all the others around here," Zen said. He reached up and pulled one leaf off. An aroma filled the air as he rubbed it between his fingers.

"Kind of a sweet smell," I remarked. Some of the women wore special water in the village that would make them smell differently; most of those were the ones removed from the warrior league. "Any way, why do you assume this tree is the different one? Perhaps it's normal and all these other trees are deformed."

The leaf fell from Zen's fingers. I turned and hit against his shoulder to return the favour as I strode past him.

"That was pretty thoughtful, what you said back there."

I turned to see Zen fall into step beside me. He held the map in his hand again, looked up, and then tucked it away in a pocket in his pants.

"If you say so."

"Alexa, you have a mind that thinks so differently. Just think what you could achieve in your life if you thought beyond your training."

"Maybe, but making a comment about a tree doesn't add much value to our village. Killing a dragon keeps them safe. Killing a thief keeps their hope. It's all a big circle, Zen, where everything relies on everything else falling into its place."

"Doesn't mean the circle can't be expanded out, though. People grow, villages grow — shouldn't that circle accommodate that as well?"

I opened my mouth, but words failed to justify my standpoint. I wanted to blame the forget-me-not but I knew he had a point. When I looked ahead, Zen had started up a small pebble path. My shoes wouldn't go well on that path, and I wished I had my other shoes still. *Darn dragon.*

We followed the path for some time as it wove around the mountain. My feet constantly slipped on the pebbles, and I cursed every time I had to catch my balance by slamming the sword into the ground. Zen seemed to have fewer issues dealing with it.

We arrived at the first cave when we took a sharp turn to the left. I gratefully stepped onto the hardened dirt as the pebbles scattered away. The cave had an opening big enough for Zen to walk into without having to duck his head. It appeared set into the mountain itself, much like the cave we had gone through after I survived the dragon attack. A pink leafed plant grew along the edge of the cave's arch. Leaves hung down in places, and yet it wasn't a vine. I'd never seen a plant with pink leaves, so many new things to discover. I sheathed my sword to free my hands.

Zen stood at the mouth of the cave, peering inside. I turned my attention to the leaves. I pulled a couple of leaves from the side of the cave and held them in the palm of my hand. They were soft, like feathers on a baby chick. I turned the leaves over to see the underside had a darker shade of pink. The veins of the leaves were much easier to see on that side as well. Lifting it to my nose, I checked for a scent of any kind. Nothing; not like the leaves Zen had crushed before. Still, I wished I had thought to barter for a new bag. I felt awkward asking Zen to put them in his. Sure, they wouldn't make any difference, but I wanted to be responsible for my own things.

"Alexa," Zen asked and I turned to look at him. "You ready to see where it goes?"

I turned back to the pink leaves. Lots of the girls liked pink, some even mixed the crushed petals of the ranna plant with water to make a thick pink paste which they then applied to their lips and sometimes to their cheeks. I had never tried it; the women who got reassigned did it, especially if they accepted a partner during the coupling. Still, holding the leaves in my hand made me want to try to make it, maybe wear it. Not that I wanted to wear it for anyone… I looked back at Zen and he nodded towards the darkness, completely unaware of my thoughts.

"Bring it if you want."

"No pockets," I replied. My hand turned over and I watched the leaves until they rested on the ground.

"You could have put them in the bag."

I shook my head. "They're just leaves."

I walked over to him, peering into the cave. I would have felt better if I could have seen some kind of light, something to assure me I wasn't about to walk into some kind of dragon lair and be burnt to a crisp. My body shuddered at the thought.

"You want to go in first?"

"Sure," I said, my hand ready to grab the sword if I needed it.

Stepping into the darkness, I felt the cool air surround me. My eyes took a moment to adjust to the change. It had curved walls of stone that appeared to be bare. A breeze came from somewhere to the right and I squinted my eyes to try and see where it possibly came from, but the only thing I could see was more darkness.

I felt something touch my neck. My hand whipped up to my neck and batted it.

CHAPTER 15

"Ouch Alexa," Zen said as he gave his hand a rub.

"I thought it was a spider!"

"You really need to deal with that fear."

"Let me deal with dragons first; they're not as scary."

Zen laughed, and I took a step in the breeze's direction. Somewhere water dripped into a pool below. The cave smelt dry though. I had expected it to have more of a moist, musty smell. My feet moved easily over to the polished rock. I wondered if perhaps water ran directly through the cave during the winter.

I reached my hand out to the wall as the light from behind faded to nothing. We must have come around a corner. The darkness surrounded us and I couldn't even see my hand in front of me. If we were attacked, I would be in a poor defensive position. My steps became smaller.

A mass crashed into me from behind. I heard Zen

mutter something under his breath. Served him right for not slowing down. With each step I took, I listened for any sound other than the breeze travelling through the tunnel and the padding of our feet on the dirt. I took another step and sunlight blinded me. My arm went up to shield the light. I peeked over my arm to allow my sight to adjust, but the light continued to bombard my eyes.

Turning my head, I saw Zen similarly shield his eyes behind me. There had been no warning as we had followed the path, and the turn of the path hadn't seemed that sharp. I ventured another glance towards the light; it hadn't abated.

"I think we'll need to just go for it," I said.

Zen's free hand reached out and caught my hand. "Just in case there's a sheer drop."

"Fair enough," I replied, though I was happy to have the reassurance.

With my arm still protecting my eyes, I took small steps in the direction of the light. The breeze died down and I lowered my arm a little. The intensity lessened and my arm fell to my side. I took another step and the view beyond the light came into view.

A blue sky sat above the landscape below. A forest of trees of varying colours spread like a blanket below. I heard a faint roar and looked up and saw a black dragon flying towards a mountain in the distance in the south. My feet had come to a standstill as I stood on the edge of the sheer cliff. I noticed a path continued off to my left, but I turned back to take in the sight.

"Wow," Zen said as he stood beside me. "That's a breathtaking view."

"It's make me think it might be possible to fly in the air one day. Can you imagine seeing such sights at a whim?"

"Something to aim for in the future?" Zen squeezed my hand.

"I think I could put that on a list," I replied. The air tasted fresh, clean, and light. I would have liked to have stayed longer, but there would be time enough for that on the way back. "Come on, we need to keep moving."

"Just a moment more," Zen said and I felt his hand squeeze mine again.

When I looked up at his face, his eyes looked ahead at the mountain where the dragon continued to hover and glide. I suspected that his attention was on the dragon rather than the mountain, but no harm could come from watching. Even I could appreciate the dragon from that distance as it flew with grace with its wings outstretched, catching the air in a way that kept it at a steady height. When I kill one, I would have to remember to take a better look at the way the wings were constructed. That could prove to be useful knowledge as we continued to fight against them.

"Okay, I guess we go that way," Zen said and took a step in the direction of the path.

His hand pulled on mine. I took one last look at the dragon before checking the ground ahead. I felt grateful to see the path of hardened dirt continued. I loosened my fingers against Zen's hand, justifying it to myself that it would be easier to climb with my arms free. He turned and looked back at me for a moment, smiled, and his grip freed my hand.

"I'll lead the way since I can read the map."

"Hey, we had that discussion before. It's not the reader's fault, it's poor map drawing," I replied.

The path wove away from the cliff edge, and stout trees with dark green leaves appeared on both sides. Grass covered the ground but had been fenced off by nature with a row of rocks beside the path on either side. *Maybe not nature, nature isn't that exact, but if not by nature, then who had taken the time to build such a thing in an isolated area such as this?*

By the time the second cave came into view, the sun shone down directly on us. The possibility of doing the journey in a day seemed unlikely, just another way the note had been inaccurate. There were no pink leaves framing this cave's entrance that looked slightly crooked with the right side higher. A vine with green leaves snaked down to the top of the entrance.

"Did you want to…?"

I shook my head, and Zen nodded. He didn't wait for me this time and was swallowed by the darkness. I knew the map would say that we wouldn't be far from wherever it led. I doubted that we should have gone there. If we'd continued on, we might have found a dragon by now.

"Alexa, hurry up," Zen's voice called out.

I sighed and walked into the cave. A soft light replaced the darkness as I stepped further away from the sun's light. This cave had something growing on the walls that illuminated. Looking up, I saw the twinkles of light all around, like stars at night. I couldn't resist. Stepping up to the nearest wall, my hand reached out and brushed against the glow. On closer inspection I saw flowers, so tiny they were half the size of my little fingernail, were responsible for the sight.

"These are so fascinating. I wonder what makes them glow?" I said.

Zen waited for me to close the distance, but said nothing. I passed him by and felt his hand brush against my waist. Taking the lead, we followed the path that twisted back and forth. The little flowers made the climb easier than the last.

Light filtered from the left side ahead, and I smiled. At least this time, we didn't have the sun attempting to blind us. I paused and turned to see how far behind Zen was, surprised to find him coming around the last bend.

"Looks like we've at the end of this one. What was next on the map?"

"Oh, hang on," Zen said and retrieved the map from his pocket. He turned over the paper and leaned it against the flowers. I could see the blue glow on the paper as Zen's finger traced over the picture. "The waterfall and then we're there."

Waterfall. I'd forgotten about that. It seemed hard to believe that a waterfall could be found so high up the mountain. We had been climbing for over half a day and the thought of a refreshing water shower sounded good.

I stepped into the dull light. We had to be on the east side of the mountain since the light shone on the side. Before me I saw a plateau of rich, green grass that reached up to my knee. My hair tickled at my face from the breeze and I looked up to see the mountains that loomed over the area. I turned around on the spot and took in the view. The mountains rose up on all sides, and yet... *How does the light filter through the doorway? This valley has too much light for such high surroundings.* Zen came into view, and I stopped turning.

"Wow."

"It doesn't make sense."

"My exclamation?"

"This place. Where is the light coming from? I mean, look above and you can see the sun over there, somewhere behind this mountain, but down here it should be in shadow. How is it that this place is like this?"

Zen's eyes darted around the mountains and lines creased his forehead. He looked around again. It wouldn't matter if he looked fifty times the answer would be the same — the valley we were in defied nature.

"It's weird," he said. His eyes then moved to the surrounding sea of leaves. "You don't think there's anything lurking in this, do you?"

"Afraid some capai is lurking?"

"Hey, stories of those critters gave me nightmares as a kid."

I laughed, though I shouldn't have. The stories we'd been told about the capai were almost worse than the stories about dragons. Capai were said to be solitary animals about the size of a human head.

Their bodies were covered in these needles, and each needle was capable of killing. The stories always included some hapless teen walking through an unfamiliar field of grass, blissfully unaware of the predator that preferred to remain concealed in the shadowed grass, waiting for its victim to come close. Once the capai chose to attack, it would barrel through the grass at such speed that the victim would hear it but not see it until it had already thrown its body against the leg. A needle, ripped from the capai and now embedded into the soft flesh of the victim, would begin to pump in the deadly toxin it contained. Paralysed, the victim would collapse to the ground and the capai would move in, baring the hundreds of sharp teeth to its prey. Almost always the victim would be eaten while still alive. Despite the number of stories we'd been told, I had never heard a single first-hand account.

With the capai stories still spinning in my head, I lifted my leg and took a step into the grass. My foot came down, and I froze to listen for any rush of movement. There were a couple of shadowed areas on the grass not far from where I planned to walk. Now I hesitated. Perhaps the waterfall wasn't in that direction.

"Who's afraid of the prickly beast now?" Zen's said in a sing-song voice.

"I'm not afraid, I'm being strategically cautious."

I turned to see his eyebrows high on his forehead. "Are you sure the waterfall is over there? I don't want to walk through this if I don't have to."

"The map says it is." Zen looked to each side and then back at me. "Besides, it's not going to matter where we walk, we're going to have to conquer that."

He pointed at the grass. I shouldn't have raised the topic of capai. Trying to be smart and brave and all that; the capai now made the damn spider look like a pet. With my attention back to where we're headed, I closed my eyes and started to walk. It's so much easier to concentrate on what you can hear if you don't have to worry about what you can see. Of course, if you walk into something then it becomes a stupid thing to do. In order to avoid looking foolish, I periodically opened my eyes to check the tree with the purple and gold leaves was still ahead.

Swoosh.

I stopped and drew my sword and batted it at the grass around my legs. Nothing appeared. I waited; I had heard something that didn't belong. The pounding in my chest spread so that the sound deafened my ears. Sweat covered the hilt of the sword as I tightened my fingers around it. *Swoosh.*

"Run for it!" I yelled.

I ran with the sword in one hand, hoping Zen wouldn't get too close. My eyes darted from the tree ahead to the grass at my feet. At any moment a capai would appear. I knew this had been a bad idea to come! The grass thinned and I could see my legs clearly as I slowed down and stopped at the tree trunk. Purple and gold leaves fell from the branches above like rain, and I spun around to see Zen clear the grass as well.

"Did you see one?" Zen asked as he bent over breathing heavily.

"I heard something."

Swoosh.

My free hand grasped the hilt and I turned. A small grey bird with tail feathers three times its size stared up at me. It opened its beak and…

Swoosh.

"What type of bird makes a swoosh sound?" I said, surely the fluff ball wasn't real.

"Apparently that one."

The little bird cocked its head to the side. It opened its beak and said, "That one."

If I hadn't been looking at the bird, I would have sworn Zen had said the words. He stepped up beside me and knelt down. I wasn't that keen to get a closer look. Something about a creature that could pretend to be something else made me uneasy.

"That's fascinating," Zen said and held his hand

out towards the bird.

The bird leaned back. Its little eyes looked at each of Zen's fingers in turn. Zen steadied his hand just away from it; it could have fitted easily in Zen's hand if it wanted to. Apparently it didn't. Its beak moved forward and bit the closest finger. It held on as Zen stood up, swearing under his breath and shaking his hand as the bird held on.

"Get it off, Alexa!"

I sheathed my sword. No need for overkill. Zen continued to spin around in a circle with his newest accessory. The bird had its tail features displayed, showing a pattern of red and gold with what looked like a giant eye in the middle.

"You're going to have to stand still if you expect me to help."

"It hurts, Alexa. Stop laughing and get it off my finger!"

Zen faced me, but he still jogged on the spot. I moved forward to his outstretched hand to see blood running down either side of the bird's beak. It had its eyes closed and had braced itself against his finger with his claws.

"Come on little birdy. The big scary monster didn't mean to frighten you. You be a good birdy and let go," I cooed and gently ran my finger over the soft body of the bird. It opened its eyes and focused on me. The tail feathers began to group together. I held my hand out below Zen's. The bird's claw left Zen's finger and tentatively touched my palm, before its other claw followed. Its neck stretched to keep its hold, and finally the beak opened. Zen stepped backwards and cradled his hand. The bird turned on my hand before nestling down; its beak still stained with Zen's blood.

"It's cute. Can I keep it?"

I looked at Zen to see a glare that gave me my answer. My lips curled up as I tried in vain to stop the laughter from escaping. While he continued to nurse his injured pride, I looked around and saw a nest on the ground near the base of the tree. I gently coaxed the bird into it and then backed away, leaving it to its domain.

"Let's get going," Zen said.

He strode past me in the direction the map must have said the waterfall would be. I looked back at the little bird and made a mental note to stop and say goodbye on the way back down the mountain. I'd never heard of a bird that could mimic, but it reminded me of a travelling show that passed through the village before my training began. The people had been different from us. Both men and women performed tricks as we watched on. One woman in the group could mimic anyone's voice or sound, she'd had this curly dark red hair that she wore loose; it reminded me of the bird's tail display. My mind focused on what I could remember of the introductions, trying to think of her name. Fiya. They called her Fiya.

I smiled at the little bird. Its eyes were closed and its wing covered its beak. "I'll see you soon, Fiya," I whispered. The bird didn't respond.

"Alexa! You coming or not?"

I made my way in the direction of Zen's voice, following the disturbed dirt and flattened tufts of grass. I wasn't as good at tracking as him, but I wasn't completely hopeless at it either. He stood there waiting on the path. The corner of his shirt had been torn, and I saw the missing piece wrapped around his finger.

"Gotta watch those little birdies," I said grinning.

"You're more worried about that bird than my finger," he chided.

"I call that justified defence. I totally approve of Fiya's instinct."

"Fiya? You named the nasty bugger?"

I shrugged. "It didn't bite me. Plus, that's one smart bird."

"How so?"

When I reached Zen, I paused and took his hand to get a better look at the bandage, he'd done a good job considering he'd used his right hand to wrap it. I tapped the bandage gently and looked up at him.

"Because that bird mimics."

"I know that."

I released his hand and took a step past him, ready to continue up the dirt track I could just make out. "So what made the swoosh sound then? Huh? Think about that."

He didn't reply, and I imagined the look on his face when it dawned on him what I had suggested. The thought gave me a creepy feeling as well, especially considering we'd have to go through the grass on the way back. Still, that would be a problem to face later.

It didn't take long for the trees to abate on the sides and more rocks to appear scattered over the path and larger ones to the side. Somewhere ahead, I could hear water moving in unison. We were almost at our destination.

When the waterfall came into view and my breath caught in my throat. The water tumbled over rocks up high from the mountain we were on. Crystal clear, the water fell down to... I peered over the edge and saw a small lake being pounded with the water as it hit the surface. It looked like that lake then continued off on its own journey as a river, snaking down and around the side of the mountain and out of sight.

A clear path lead around to the waterfall and I felt relieved that it was a comfortable width and I wouldn't need to second guess where I put my feet down as I walked. Zen stood silently beside me, watching the flow of water.

"We need to go through that, right?" I asked.

Zen nodded without moving his gaze. The mountain adventure we were on certainly attempted to reward us with spectacular views, if nothing else. Leaving Zen to stare, I walked on the smooth stone ledge. The side of the mountain continued to ascend on one side. I looked up to see the blue sky remained, but couldn't find the sun to get a feeling for how long we had before night would fall again.

I approached the waterfall, feeling the wet spray on my face and hands. The closer I walked to it, the clearer I saw the darkness behind the waterfall, the path leading behind the water. I made my way behind the waterfall, careful to avoid the water that would surely have pulled me down to the lake with it. When I peered into the cave, there was no need for glowing flowers or setting some naja on fire because I could see exactly what whoever left the map had wanted us to see.

CHAPTER 16

The truth about the dragons supposedly sat before us. I didn't doubt that the place we stood staring would indeed tell us something about them. Framed by the cave opening, a temple with a beautiful tended garden surrounding all sides of it beckoned for us to come nearer.

Zen went to step around me, but my arm blocked his path. It looked enticing, too enticing. From where we stood in the cave, the sky wasn't visible, but this seemed like dragon property to me. I took the lead after drawing my sword, wanting to be prepared for anything unexpected. When I reached the edge of the cave, I took the chance to check the sky. I couldn't see any dragons hovering above, waiting to make us a meal.

I relaxed my shoulders a little, but kept my grip on the sword. I walked around the path and watched for any sign of movement in the low bushes on either side of us, for any sound that didn't belong. When we reached a closed gate, I crouched in front of it. My fingers traced over the bent metal that formed two dragons facing each other, only torn apart whenever the gate would be opened.

"There has to be someone here. There's no way this naturally looks like this," Zen hissed as I stood up.

"We won't find out anything unless we go to the temple."

"A temple for dragons; why would they need a temple?"

"Why did our elders have the Hidden?" I countered.

"Fair point."

Still, despite my argument, I felt eyes watching us and I drew my sword to be safe. The eyes of a giant stone dragon that sat in the middle of one of the intricate gardens glared down at us as we passed it by. Each time a breeze disturbed the leaves, I paused to watch, check. I glanced behind us to see we'd made little progress from the gate.

Turning, I tried to quicken my pace a little. I felt vulnerable even though the trees blocked out some of the sky, even though I heard nothing out of the ordinary. My shoes slid on the loose stones as I finally got within reach of the veranda that appeared to be around the edge of the entire temple. I watched the panels of the wall. I had heard about such things, but never seen them. One flew open.

My sword high, I adjusted my footing and waited for something to emerge from the shadows of the temple. The panel had been opened about halfway, but a baby dragon might get through. *Did baby dragons exist? Of course, they would have to, wouldn't they? Otherwise dragons...* I shook my head; there would be time to ponder such things later.

I pursed my lips together and exhaled slowly. My eyes narrowed on the darkness. Heart beat fast; I waited. A slippered foot appeared from the darkness, followed by a tall man in a long black robe. His hands were hidden away in the oversized sleeves that hung in front of him to at least his knees. *Never trust a person if you can't see their hands.* Training. I had to remember my training.

He raised his head up to the sky. I resisted the urge to follow the man's lead; Zen probably looked up, but I heard nothing from him behind me. The man continued to focus above as his sleeves parted. I licked my lips and tightened my grip on the hilt. His hands emerged as his sleeves fell to his shoulders as he raised his hands up to the sky.

"Welcome to Dragonia Temple," the man said. His hands returned to their original position, and his chin lowered until his gaze met mine.

From where I stood, his eyes looked bright

green, but perhaps that was how the light hit them. His greying black hair flowed freely around his body to his waist.

"Who are you?" Zen asked from behind me.

"I am Uhandra, one of the keepers of the temple. You will come to no harm here; you have my word on that."

"A person's word means little to someone who doesn't know them," I said.

"True, true." Uhandra nodded. "However, you have come to our home and we welcome you. If you are unwilling to accept that, then you know the way to where you have come from."

Uhandra looked up to the sky once more and began to turn around. I lowered my sword but didn't put it back in the harness. The man might not appear to be an immediate threat, but that could change. Zen brushed past my shoulder and strode to the veranda. He stepped up onto it with ease before he reached out and touched the man's sleeve. I wanted to yell at Zen.

"Wait, we've come to learn," Zen said.

Uhandra turned to look at Zen. His face transformed from indifference to warmth as a smile spread across his face. He reached up, placed his hands on Zen's shoulders, and nodded. Why Zen showed no hesitancy annoyed me.

"Come, we are always happy to impart the knowledge we have to others."

Uhandra looked at Zen a moment longer before he spared another glance at me. My fingers tightened around the hilt of the sword. Uhandra removed his hands and clasped them in front of his body.

"Come children."

Children? Did I look like I was five? My teeth clenched together as Uhandra turned and began to walk through the doorway. Zen followed him, and I shook my head. His constant curiosity about dragons frustrated me. I released the breath I held and sheathed the sword. I assumed they wouldn't let me into the temple if I wielded it anyway. Leila always insisted knowledge lead to higher quality strategies, but this wouldn't have been what she meant.

My shoes made little noise as I approached the veranda. A sneak attack would be something to be aware of. When I reached the veranda, I wasn't able to just step up onto it with ease and dignity like Zen. I braced my hands against the wood and pushed myself up. I twisted my body until I could sit on the edge. My feet dangled as I caught my breath.

I couldn't deny that the view looked beautiful. Any other place or time and I could see myself happy in such an environment. Somewhere behind me I heard Zen and Uhandra. Their voices were muffled.

Either they didn't want me to hear or they were further into the temple.

With a growl, I stood up and walked to the door. I paused at the threshold with my desire to draw my weapon high. I glanced around at the calmness of the garden and the spaciousness of the wooden veranda. My gaze fell on the darkness inside the temple.

"Bloody dragons," I muttered and stepped inside the temple.

Despite looking dark from the outside, I found the inside light. The temple comprised one level for this room, with the ceiling made of some type of clear material. It looked like glass, but having lifted a pane to fix the window in my cottage after a wild sword swing, I knew they were heavy. The support beams didn't look strong enough to hold such a weight. Through the ceiling I watched the sky redden. It looked beautiful, even though part of me waited for a dragon to swoop in and attack. But nothing untoward happened.

I tore myself from the view and saw that the walls were lined with paintings. Each painting measured twice my height, and each one depicted a dragon. Some were in flight, some were asleep; mostly they were what I would call "a pretty painting to cover a mark on the wall". I stepped back and observed all the paintings that lined one wall together. Maybe when viewed together they would make more sense, but if there was a meaning behind them, it went beyond me.

Apart from the paintings, there wasn't much more to the room itself. The wooden floorboards stretched beyond the walls into the next, divided by the same sliding panels that stood on either side of the doorway I entered through. I heard Zen's muffled voice beyond that panel door.

In the next room, I found Zen seated at a table. The table stretched the length of the room itself and it was larger than my entire house. More paintings lined the walls, though unlike the bright and vivid colours in the previous room, these ones were more subdued. Most were in black ink and depicted dragons with green and red paint for the leaves and flowers. I liked these paintings better despite the subject matter.

Zen raised his head and beckoned me over with his hand. I took the seat next to him and heard my sword clatter against the bench seat as I did so. I didn't get a chance to say anything before Zen pushed a book towards me and tapped at a section.

"Isn't this interesting? It's about dragon behaviour."

I grimaced. Uhandra sat opposite Zen and smiled at me. That didn't help. "We just got here and you've already found something to catch your attention?"

"Come on, look."

I faked interest in it. The neat writing spread out beneath yet another picture of a friendly looking dragon. I read a few lines that spoke of dragons' gentle nature. *Oh please.*

"Alexa, if this is the true behaviour of dragons, then just think of the possibilities if we can communicate with them."

"It's one book in a temple that seems to hold dragons in high esteem. If you ask me, I think anything you read here is going to be dripping in bias."

I pushed the book back towards Zen and folded my arms in front of me on the table.

"Do you not believe in the good that exists within everything and everyone?" Uhandra asked.

I raised my eyes to look at him. "Sometimes that small good has to be sacrificed for a greater purpose."

"You don't think it is worth holding on to?"

"I don't know what type of life you lead up here, nor how much time you've spent down there in the real world, but let me put it in a way you might be able to understand. I believe in goodness, I believe in protecting those that work hard to be part of a society and support each other. If any of those people suddenly turned on others, when no harm had been done to them, and hunted them down, slicing through their flesh and burning them alive in a slow and painful death — then I don't care if they have any good inside them or not. At that point they've ceased to be entitled to being considered for anything except death." Confident, precise. Leila would have been proud of that.

"But what if that person had been forced to do that? Would you still have the same attitude?" Uhandra asked. His fingers intertwined with each other as they lay on the table before him.

"That person still had a choice. If they weren't such a coward to face death themselves, then the killings wouldn't happen. It doesn't matter if you're forced to do something or not, you're still responsible for your own actions."

"So if your mind became infected with something that caused you to think and do unimaginable things, you would be brave enough to sacrifice yourself to save others?"

"Of course I would."

"What if it was him? If your friend suddenly turned into the monstrous killer in your mind, could you kill him?"

I heard the extended pause. Zen whispered my name.

"If Zen meant harm to others, then yes, I would kill him because I feel that's what he would want. I don't think he would want to be known as a killer."

"Really? You'd kill me without trying to help me?" Zen asked.

I watched my fingers as they traced along the patterns in the wood of the table. Zen's hand reached out to still mine. I didn't want to look at him. It hadn't been a nice thing to say, but I would kill him because I cared.

"Sometimes the situation doesn't allow for help. My duty is to protect the village. I swore an oath to that," I said.

"She speaks from practicality, Zen. It would seem that is how she has been trained to behave and think. We shouldn't judge her for that, even if it is in fact contrary to her own feelings," Uhandra stated.

"Doing the right thing means putting your feelings aside," I stated, determined to get my point across.

"Putting your feelings aside means ignoring a piece in a larger puzzle. Without that piece it is incomplete," Uhandra countered.

"But still complete enough for the big picture to be seen," I said.

I looked up to see the corners of Uhandra's mouth twitch. Not quite a smile, but I sensed one lurked.

"You aren't afraid to put your opinion forward. You, Zen, you listen more and I believe consider possibilities. Your mind is more open to challenging old ways and embracing new ideas."

"You've known him for a matter of minutes and you think you know him," I said.

"You are not without new ideas yourself Alexa, but you have difficulty in pushing for change. You have that power and yet you don't use it," Uhandra said and watched me. "Something in both of you wanted to come here. You could only know about this place if someone told you and provided instructions. No one forced either of you to journey up this mountain. You are not without hope."

The sound of metal hitting against metal rang out from somewhere. If stars could make noises, then I imagined that was how they would sound. I turned my head towards the panels. People started to move past, they didn't speak, all I heard was their feet as they padded softly on the floor.

"We are preparing to eat our evening meal. You are both welcome to join us and spend the night as well." Uhandra stood with his hands still perched on the table. His attention turned away from me and to Zen. "We have an extensive collection about dragons; I would be honoured if you would join me after the meal."

"I will; thank you."

I looked over at Zen but felt invisible at that moment. He looked at Uhandra with something I hadn't seen on his face before - admiration. Perhaps I wore a similar look when I had been younger and had thought that Leila's skill would mean she could never be defeated. Of course, when I won during the training sessions, I knew no one could be invincible. A sober thought given I wanted to destroy the dragon population single handedly.

Uhandra walked to the panel and slid the remainder to the side. Zen got to his feet and joined him in the doorway. More people, more men, in robes the same as Uhandra walked past them and down what looked like a passage-way. All my life I'd known my place and felt like I belonged. Here though, here I felt like I stood in a world I didn't belong to and wasn't supposed to know about. While Uhandra hadn't been unwelcoming, I didn't feel wanted either.

Zen turned and looked over his shoulder at me. I hadn't moved from the bench. He held out his hand, before Uhandra moved into the passage-way and joined the others.

"Come on, Alexa," Zen said.

"There's something about this place that's..."

"We can't do anything. They're offering food, and a place to sleep with no payment required. We're lucky, let's not come across as being ungrateful."

"I'm not ungrateful, I'm cautious."

Zen walked back to the table and stood across from me. He placed his hands on the top and leaned forward. "I think you're jealous."

I broke away from the eye contact and went back to studying the patterns on the table. "I'm not. I just don't trust him."

"Alexa, seriously, you came all this way up here. Let's make the most of it before we continue on. We might learn something…"

"We'll learn nothing Zen. I'm guessing these people see dragons as some kind of wonderful creature who can do no harm. I'm not interested in hearing the excuses they have."

"You're uncomfortable."

I looked up and saw a smile on his face.

"It's not funny, this place is just so, so…" Words failed. "Zen, I'm warning you."

"Come on, Alexa. I'm hungry, so I'm going to go where they've gone. Up to you if you come."

He didn't give me a chance to object and left the room. I sat being watched from the walls by the dragons. I placed my hands palm down on the table and slid them to the edge. Leaning back, I gripped the edge of the table and looked up through the clear ceiling. More stars than I'd ever seen before interrupted the dark sky. Danger lies in beauty though.

"Bugger you, Zen," I murmured.

I walked down the corridor alone. Panels lined the walls on both sides to conceal whatever lurked behind them. The sky above disappeared as the ceiling became solid. I couldn't hear any movement, but I assumed another floor held more secrets above me.

In the end I followed my nose and the chatter to find the room. The panel stood wide open and inside I could see men as they sat on both sides of a table in their bright robes. Zen's earthy colours and difference in material made him easy to find. Beside him, there sat an empty space.

I hesitated. I had never seen so many men in one place, with no other female in sight. My gaze went from man to man. They varied in ages from my age to the very old, much older than Kaera had been when she died two winters before.

Leila trained me for many things. Being in a room full of men without another female was not one of them. The aroma of food implored my brain to listen to my hunger, but my feet remained still. Bowls were being brought into the room through a panel on one of the longer sides of the room, opposite from where Zen sat. I licked my lips.

The murmur of chatter ceased. The men closed their eyes and looked up at the ceiling with their arms raised. I felt compelled to look as well and saw a painting that covered the ceiling. Two dragons, one black and one white, greeted each other on a mountain. The style of this one differed from the previous two rooms. It appeared detailed where the dragons were concerned, whereas the surrounding scene went from detailed to more of a blur of colours to allude to what it might be at the edges.

"Dragon brothers, we thank you for the protection you offer, for the loyal service you perform, for the cure that will one day be brought to end the burden and set all free. Dragona."

My gaze returned to the men, but I couldn't work out who had said the words. All in the room repeated the last word and lowered their heads. They started to eat the food in front of them.

I looked back down the corridor in the direction I'd come before I glanced back at Zen. He sat engaged in conversation with those around him while he ate. I'd never seen him look so comfortable. Yet, I had never felt so uncomfortable.

This isn't my place. I headed back the way I had come. My pace quickened the closer I got to the room I had entered the temple through. The further I went down the passage-way, the more the panels blurred. I tried to remember if panelled screens had been on my left when I had first entered the hallway. It had been standard training to know as much as you can about an unfamiliar environment, and yet I couldn't remember a thing.

My feet paused in front of one panel, and I slid it aside. An unfamiliar room lay in front of me. More dragons on the walls and a giant painted black dragon on the wooden floor. Above me I saw the ceiling of stars and sky above me. At least I had to be close to where I entered. I stepped into the room, closed the panel behind me, and headed to the side wall. Another panel and I entered another room. Room after room I did this until I finally arrived in the room I had first stepped into. I took the last few steps until I found myself outside in the freedom with the night air.

Instinct made me want to move away from the temple, to put more distance between those men and me. I wandered into the gardens and sat down at the feet of one of the stone dragons that towered above me. I could see the temple if I looked over my shoulder. I thought of Zen, but my fear inside wasn't for him.

I pulled my knees up to my chest and wrapped my arms around my legs. Somewhere I could hear the sounds of cicadas as they chirped with joy that darkness had arrived. I had spent a lot of time alone on training exercises when I had been younger. I'd never had an issue with being alone, but having company had always been a slight comfort. Despite Zen being so close, I felt alone.

My hand reached up to my face. *Where had they come from?* I wiped away the tears that trailed down my face. Zen's face faded away in my mind and instead I saw Leila. Leila when she taught me how to pick up a sword when I turned six. Leila, who taught me how to line up fruit and impale each with an arrow. Leila, who taught me to braid my hair so that it wouldn't get in the way as I charged towards my target.

She had taught me so many things. Maybe I never realised how many. I certainly hadn't appreciated it until now. Now I wanted nothing more than to hear Leila rebuke me for not following instructions, chastise me for sloppy work, embrace me... though that had been rare. Shows of affection were uncommon; they were seen to be a weakness amongst the warriors and the elders. Those cut from warrior training and who were coupled were free to hug, hold hands, and kiss.

With my eyes closed, I wished for the memories to fade into the surrounding darkness. All those days were long gone and I was so far from home. I leaned my head onto my knees. At least the fabric would soak up any stray tears.

CHAPTER 17

Dragons circled above me. Around and round, yet they went nowhere. I reached up to touch them. They seemed so close. My hand looked small, chubby. I moved my hand in front of my face. They looked weird. Someone close by hummed a lullaby.

I turned my head with some effort, unable to lift it from the softness of the pillow. A woman stood with her back to me and rocked back and forth. She looked like a giant. My hand reached up. Why was the woman so big? Or... Why was I so small? She turned as my hand reached for her.

"Alexa."

I opened my eyes with a start. The darkness remained around me, but the image of the woman had frozen in a half turn. I just wanted to see her face. It seemed so familiar.

"Alexa," Zen repeated.

I felt his shoe nudge mine. The woman vanished. *Damn Zen.*

"What?" I grumbled.

I wondered when I had laid down; I didn't remember doing it. My harness remained buckled in front, and I felt the sword as it pressed into my back. I stretched my arms up. At least I had slept. Zen crouched beside me.

"What happened to the food? I really thought you would have put anything else on hold to eat something."

My arms lowered and I sat up. "I saw that room differently."

"What? So you came there?"

"I haven't eaten all day. Of course I bloody came there," I said. My stomach added to the message.

"I saved a seat for you."

"I know you did. I saw it, Zen." I sighed. "You don't get it, do you?"

"Get what?"

"It was a room full of men Zen! Strange men! And I was the only female! How the heck do you think they made me feel?"

Zen's mouth opened, then he closed it. He sat down beside me. I shuffled over a bit and propped myself up against the statue.

"I never thought of that. Intimidating I'm guessing," Zen said.

"That and more."

I didn't feel like arguing about it anymore. Perhaps my grumpy mood could be blamed on the lack of sustenance.

"Did you speak with Uhandra?"

"That's why I came looking for you. They've all gone to bed, but he showed me this massive room of information. Come on Alexa, you should see it and the information it has."

"Does it have anything helpful? Like how to kill them all without putting myself in mortal danger?"

Zen smiled and put his arm around my shoulders. "You'll only find that out if you come and have a look."

"Only because I have nothing better to do."

"Come on."

Zen stood up and reached out his hand to me. I took his hand and he pulled me to my feet. His hand held onto mine even after I tugged at it. He switched my hand from one of his to the other and held it as he led me back into the temple.

He probably doesn't want me to get lost. That would make sense. He led me back into the temple, through the same room as before, and then back into the corridor. I tried to count the number of panels. Note the number of turns and the direction in which we went. A staircase sat in the middle of the hallway that widened out on both sides to accommodate it. My eyes followed the steps as they ascended up in a curve to the next floor. That wasn't where we were headed though.

Zen walked around them and to a room behind it. He slid the panel aside. My first instinct was to check out the ceiling. I liked the clear ceiling, but in this room wooden boards covered the length of the room. There were no dragon paintings on the walls here, there was no room. Each wall was lined with varying bookcases. One wall looked to have books that were bound properly. I had never seen so many in one place, but Leila had told me once that some places outside of the village kept such large amounts. A secret I had to keep, but one I hadn't believed until now.

The shelves on another wall had rolled up papers, though from where I stood inside the door I couldn't tell what was on them. Another wall appeared to contain paintings, each in an alcove with a cloth draped over them. It figured they had to have paintings somewhere in the room.

"Over here," Zen said.

He pulled me towards a small table in the middle of the room. A couple of books lay at one end, but an unrolled parchment covered the majority of the surface. We came to a halt beside the table, and Zen released my hand.

"Uhandra says that this is one of the earliest records of the temple here. It's from before the burden. This is showing that the dragons lived high in the mountains here." My eyes travelled to where he pointed. It looked like some kind of map. "Villagers lived down here. To me, it looks like it could be talking about this very mountain we're on and the village we stopped at."

"How convenient," I mumbled.

"Come on Alexa, don't be like that. There's more too," Zen said and reached for the books.

"Oh I'm sure there is."

"Sit on the chair."

I turned around to see a long chair of sorts. I hadn't seen anything like that in the village, nor any that we'd visited. The chair was big enough for at least two to sit on, maybe three if everyone breathed in. I'd barely sat down when Zen joined me. A book landed on my lap and he opened it before he flipped through the pages. He stopped on one with a painting of a black dragon staring at a white one. *I've seen that before.*

"This dragon, the white one; this is the story of how she brought the burden to the dragon."

"Of course a bunch of men living on a mountain would have to blame a woman for all the mess." I folded my arms across my chest and leaned back into the chair.

"Give it a chance?"

"Do I have to?"

"I'm asking you to."

I looked over at him. His big green eyes stared at me, and I felt my resolve run and hide. How could I deny listening to my best friend?

"Okay, but I'm listening under protest, just so you know."

"I'll take it."

I sat up and leaned in closer to the book. Writing covered most of the page, some of which I could read, but many of the words were unfamiliar.

"Give me the short version in a language I can understand."

"Yeah, strange looking words, aren't they? I asked Uhandra about them, he said that is how the writing system used to be. He showed me a couple examples of how double letters came to replace these other symbols and how..."

"Zen, the story."

"I found it interesting."

"I can tell," I said, and managed a smile.

"Alright then, apparently before the burden

everyone lived peacefully. Dragons didn't attack and people didn't attack them either. Then this woman here…"

"That's a dragon."

"I know, but it was a woman."

"Then why does she look like a dragon?" I pointed out.

"Can I just tell the story?"

"You are."

"You're impossible. She was a dragon at first and she fell in love with another dragon, this one." His finger tapped the black one. That seemed obvious even to me, but I didn't interrupt. "The problem was he wasn't interested in her at all. This says that she tried everything to get him to agree to be her mate, but failed. So she went to the mountains in the north and met a human who told her that there were plants that could teach him a lesson. She agreed, and this human made a drink for her, which she was only to drink afterwards. So she returned here with this plant mixture that had been placed into a sweet drink, but she didn't listen to the human and decided to add something more to it — her blood."

"Ew. You know that's disgusting, right?"

"Sure it is."

"Then don't sound so happy about it."

"Enthusiasm isn't always about happiness. Anyway, stop interrupting." Zen looked at me and I shrugged. "So she convinced the male dragon to drink this mixture as a parting goodbye."

"He wasn't too smart then, was he?"

"And then she returned north, as she had agreed to do to meet with the human. The human gave her a second potion to drink, and it transformed her into a human. The book says that she stayed with this other human until one day she confessed she added her own blood. The other human was incensed and told her to leave. After that there's nothing more about what happened to her."

"And so what happened supposedly because of this blood being added?"

"Ah, you're curious then?"

I whacked the book underneath with my hand and laughed as Zen struggled to keep his hold on it.

"I get it. Nothing happened at first. The dragon went on and found a mate, and that's when things changed. The egg hatched and it wasn't a dragon, it was a human."

"Whoa, that makes no sense because then we wouldn't have dragons now."

"It seems that when they get older something triggers them to transform into dragons. The book says the burden stems from that change from human to dragon they go through. It affects who they are and the mixed blood drives them mad until they can't control their own actions anymore."

"So the blood makes them kill humans in some kind of weird revenge for something that was in fact the fault of a dragon in the first place?"

"Exactly."

"Oh come on. And what, this can be reversed how? Let's say this book isn't full of shit, though I still think it is. This book says nothing about what plants were combined to make the potion, let alone how to reverse any of it."

"But it shows there might be a way to save the dragons."

"Might, Zen. These people could have written anything in those documents to make it look like it's some ancient record. If the answer was here all along, why didn't these men solve it? Huh? Answer me that? I mean, how long has our village been fighting off the dragons? We can't listen to all this."

"Ah, you're just hungry."

"Yes, and I want to get out of here."

"We'll leave in the morning."

"Good."

"Maybe. Depends, that was a big climb up. A few days wouldn't hurt."

I rolled my eyes. *Seriously?*

"They've made up rooms for us. Come on, I'll show you."

We left the room and headed back to the staircase. Zen stepped up onto the first and paused. He reached back and grabbed my hand. *Did he sense my hesitation again?* We walked up the stairs to find several corridors going in all directions.

"This way," Zen said.

He led me down a corridor behind where the stairs ended. He slid open a panel and a mat lay on the floor of the small room. The room contained nothing else other than the mat.

"I'll be in here."

I turned to look as Zen let go of my hand, but my fingers curled tight around his. Behind those panels would be more men. These panels had no locks on them, and there was nothing in the room that could bar entry.

"What's wrong?" Zen asked.

A weakness or necessity for my safety? I wasn't sure that it mattered. My gaze went to the mat again. I couldn't even look at Zen.

"I don't want to be alone in here," I whispered.

"I'll stay here then," he replied. "Let me move my pack."

I let go of his hands and stood there. He slid the panel back of the room opposite and emerged with his pack and sword. When he reached me again, I felt his fingers curl back around mine and tighten.

We stepped into the room, and Zen slid the panel across. When I looked above, I saw the clear sky above with the stars scattered across it. I felt comfort in that. When Zen released my hand, I undid the buckles on the harness. There wasn't anywhere practical to leave the sword, so I placed it next to Zen's in the corner.

I laid on the mat and stared up at the stars and wondered how much they must have seen in their own lifetimes, how many questions I had that they could answer. They knew the truth of the past and present. Zen soon joined me on the floor and he nudged me. I raised my head and he put his arm out as a pillow for me.

"Are you okay?" Zen asked.

"Yeah, I think so."

"It's kind of like the other night on the roof."

I smiled. "Yeah, except most of that's a fuzzy blur."

"True, I enjoy being able to remember much better."

I rested my head against his body, but continued to watch the stars above.

"Alexa?"

"Yeah?"

"About the coupling. I won't be choosing anyone when the ceremony comes around."

"You think the village will still have the ceremony with the elders gone?"

"It doesn't matter to me."

"Aw, they'll still have you, Zen. Village tradition will continue."

"Alexa, I don't want to choose any of those other girls. I know who I want to choose, tradition or otherwise."

I felt his hand move to my back. My heart quickened as I turned my head to look at him.

"Zen..."

He shook his head.

"I don't care about tradition, Alexa. If you will have me, you are my first and only choice." His other hand reached over and cupped the side of my face. "I love you, Alexa."

"We've been through this before. I'm a warrior, Zen, I'm not allowed to..."

"Most of the elders are gone, Alexa. Here, there is no one to judge, no rules we have to follow."

"But..."

"Haven't you ever thought, maybe, of being anything more than friends?" He sat up and his arm slid beneath my hair until his hand cupped my head.

"I... Maybe... But..."

His closeness wasn't unwelcome. No matter what, I always felt safe when he was near. The little I could remember from the night on the roof seemed like a distant memory.

"I don't need an answer Alexa, I just need you to know how I feel."

I nodded. *What are the right things to say? Should I say something even though I don't know what's going to happen?*

We settled back down, but I was aware of his every movement long after he fell asleep. The stars had no answers to my question.

CHAPTER 18

I hunched my shoulders and relaxed. The sun seemed overly bright above, and I used my hand to shield my eyes. From the yellow glow, I saw the silhouette of a bird. *Was it a bird?* It flew to the right, and I looked away as the light invaded my eyes. White light with stars took over my vision as I shook my head.

The ground came into focus, but no grass as I expected. Smooth wooden floorboards with a slight shine to me. I couldn't feel any heat on my back, and I soon saw why. Above me, a ceiling shielded the sun's light. Clear windows and yet they protected so much better than the ones in the village.

"Alexa?" Zen said.

I glanced around the room with dragons painted on the wooden boards. They moved as I watched. Their powerful wings beat up and down. In the sky, the two black dragons flew before another joined them. A white dragon. The three flew with synchronised movements. There were no clouds in their way.

One black dragon turned to look at me. Its eyes flashed from green to brown to black. The other two dragons faded away as the dragon with black eyes headed for me. My heart pounded in my chest.

"It's just a painting. It's not real," I said.

The dragon flew from the wall and towards me. I fell to the floor. A rush of air sent my hair flying, and I reached out my hand.

"Wait, dirt?" I lifted my head. "What?"

"Alexa?" Zen said.

I heard the beat of wings above. My hands pushed against the ground and I ran for the trees. Fabric on my sleeve snagged on something and I stumbled forward into the shadows.

When I turned, I saw the black tail disappear. Then the dragon landed where I had been. It looked my way with its black eyes and I shuffled backwards along the ground. My arm ached. I felt something trickle down my hair. The dragon moved forward, but couldn't fit through the trees.

"Alexa?"

The forest faded and wooden floorboards came into view and a hand. *Why was there a hand near my face?*

"Are you awake?"

"I am now," I said. "I think."

"You think?" I felt his arm wrap around my waist.

"Weird dream, that's all."

"Do you want to talk about it?" he asked.

I shook my head. "It was just a dream."

I rolled over and saw the smile on his lips. His arm still lay over my waist and caused a mixture of feelings to bubble away inside me.

"Promise me we only stay today," I said.

"Promise." Zen continued to watch at me. "Alexa?"

"We should get up. I can already hear movement in the temple."

I stood up and moved to my clothes. By the time we left the room, we still hadn't spoken further. I followed Zen to the room and sat close beside him. Men filtered in through the doors in identical robes and I shuffled a little towards Zen until I couldn't move any further.

"Relax. The food is good," Zen said.

He wasn't wrong about the food. I finished the meal and resisted running my finger over the plate. Uhandra came to sit opposite us as the men left to do whatever it was they did.

"Are you staying?" Uhandra asked.

"Just for today, but in the morning we will need

to leave," Zen said.

"We're honoured you will spare the time for today then. I found some books you might be interested in last night and put them on the table ready for you. Alexa, will you join Zen and I?"

I felt torn. I wanted to stay where Zen was for comfort, but the thought of being in the room surrounded by books filled with dragon lies made my head hurt.

"Actually, do you have something I could put a few flowers into? I noticed yesterday you have ones I haven't seen before."

"Most definitely Alexa. Would you like some paper too? A pencil?"

Uhandra's enthusiasm oozed; mine wasn't so keen. "Sure."

He turned his body towards the door. "Matthias, Matthias come here."

A man entered, and I felt Zen's legs tense. Matthias' jaw clenched as well as his gaze focused on Zen even as he spoke to Uhandra. He nodded and left the room.

"Are you alright, Zen?" Uhandra asked.

"Yeah, fine. I was just thinking about what we looked at yesterday."

Matthias brought a small box, paper, and pencils

to the room before he excused himself. Uhandra stood as well.

"I'll meet you in the room when you are ready, Zen."

Uhandra nodded at me before he left the room. I turned to Zen and prodded his leg with my finger.

"What was that?"

"What?"

"You, when you saw Matthias, you went all... I don't know... You weren't you."

"It was *him,* Alexa."

"Who?"

"The man who came to the village."

My gaze drifted back to the doorway.

"We can leave now," I said, but Zen was already shaking his head.

"No, let's gather the information we can. You sure you'll be okay on your own?"

"Sure, I have a sword, and besides, they don't seem to linger much outside. I know where to find you." That was a lie. I knew the room he would be in, but I doubted my ability to find it on my own.

"Okay, as long as you're sure. I'll pop out to check on you though."

I nodded. I collected the supplies, and we parted

ways in the corridor. The smell of the flowers made it easy to find my way to the outside. Their scent was strengthened by the sun as it warmed them.

I spent a good while in the garden and collected different flowers. Zen could look at them later. I hadn't bothered to use the paper. Instead, I had folded it so it sat flat in the bottom of the little box. When I approached the statue I had sat at last time, movement caught my eye

The orange robe moved down a path in the garden. Black hair loose. A lot of the men looked similar, but the walk looked like Matthias'. I had noticed when he entered he favoured his right leg.

I placed the box and pencil at the base of the statue. This situation justified my harness and sword. I moved down the path, careful to keep as low as I could. Most of the plants weren't large enough to conceal me if he turned around. He didn't though.

The path curved around the temple and I noticed the plants were higher in this section. Better for me. Up ahead, Matthias paused and I crouched down. He turned slowly and I saw he had books in his hands. *What was with these men and books?* I stayed as still as possible.

When he turned and continued, I sighed with relief. I thought he had seen me the way he stared. Matthias continued on the path until a stone wall appeared with a metal gate. The wall reminded me of the stone used to build the Hidden.

Matthias held the books in one hand while he reached for something on the wall. I squinted and tried to see what it was. As his fingers picked it up, a flash of light caused me to look away. I blinked as spots flickered across my vision. The sparkly dots continued to float over everything. I squeezed my eyelids tight and rubbed my fingers over them, then opened them slowly.

The dots faded, but Matthias was gone and the gate closed. I could see beyond the metal poles stones covered the ground.

"Probably wouldn't have seen anything anyway."

I milled around and picked a few flowers in case anyone questioned why I was there before I returned to the statue. Zen stood there, waiting.

"Where were you?"

I held up the flowers. "Why?"

"I was worried. Everything okay?"

I tried to slow my blinking down. "Yeah, a bug needs to adjust its senses. Flew right at my eye."

Zen stepped forward and turned my face up. "I can't see anything. Maybe you should ask Uhandra if there's someone here that can look at it?"

"It was a bug. Those tiny annoying creatures that

are blessed with extra loud voices."

"You're sure?"

I nodded. "I think I will come back inside though. It's hot out here."

"Good. Uhandra is getting us some refreshments in the room. Plus," he smiled and leaned closer. "I can bore you with the new books he found."

"What did I do to deserve such treatment?"

His hand fell away from my face and he picked up the box.

"Those are nice," he said as we walked back to the veranda.

"I thought so too. Give you something to do if we get back to the village."

"If? Not when?" he asked.

"If, you know, as in *if* we survive."

He looked disappointed with the answer. Inside, I relished the cool air. I stopped at one bathroom to splash my face with water and rid my body of other things. When I emerged, I felt I could almost deal with spending the afternoon surrounded by books.

That had been optimistic to think. I enjoyed the snacks that Uhandra had brought to the room on a tray. He came and went all afternoon as Zen devoured book after book and I used the paper to draw random things.

As we curled up on the floor to sleep that night, I just wanted to be gone from the temple.

CHAPTER 19

I walked away from the dragon temple and sensed a weight lift from my shoulders. Zen had privately spoken with Uhandra while I waited outside beneath the dragon statue again. I'd picked a couple of the flowers to pass the time and awkwardly held them in my hands. The girls always held bundles of flowers for the coupling ceremony. I tried to imagine myself holding one of them, the green leaves around the edge fanning out to frame the rich red hadrana flowers with the odd piece of white kajan flowers.

Hadrana flowers had never been my favourite. They began life as small buds that slowly opened with one petal at a time. Those on the outer edge were much larger and overlapped the next petal as they became smaller and smaller, forming a spiral into the centre of the flower. Most girls in the village adored them, even fellow warriors, but I found the smell pungent. The petals themselves always seemed to leave some kind of residue on the tips of your fingers, even though you couldn't see anything. Its leaves weren't much better as each light green leaf flared out to sharp points along each side. It was common for the men who picked them to return with hands covered in scratches. Once, I had tried to pick one and a leaf had brushed against my skin. A red rash appeared there within minutes and no amount of help from the medicine man made it go away. For a week I had to just put up with the intense itchiness of it and vowed to never go near them again unless I had a sword or a fire torch.

Kajan flowers I had no issues with. They were tiny balls of fluff. At least, that's how they appeared to me anyway. The little fluff balls dotted the stem, and the purple leaves only grew at the very base, far larger and out of proportion with the rest of the plant. Still, at least they didn't stink up the place or make me contemplate cutting my hand off.

Zen came out of the temple, and I abandoned the flowers at the base of the statue. Maybe when the dragon threat passed, I could return and document them with Zen somehow. He liked to record anything new he found in great detail in his books. A few times even the elders had gone to him for information, which was why they provided him with a supply of the blank books in the first place.

"We should make it to the bottom before dark, you think?" Zen asked from behind me as we passed through the first cave.

"Hope so. I mean, usually it's quicker returning than going anyway. We know what to expect."

"Hope you're not still thinking of bringing that vicious bird."

I stepped out of the cave and felt the spray on my face from the waterfall. I walked along it until the path headed down the mountain again to where I had last seen Fiya.

"If Fiya wants to come, then I will."

We said no more as our feet skidded on dirt as we descended towards the field of grass again. My eyes focused on that grass and considered whether a capai lurked there or if it was just my imagination. I reached the tree before Zen and stopped to look around. The empty nest sat on the ground, and I looked around for any signs of Fiya.

"Fiya, Fiya," I whispered not, wanting to frighten the bird.

"Alexa." Zen sounded impatient as he came to a stop beside me.

"Hey, I told you I was going to look for Fiya."

"What did I say?" he said, and raised his hands.

"It's not what you said; it's how you said it."

Zen pointed his finger to himself. "Me? I haven't said a word since the waterfall."

I turned away from him and brushed my hand

over the grass to see if Fiya had hidden away somewhere in there.

"Alexa!"

"Zen, I..." I said.

"It wasn't me!" Zen replied.

I smiled. "Fiya? Where are you are hiding little one?"

The grass near Zen changed as red and gold tail feathers fanned out. The bird walked through the grass towards me where I had crouched down. Zen stepped back as the last blades of grass parted and Fiya appeared. She stopped for a moment and looked up at Zen. He rubbed his bandaged finger. The bird looked away and toddled over to me, relaxing its tail until it dragged on the ground behind it.

"Hey little one. I'm going back down the mountain now, you can come too if you like."

I held my hand out in hopes that Fiya would hop right on it. She scratched at the ground a little before she flapped her wings and flew onto my hand.

"Looks like we have a guest with us."

"You don't even know what it eats. You can't even take care of yourself properly."

"I can learn, and I think Fiya is capable of taking care of herself. Aren't you, girl?"

"What makes you think it's a girl?"

"Because she bit you," I replied, and stood up.

I lifted Fiya up onto my shoulder where she turned around several times. She settled onto my shoulder and draped her tail down my back. I stroked her head and saw Zen shake his head, but a smile remained on his lips.

"Come on, bird girl, let's get off this mountain and back amongst people before you decide birds are better. You can go first again."

The grass swayed in the breeze. Somewhere, some birds chirped. I waited for any swooshing sound but heard nothing.

"Okay Fiya, you ready to run across this?"

Fiya opened her mouth and let out a roar. Despite seeing her beak open and having the sound blast into my ears, I still looked up, just in case there really was a dragon about to attack. The sky, while still pink from the early morning, remained clear of dragons.

"Good Fiya. Who knows Zen, maybe capai are afraid of Fiya?"

"Alexa."

I smiled and drew the sword over my right shoulder, just in case. After inhaling a deep breath, I bolted for the grass. It slapped against my legs as I tried to keep as little contact with the ground as possible. I glanced at my shoulder and saw Fiya holding on with her claws.

Halfway across and I heard it. It wasn't Fiya. *Swoosh.* A lump formed in my throat. I tried to run faster, but a stitch stung my side already. Heavy footsteps behind me grew louder. Zen grabbed my elbow as he passed and pulled me. My feet stumbled amongst the grass.

"Faster Alexa!"

A roar deafened me. I could see Zen saying something, but nothing reached my ears. I turned to see nothing behind me, but Fiya had stretched her legs, spread her wings and had her tail feathers on display. Her beak opened, but I heard nothing.

My foot caught on a tuft of grass, and my arms flailed as I tried to regain my balance. Zen spun around and caught me around the waist and dragged me the last few steps to the entrance of the cave. He lowered me onto a rock, and I leaned forward to catch my breath.

I checked my shoulder to see that Fiya had settled back onto it. Her feathers relaxed as she snuggled down and tucked her head under her wing, with her eyes firmly closed. Fiya's state of calm felt in direct contrast to my own. My legs twinged up and down as my heartbeat slowed.

I sat up straight and saw Zen nearby on the ground. He held his sides with his hands and stretched his legs out. His lips moved, then paused. I shook my head. Zen's forehead creased, and he pointed to his ears. He was right; I couldn't hear anything. A new panic rose inside me.

"I can't hear anything!" I think that's what I said aloud, it's what I intended to at least.

"Alexa, it's okay," Zen mouthed slowly. He got up, knelt down in front of me, and took my hands in his. "It's okay."

I shook my head. It wasn't okay. I needed my hearing to be a warrior. *What if it never comes back?*

"Come on, we'll take it slow."

He stood up and pulled me up to my feet. I bit my lip. My hand reached up and I used the back of my hand to wipe my face. Zen's arms wrapped around me, and he pulled me close against his body. I buried my face into his shirt as tears flowed from my eyes. My fingers balled up some of his shirt as he rested his chin on the top of my head.

Eventually my tears dried up. At that point I should have pulled away from Zen, put the distance between us, but I didn't want to. I liked the way I felt safe in his arms, the way he always looked out for me; perhaps this is what he meant when he said he loved me. Eventually I had to let go of the comfort. We still had to get back down the mountain, and I didn't want to get caught climbing in the dark, especially if my hearing didn't return.

I allowed Zen to lead, and watched carefully where he stepped as we headed through the cave. We stopped briefly on the other side and then continued on the descent. Fiya remained asleep on my shoulder, seemingly unaware of everything that happened around her.

By the time we exited the last of the caves, my legs had started to ache. The sky had darkened, and clouds covered most of the moonlight we would normally have. We still had the rest of the mountain, plus the forest to get through. Another night in the open seemed inevitable.

CHAPTER 20

We had made it back to the town in the late afternoon the day before. Zen had used some of the gold to get us a room again at the inn. It was a relief to rest. My hearing had returned, but my body ached by the time I went to bed. I had hoped I'd feel better when I woke, but whatever my body was suffering from had other ideas. My head continued to thump no matter how I put it on the pillow. Fiya sat in her basket beside my bed eating a piece of bread Zen had offered her earlier.

With some effort, I turned over in bed. My face contorted as I winced at the incessant ache at the base of my back. I had already tried sitting up, but nothing seemed to help. I reached down and rubbed my hand over the lower part of my stomach; I hoped it would soothe it enough to give me some respite. It didn't.

Zen entered through the door with a cup in his hands. Curls of steam danced above the rim of the cup as he gave me a half-smile. I could see the dark circles beneath his eyes and the creases that lined his forehead.

"I thought something warm might make you feel better."

I pulled myself up in bed. Something felt wrong, very wrong. I reached between the sheets and ran my hand over the wetness I had felt on the back of my legs. When my hand emerged, my fingers were stained with blood. I opened my mouth, but didn't know what to say. The cup clattered to the floor, and Zen had already crossed the room to the door.

"I'll find a medicine woman," he said.

The door closed. I turned back to the blood. I knew blood; I knew the texture of it, the way it pooled, the sharpness of the taste. This blood wasn't like the same as that from a wound. I raised my hand to my nose and jerked my head back. I had smelt nothing like that before I lifted the blanket to see a patch of blood on the sheets. It wasn't huge, but my breath quickened. My legs had no signs of injury and yet... I reached between my legs to find the underwear damp. My fingers stained darker when I looked again.

Footsteps thudded on the stairs. I hurriedly threw the blankets over me and tried to wipe some of the blood off onto the sheets. My gaze fell to the mess on the floor where whatever Zen had bought me had formed its own puddle; the pieces of the cup lay scattered.

The door opened and a lady entered with a smile on her face. *How can she be smiling? Didn't Zen tell her what's happening to me?*

She placed a bag at the end of the bed and rolled up the sleeves of her pale green dress. When she began the second one she turned around to Zen, who stood just behind her watching the end of the bed, biting his lip.

"Time for you to leave," she said, and shooed him with her hands.

"I'm staying. If something is wrong with Alexa, I want to…"

"You will do as you are told, young man. Now out, there's nothing at all wrong with her. Out."

When Zen hesitated, she pushed him with both hands so that his feet skidded on the floor. He looked up at me and I shrugged. The woman closed the door on him and then turned to me.

"He comes to me all in a panic about such a thing!" she said, and grabbed a chair as she walked back over to me. Sitting on the chair, she wiggled a bit before smiling at me. "I'm Maeja, the local medicine woman. You know what's happening, don't you?"

"I… I'm bleeding."

Maeja's smile faltered. "But surely you've been through this before? By your age, many times."

I shook my head as my fingers played with the edge of the sheets, twisting them until they became hard.

"But surely, you and your fellow…"

"We're not together," I said.

Maeja raised her eyebrows. "You could be if you wanted to, child. You're one of the girls from the north, aren't you? The ones they train to fight, perhaps?"

"Yes, we come from the valley."

"Ah, I have heard a little of the place that's deep in the valley. They keep many strange ways in that place. Do they have you eat something every day? Or drink it perhaps?"

I thought about my routine. "There is a tea we're supposed to drink every morning, but I lost my supplies several days ago when a dragon attacked."

"You've been drinking it for many years then?"

I shrugged. "Since I was about ten or eleven. Why?"

Maeja sighed and shook her own head. "It's dangerous to drink that tea continuously. They warned the elders there about that practice. So many healthy young women who grow up and cannot have children. You seem to be lucky. Your body is already trying to put itself back on track."

"I don't understand."

"Child, you bleed when you are not with child. Once a month roughly it happens for a handful of days."

"But I can't be feeling like this. I have things I need to do and how am I supposed to do anything?" I complained.

Maeja laughed. "Ah, so young. It is not the end of the world. You learn to manage them, you learn how to predict when it's coming and plan accordingly. First though, I assume you've gotten yourself into a bit of a state. I've already asked the serving boy to run a bath in the next room for you. We'll have you changed and I'll show you how you manage with some cloths."

She leaned forward as if to stand. I reached forward and put my hand on hers. "Please, I have things to do. Teach me yes, but I need the tea, or something like it. I need something at least until I've done what I need to."

"If you continue with the tea, you may pass the point of being able to be a mother. Think about that as you soak in the water. If you still want the tea after, then I will provide you with only enough for two months."

I nodded. She sounded like a fair woman. A knock on the door to the side of the room drew our attention.

"Thank you," Maeja said, and then turned to me. "Come on, let's get you out of those clothes and sheets and get you cleaned up. No need to be embarrassed, it's nothing I haven't helped young girls with many times before."

Despite all my training and skills I had, I felt embarrassed by my body. Maeja ushered me into the adjoining room, where a steaming bath of water waited. Such a thing was rare in back home and a privilege of the elders and those who achieve a high standard. I had twice had the chance to have a warm bath. The first when I gained the status of warrior-lead after a hunt, which saw me locate fourteen of the twenty hidden flags. The second, when I went from warrior to the elite of the warriors and the next in line to be considered for elder positions.

Maeja followed me into the room and waited while I stripped off my clothes. I cringed at seeing the bloodstains, but Maeja didn't show any sign of the repulsion I felt. Maeja gathered my clothing on the floor and I eased myself into the warm water. A fragrant bar of soap sat on a small table beside the bath. I wanted to use as much as I could to cloud the water to hide any trace of blood that might mingle with the water. The thought of a boy emptying the water caused my cheeks to burn.

"I'm going to have these seen to straightaway. Do you have another outfit?"

"They're all I have," I replied.

"I will have a word with the young man and see about purchasing you what you need. Until then, just relax."

The door closed. I knew the door only led to my room. I glanced at the other door and wondered if it had been. My eyes focused on it until I climbed out of the bath and tiptoed over to it. I tried the handle and let out a sigh; locked. By the time I got back into the water, I could see the water trail I had left across the floor. Thankfully, it only looked like water and nothing else.

I washed my body with the soap and cloth. The scent filled my senses but I couldn't place what it was or where I'd smelt it before, but it had a scent of familiarity. Once clean, I closed my eyes and tried to relax. The warm water and steam felt good, and I sunk further into the water. My headache eased.

My body remained relaxed until a knock as the water sent water across the room as I tried to ensure that the water covered my body. Another knock at the door.

"It's Maeja, child."

"Come in," I said.

She entered the room with a basket and I strained my neck to see what she brought. She took a towel from the top of the pile and shook it out before she held it up for me. No one had done that for me since I was little.

I pushed myself above the water's surface and used my arm to cover my breasts as I stepped out of the tub. My gaze focused on the puddle of water at my feet as the drips settled on the wooden floorboards. Maeja wrapped the towel around me and smiled. From the basket beside her, she pulled out several pairs of clean underwear and folded pieces of fabric.

"I have brought you these cloths to use while you have your time. You need to change them regularly otherwise they get this smell and wash them well, best if you can dry them out in the open somewhere in the sun. Your young man provided enough for me to buy this outfit, too. It's probably not your usual style, but this is more common for women to wear here."

I watched as she turned back to the basket and pulled out a dress. *At least it isn't white*. The dark pink dress had hems of darker pink with gold like stitching. The neckline featured a string of white flowers.

"Thank you."

"No need, your young man picked it out, he was very keen to be helpful." Maeja placed the gown back into the basket. "He's worried about you. I've told him not to, but I think he needs to hear it from you."

"When I work out the right words, I'll talk to him."

"Child, he doesn't need the right words. I don't know about how things are in your village, but let me tell you this, if I saw a man look at one of my daughters in such a way, I would hope she noticed."

I looked away from Maeja. *How can one woman know so much?*

"He said something to me," I said as I fidgeted with the towel.

"I can guess, but it might be easier to just tell me."

I nervously wiped my body again, even though I felt sure it couldn't get any dryer.

"He said he loved me."

"And you don't feel the same way?"

"I don't know. My job is to fight, to protect... It isn't my place to take a man."

"Your place? Child, I think he would do anything you asked. Don't take too long to see that. They trained you to not understand your own feelings because they said that would make you a stronger warrior, but that's wrong. What makes you strong, no matter who you are or what you do in life, is the way you allow others into your heart. It's important to have a reason to fight because the heart will always lead you to make the decision that's right in the end. Now, get yourself dressed before I have to put you back into the water again to clean."

With that, Maeja abandoned the basket and closed the door. The underwear and its fresh addition fitted fine, although when I walked back to the basket to grab the dress it felt like I had some weapon hidden away. I felt sure I walked funny and couldn't help but brush my hands over my bottom to check the extra thickness wouldn't show. It wasn't something I wanted to get used to. She might be all for having children, but many women lived happy lives without them. I slipped the dress over my head and it fell around my body. The line of the skirt at least meant that it didn't cling to me, and I felt confident that even if I walked like an injured duck, the reason would remain concealed.

I folded the towel so the folds of it concealed the blood. In the basket I saw Maeja had brought a little pot with a familiar grey powder. I smiled with joy as I picked up the jar and replaced it with the towel.

I cast one last look at the white-pink water in the tub before I grabbed the basket and left the room. Zen sat on the bed with his head in his hands. His hair had loosened from its tie and strands fell over his shoulders. He looked up when I entered and crossed the room with just a couple of strides.

"Here, let me take that," he said.

Zen tugged the basket free and placed it on one of the wooden chairs.

"Do you need to sit down? Or do you prefer to stand? They're cooking food soon downstairs, unless you'd rather eat here…"

Maeja hadn't been wrong. "I'm okay Zen, really."

"But you were bleeding, and you weren't injured," Zen whispered.

"I know. Maeja has explained. I am fine, really."

"How can you be fine if…"

"Shh, I am going to be fine. In a couple of days I'll be back to normal."

Zen nodded but didn't move. His eyes focused on my face. It looked like he wanted to say something.

"You'd tell me if you weren't, wouldn't you?"

I reached out and placed my hand on his arm. The sleeve of my dress fell back from my wrist and settled around my elbow.

"With this, yes, I would tell you if there was something wrong, but Maeja has explained things to me and apparently I'm fine."

He didn't look convinced, but nodded all the same. "You look really beautiful."

"It's the dress," I said and lifted one side of the skirt with my free hand.

"It's never the dress," Zen replied. "You think you might want to eat something then?"

"Yeah, I would like that, but none of that drink this time."

"Come on then."

CHAPTER 21

Together, we walked downstairs. The number of people who turned to look made me shift nervously. I kept thinking that they knew my secret, but after several comments about the dress, I relaxed into the chair. Zen had gone to order, and I wondered how much gold he had left to pay for things. I hadn't intended for us to need to restock so early in our journey. He said nothing as he returned and sat at the chair beside me, closer than he would have at home at the round table we sat at.

"Do you want to head off straight away, or stay a few days…"

The question hung in the air. I had thought about that in the bath. Part of me longed to stay in the room until the bleeding passed, but then we would spend additional money and lose valuable time in reaching the mountains. It made more sense to push through, even if I had to go slower than before.

"We'll leave in the morning. It could take another five or six days to reach the base of the mountain in the distance."

Zen nodded. He didn't question it and I appreciated that. When the plates of meat with plants on the side arrived, I took a moment to appreciate the smells. After such little food up the mountain to the dragon temple, I hadn't enjoyed such a spread since Zen had cooked back home. I showed my approval for the food by polishing off every morsel. I wiped the plate clean with the bread I had kept aside from the beginning of the meal.

"Should we..." I began.

The doors of the building swung open, hitting the walls on either side. Three women stood covered in dirt, one had bloodstained clothes. In her hands lay a small child. His head hung limp and his eyes were closed.

"We need the medicine people, straight away!" the woman carrying the child demanded.

A girl came out from behind the counter. She hurried around the group and out the doors. The woman moved over to a vacant table and laid the bleeding child on top of it.

"Hey, you can't do that. We serve food in here!" the barkeeper said and tossed the cloth over her shoulder.

"I'll do as I damn well please when a child is dying. Here." The woman unclipped a small pouch from her belt and tossed it towards the barkeeper before she moved out from behind the counter. I watched as the barkeeper opened it before pulling the strings tight and tucking the pouch down between her breasts.

My eyes drifted back to the boy on the table. I couldn't see where the blood emanated from. I leaned closer to Zen to get a better look without being too obvious.

"Why is no one helping?"

Zen shrugged and leaned in closer. "You stay; I'll see what I can do."

He stood up and walked around the table. The two other women moved quickly to block him from getting any closer to the child.

"You don't come any closer," the woman with the long black hair stated, and pulled a dagger from her belt.

My gaze looked to the ceiling, to where my sword lay beneath the bed, utterly useless for me at the moment. I debated whether to join Zen, but my back ached, and I wasn't confident with the extra padding between my legs. A sword would be easier than fighting against a dagger with my body and skill. It seemed a poor excuse.

"I only want to help..."

"You're a man. What would you know other than

how to inflict pain onto others?" she spat back in response.

Zen's hands went up in defence as he shook his head. "I'm only trying to help."

The third woman stepped forward and blocked the partial view that remained of the boy. Her hand stretched towards him and her other near her hip. I couldn't see a weapon, but didn't doubt that she had one. I stood up and instantly regretted it. It felt like someone poured a bucket of water between my legs. I hoped no one would notice anything, since the wall was behind me.

"Zen, come and sit down," I said.

He turned his head towards me and nodded. Zen stepped away from the women as Maeja sent the doors flying into the walls again. She hurried over to the woman closest to the boy and set a basket down on a vacant chair.

Zen continued to walk backwards towards me and I sat back down on the chair when neither of the women went for him. My eyes looked around the room at the other men who sat at tables, all of them busying themselves with the grain of the wood on the tabletops. I doubted this was the first time they had been told to back off, or accused of being the bearer of pain.

"What do you think she meant by that?"

"Who knows, remember men aren't trusted back home either. Though, those ladies seem to have a deeper hatred for you all."

Maeja nodded towards the first woman. From what I could see, she picked up the boy again and the four women left the inn. The doors hadn't swung back in place before the young girl who had gone for help appeared with a bucket. Without being told, she dipped the cloths into the water and attacked the stains on the table and then the floor.

"Come on, do you want to go back upstairs and rest?"

"No, I'm curious about the boy," I replied.

Zen leaned forward and rested his folded arms on the table. "On this occasion, Alexa, that's something I can't help you with."

I reached out and touched his arm. "That's okay. I think maybe I'll head over there in a minute."

"You sure..."

"I'll be fine, Zen."

I pushed myself up from the table and braced for the same feeling as before. Before I could check on the boy, I needed to check on myself.

"I'm just going to go... wash up first."

I didn't wait for a response and ascended the steps two at a time until I closed the door behind me with a soft thud. I took a deep breath and debated whether to take the dress off or just hitch it up. Decisions! I took it off; better to be safe. I turned the dress around just to check that I didn't have blood everywhere, but it looked as it did when Maeja handed it to me.

I took the bucket of water out from under the bed meant for hand washing before I removed the cloth and dropped it in. I'd deal with it later. At the moment I just wanted to check on the boy.

With the fresh cloth in place and the dress back on, I stopped to check on Fiya. She looked up at me and flew onto my shoulder; I wouldn't be alone after all.

I headed downstairs and gave Zen a wave as I headed for the door. Outside, the street didn't have any lights to help me find Maeja, and only a few people lingered at the front of houses. I walked down the dirt road and at each of the houses before I paused before one with a familiar symbol above the door. Two crescents intersected just down from the tips.

Others might have stopped and knocked, but it wasn't required back home. I opened the door. The empty corridor in front of me soon filled when the woman with long, curly black hair appeared.

"What do you want?" she demanded.

"The boy, I wanted to see if there was some way I could help. Maeja has been very good to me," I replied.

The dagger lowered. "You were with that thing." The woman spat onto the floor.

"You don't like men?"

"Clearly you don't know the truth about them, but there is time for you to learn."

"Learn what?"

The woman sneered before she shook her head. "Tell you what…"

"He's alive," the blood covered woman said as she exited a room on the left. "Who's she?"

"I'm Alexa," I responded.

"What do you want?" the new woman asked.

"I was concerned for the boy, the injury he had."

The woman pushed the other aside and stepped towards me. I stood my ground. She paused just before me and wiped the blood from her hands onto a cloth.

"Injury? Interesting choice of word."

"I speak as I find."

"You're not from here and I doubt that dress would have been what you would have chosen."

I broke eye contact to look down. "You're correct

on both."

"Why are you really here?"

I smiled. Not much seemed to get past her. "You wouldn't let my friend help, I wondered why."

"You wondered why all the men stayed away and why we refused help from your... friend?"

"Yes."

"Give me some time to clean up and I'll happily tell you."

The woman walked into a room close by and closed the door. I watched the woman with the black hair turn to her companion that had joined us during the interaction. "I guess that means I shouldn't kill her. Follow me."

I did as the black-haired woman asked and followed them back down the hall. I looked into the boy's room as I passed, but could only see Maeja as she mixed something beside a table. The only sign of the boy was the small feet that stuck out from under the end of the blanket.

We walked outside to where a table and several chairs sat. The black-haired woman gestured for me to take a seat, and I cringed at the thought. The sitting didn't seem to be the problem, but the sitting and standing up... Still, I sat and watched as the other two did the same.

"I'm Tapaja," the black-haired woman said, and tossed a few curls back over her shoulder. "And this is Janara. She doesn't talk; the dragons took care of that."

My gaze moved to Janara. She didn't look that different from Tapaja, except her hair had brown streaks through it. That's when I saw it, the scar that ran from her left ear, around and down her neck. The initial wound must have been deep in order to have scarred over like that.

"They trained me to fight the dragons; it's why I'm here."

"Few dragons in these villages, they like to prey when you're alone in a forest, or trapped on a mountain. So why here?" Tapaja asked.

"We had to come to get supplies. We had planned to move further south in the morning."

"What, with the man?"

"I've known Zen since I was born and I trust him."

"You trust until secrets divide. Were you never told that men should not trustworthy? How many men have you seen your entire life? Ten, twenty, I'd wager no more than thirty. No matter where you go in this cursed kingdom, men disappear. Of course, there are a few that remain, but that's necessary to their ultimate plan."

"Plan? Who, the men or the dragons? Men here differ from inside the valley we are from."

"Janara, the poor fool really trusts him."

"With my life, Tapaja."

"So did Janara. Where was her man when the dragon pounced on her? Oh, he was running for the trees, screaming like a little kid. Even after the dragon left, he didn't bother to check on her. A man, Alexa. A man who had declared he loved Janara, no matter what. A man who soon found another woman to love."

My gaze moved to Janara. Her nose twitched, but no other emotions showed. Either she had pushed her memories of the day away or she'd heard the story enough times that it no longer caused her pain. Maybe one day I could remember the day the dragons attacked without emotions to cloud my thoughts.

CHAPTER 22

"So tell me, Alexa, why do you trust him? That man?"

The last word she spoke in a malicious tone. I could have told her all the great things about Zen and she would find fault with every point. I decided a change of subject would be more productive.

"Dragons attacked our village. Many of our elders were wiped out. There's only the rest of us left, we thought... I thought... I had to do something."

"So are you and this man going to head off into the mountains and do what? Kill the dragons? I was young like you once and just as foolish. We have suffered dragon attacks in our homes too. A wound like my sister's is one thing, but the wound a man will leave when he betrays you will cut far deeper than anything you have felt."

"Did you kill the dragon that did it?" I asked.

Tapaja smiled. "The closest thing to a dragon. The one responsible is dead, and that mattered to me even if it solved nothing of our problems."

I raised my eyebrows at the comment. The answer made me uneasy. Either it had been a dragon or it hadn't. As much as I hated dragons, the thought of a mistaken identity didn't sit well.

"And the boy? It was a dragon?"

"Dragons are many things, Alexa. You do well to remember that," Tapaja said.

The wounds on the boy resembled those I'd seen during the last attack, but I had noticed some minor differences. Bodies of the attack had wounds with ragged tears on the edges. They were deep, and in some bodies the bone was exposed. The child's wounds bled, but they weren't deep, and the slashes were clean.

I shifted in the seat. "What else would have done such a thing?"

A smile crossed the Tapaja's face. She leaned back in her chair. "Men Alexa, men who protect the dragons. Haven't you ever noticed that they just vanish? Those that remain differ from those that don't. But where exactly do you think they go? For what purpose do you think they go? I'll tell you something — it's all to do with the dragons."

Footsteps in the house drew my attention to the back door. I glanced over to see the redheaded woman as she stepped outside. She had changed into fresh clothes and no longer had skin stained with blood. She sat down in the spare seat.

"You don't look convinced, Alexa," she commented as she sat down.

"Does the child rest well, Kalana?" Tapaja asked.

"For the moment," Kalana replied. "You're not convinced, are you Alexa? You look at us as if we are trying to scare you with a story. Cautious and hesitant to believe and yet... yet deep down something pulls at you."

"I don't know. I mean, the men must have a purpose for leaving, but I don't know why some would remain. I mean, if there was some big thing going on, wouldn't they all go?"

My own words would have found me in confinement if Leila had ever heard them. Some men disappeared without explanation. A handful stayed to do menial work, and then there were those designated like Zen. He would be coupled unless he disappeared before the ceremony. In the warmer months, sometimes an elder would arrive with a carriage filled with children. They gave those children to the couples that had none of their own to be raised.

"Men start as innocent until they know the truth," Tapaja said.

"She doesn't know yet, honey. Look at her face." Kalana pointed at me.

"Then tell me. If it is something I should know."

"Alexa, if I were to tell you all the secrets of this kingdom, you would believe me even less. You would leave this house thinking I lived in my head and not right here and now. Some things in life you must find out in your own time."

"Then tell me, if all men are part of some plan, then why do some remain?" I asked.

"So many of the men disappear when they come of age. Many a woman has lost her heart and the man. Never to see them again. What did the elders tell you about the disappearances?" Kalana asked.

"Our elders never said."

"I guess the elders have strict rules. You are from the valley where people dare not go. The elders there know the truth and I suspect they even know things we three ladies don't."

"Tapaja said secrets are why men can't be trusted. If that were the case, then what about the elders? They were women. Why should they be trusted?"

Kalana leaned forward. "The secret a woman keeps differs from the secret a man keeps."

I hadn't been completely honest with Zen about the bleeding, but that wasn't a secret. I felt conflicted by the thoughts in my head. These women must have seen things I hadn't, but they seem committed to what they saw as the truth and I wondered if it was clouded. Like my emotions clouded my impulsive decision to leave the valley.

Kalana tossed something my way, and I caught it in my hand. I opened my palm and saw the tip of a claw, a dragon claw.

"I will tell you this, Alexa. Some men disappear because their secret must be kept but those that remain are there to relay information to those that would destroy all humans."

"But then those left behind would be destroyed too. Wouldn't they?" I looked at the claw. "The men in our village have always been good to us."

"Of course, because if they were mean and cruel, you wouldn't trust them. You wouldn't feel at ease in their presence. People say far more in the company of friends than foe," Kalana said. She leaned back in her chair.

"Think about it, Alexa. Do the men in your village ever disappear for just a few hours and not say where they've been? That's the start of the deceitful behaviour. Men are always going off to do something behind women's backs. They're always planning and scheming something." Tapaja twisted a strand of hair around her finger. "Tell me Alexa, when the dragons attacked, how many of the victims were men?"

I pursed my lips. "I'm not in the village enough. I spend so much of the time on the training field so I don't see what men do during the day — except that anything I need done is by the time I return."

"And the last question I asked?" Tapaja said.

"But that... You can't say that the dragons only attack women. I mean, yes on that day women were the only victims, but that was because the hunt was targeted. All warriors are women..." I sounded like Zen. I had just defended why the dragons only attacked the warriors, even though Tapaja was right.

"Why attack those with swords when an easier prey is a village full of unarmed men?" Tapaja smiled and turned to her sister. "All in the details."

"But..." I tried to think of an explanation.

"Please enlighten, as you seem to know something that we don't," Kalana said.

I leaned forward a little and rested my elbows on the small table that sat in the middle of us. "I've heard stories and about a woman and a dragon and that things didn't go as the woman hoped. Then they claim she infected the dragons somehow, and that's why we fight them now. I don't know how much of that's the truth though, but it was something I heard."

"And you bothered to take the time to listen to such rubbish? I bet it was a man that spun that story, testing it and watching for your reaction as a woman. That's one thing they do to see if it's plausible enough to spread through the outlying villages in the valley.

You know there are even some women out here who are sympathetic to the dragons." Kalana turned to Janara. "Could you fetch me a glass of water, sweetie?"

Janara nodded before she moved inside the house.

"Tell me this then, Kalana. If the dragons don't attack men then why injure the boy?"

"I wondered how long it would take you to get there." Kalana took the glass that Janara had brought to her and took a sip. "It's quite simple, that's not a boy in there, it's a girl."

"What?"

"We seek children we feel are in danger of the influences of men and find them homes with powerful women who will raise them right. They had disguised her as a boy, thinking we wouldn't notice. It wasn't safe for her to remain where she was. When the dragon attacked us outside of the city, that proved it."

"That's why you wouldn't let Zen near her. He would have recognised it wasn't a boy."

"And don't you go running back and telling him. She is safe at the moment. Tapaja has a home for her to go to."

"What of her family though…"

"She will have a family that can protect her."

"Are you sure that is the truth, or is it what you think is the truth? I was raised without either of my parents, but to be taken away by force…"

"Seems to me you've been spending far too much time with that man. You left the village to seek revenge. I can see that. You remind me of myself once upon a time," Kalana said. She placed the empty glass on the table. "Yet now, where is your resolve? Why are you questioning things? Your elders might have been a little odd, but they knew something."

"The burden though…"

"The burden is a tale the dragons tell. A pretty tale it is, but not one of truth. Who writes those tales? Dragons and the men who stand by them. We must protect this next generation from those lies but you and your generation need to be strong enough not to give in to the corrupt tales to make you doubt their evilness."

"You sound confident in your opinions, but an opinion is not a fact," I said.

"Alexa, you don't need to believe what we say. Why don't you just follow that man of yours around; see what he does when he thinks you're not with him. It will never matter what conversation you have, pay attention as he will always want to convince you of the good of the dragons, no matter what."

I chose to bite my tongue rather than continue. It felt like this was an argument where one side had already declared themselves the winner. Still, as the conversation turned to other chatter, their words repeated in my mind. They weren't exactly wrong about Zen. He didn't side with the dragons it was just he wanted to understand and think the best of everything and everyone. The dragon temple, given a chance, I suspect he would have stayed there far longer than we did. Was that curiosity or something more?

"You must've been at on a mountain recently." Kalana pointed to Fiya; she sat asleep on my shoulder.

"We climbed the mountain over there," I said. I pointed in the general direction. "We wanted to get a better overview of this part of the kingdom and where things were."

A blatant lie. I reached up and scratched Fiya's head.

"Do you know what type of bird that she is?" Kalana asked.

I shook my head and she smiled.

"She's a teraca. They are best known for their ability to make the sounds of other creatures. You might have even heard to do that already."

I nodded my head. "I had noticed that she could

pretend to be other people and creatures. I thought she would be good company wherever I go."

"She won't go with you." Tapaja said. She walked over to me and gave Fiya a pat. "She is a mountain bird. I'm surprised she has stayed with you for so long. They prefer the air up high. You need to prepare yourself for when she leaves."

"You never know, maybe she will stay."

"You keep telling yourself that, Alexa."

Tapaja moved towards the door and signalled to her sister. Together they went inside Maeja's house.

"She tells you because she doesn't want you hurt, Alexa."

"You're right. There is a choice with everything in life, Alexa. It's just whether you're willing to open your eyes and see the truth that is right before you." Kalana smiled. "You shall have to excuse me as well. It's been a long day and I need to rest. Perhaps we will walk the same path soon."

I sat there alone at the table for a while. The cool night air felt pleasant against my skin. I smoothed the skirt on the dress. This wasn't who I was; perhaps it was how Zen wanted me to be.

With that thought, I decided to return to the inn. I passed several closed doors as I walked down the passage. Maeja appeared too busy to interrupt as she tended to the girl.

Outside the house, I walked towards the inn. A few people chattered in conversation as I passed them by. Ahead of me a man walked. His long black hair danced in the breeze. As if he sensed me, he paused and turned around.

A smile spread across his face, and he nodded. "Good evening Alexa. My, you look a beautiful sight tonight."

He didn't wait for me to reply as the darkness concealed him. I needed to get back to Zen.

CHAPTER 23

I ran up the stairs and opened the bedroom door. Zen threw the blanket over himself on the bed, but not before I had seen his hands. My feet skidded on the floor, and my gaze narrowed on him.

"What was that?"

"Nothing," Zen said.

I know what I saw. He pulled his hands out from underneath the blanket, but a conspicuous bulge remained. I walked over to his bed. I would retrieve what I had seen, and my mind couldn't think of a subtle way to do it.

"You've never hidden stuff from me before."

"It's nothing Alexa."

My hand darted under the blanket. My hand brushed against his pants as I felt for the book that I had seen. Zen leaned back against his pillow as I pulled the book out from under the blanket. The binding was unmistakable; I'd only seen it in one place. I looked up at him with my mouth open and tried to find the words, especially after what I had just been told.

He took a book from that place? Why would he do that? Why carry it down all the way down that mountain?

"What were you thinking, taking this from that place?"

Zen's legs swung over the side of the bed. I turned the book over in my hands as he reached up and pulled me down beside him. I felt the softness of the bed beneath me. Zen pushed the blanket aside and shuffled beside me until his leg leaned against mine.

"He offered the book, and I said yes. I actually bought back a couple. It's not that big a deal. You know me; I've always enjoyed reading and learning."

Kalana and Tapaja's words wouldn't let up in my mind. "It is a big deal Zen, why can't you see that? This version of events that we've been told, that dragons are actually good and we should all trust them and how they're loving and... Zen, how can you be sure that these stories aren't just trying to trick us?"

"Alexa, I just want to learn. I don't believe everything I'm told or what I read." His hand reached out and covered mine as they rested on top of the book. "If we never go outside of our own thinking and learning, then what is the purpose here? We would accomplish nothing except to go around and around in the same circle. I don't want to keep going in circles. I want to create my own path. I want you there by my side as I do."

Zen's head leaned against mine. I felt his hair brush against my skin. *Why am I so aware of him?* I closed my eyes for a moment. A new pathway might sound good to Zen, but I had never been keen on the unknown. We had both lived under the rules of the elders and even then we had broken many of the rules. I wondered what Leila would think if she could see me now. Would she rebuke me if I confessed to her that feelings stirred inside of me for Zen were more than care of a best friend?

"How's the boy?"

"The boy? Oh, yeah they think he'll be okay," I said.

I opened my eyes and looked across the room. I could feel his hand as it rested on mine.

"Did the woman say what might have caused those injuries?"

I hesitated at that. Another truth to conceal. Another secret to keep. As a woman, we're allowed secrets. The elders had been clear about how all females were superior to the men. I felt guilty that I didn't want him to have secrets from me and yet I had many I kept from him. The words of the women also repeated in my mind. It didn't help that I had suspicions about their story of a dragon attack.

"Apparently it was some kind of wild animal that attacked."

The fingers on my free hand ran down the spine of the book. His hand squeezed mine. How much danger could reading a book create? I pushed the book back towards him and felt the engraved cover as it slid out from under my hand.

Zen's hand moved the book to the bed beside him. "You're not happy I'm going to read it, are you?"

"I don't like how they've got you drawn into their world and that you said nothing to me about the books."

"I could have said something, but then you would have tried to convince me not to bring the books. Tell me Alexa, what's so bad about bringing these books here to read?"

"Because you took them from the temple." I tucked a strand of hair behind my ear that immediately freed itself. "At some point in the future you'll need to go back and return them. It means that you're going to climb back up that mountain and go back through that field and to that temple to see those men again. It makes me uneasy."

"I can understand being up there in the temple

making you feel uncomfortable, but why be afraid of me going back? I admit I found it liberating being around so many men with new ideas. Conversations about things I never knew or stopped to think about. For those couple of days, Alexa I wasn't being told I wasn't good enough because I was a man. I was in a place where I felt like somebody, somebody who mattered. Can't you understand that?"

"You matter to me Zen, that's why I fear those books. I fear the ideas you will get and that maybe when I return to the valley I will be alone."

Unlike Zen, I had never been told I was useless. Leila had criticised me many times, but all that helped me to improve. I felt more confident around women though, so perhaps that was what he meant. That feeling of having a place.

"No matter what Alexa, you won't return to the valley alone."

Zen sounded more confident than I felt. I could almost visualise myself as I walked back into the village.

"Alexa?"

Zen's hand reached up and caught the disobedient strand. He tucked it behind my ear and smoothed the strand against the rest of the hair. I felt his fingers brush against my cheek. I closed my eyes as his scent comforted me.

"Tell me we're okay, Alexa."

I exhaled slowly. We were a long way from home and he was all I had. As much as the books made me uneasy, we had left for a reason and I would rather journey with Zen than by myself for as long as possible.

"We made a promise; I'm not ready to break that."

He wrapped his arms around me and drew me close. He'd hugged me many times, but my heart had never pounded so hard.

"I'll stand by you no matter what, Alexa."

I felt him kiss my hair. I'd see men in the village do that, the ones that were coupled. A change of conversation was needed.

"When I was coming back here, I saw someone in the street that I didn't expect to see."

"Really? Who?"

"Ojerren."

I felt his hold release. "Ojerren? Back here? Really? I thought he said something about returning home. Wasn't that before we headed up the mountain?"

I nodded, though I hadn't paid attention to much of what Ojerren said.

"Well, obviously he didn't and something caused

him to come back." My tone sounded more accusatory than I anticipated.

"What is it that you've got going through your mind?"

"Amongst other things. When we left the valley, I didn't expect for everything to be so different. At the same time, I get this feeling about Ojerren. It's off being there is something that seems so familiar about him and yet... I feel he's purposely hanging around because there is something he is up to." I looked over at Zen. "Or maybe he's come back for someone."

"Alexa, I think you're just being paranoid," he said.

I shook my head. "No Zen, my training tells me that something is up. This is no coincidence, but we need to find out more information. We need to know who he is."

"Do you want to spy on the man?"

"I don't think we have any other choice. It was him that kept going on about the dragons and how they might be good. I don't believe that some random person left us that note to head up the mountain. I think it was Ojerren." I looked over at Zen. "Maybe he is a member of the temple. Oh I don't know, but he's mixed up with all this and the reason we got distracted."

"I don't know. He's smart. Let's say it was

Ojerren who planted the note. Think about it. He was able to sneak up on both of us and put that note there."

"Well we weren't exactly ourselves that night." I cringed at the memory.

"True, and this morning you were..." He let the sentence hang and I felt the warmth rise in my face. I hoped the dim light in the room would conceal it.

"I think sleep is what we both need to have before we do anything more. Whatever the reason for Ojerren being back here, I don't think he's going to do anything until tomorrow at least," Zen said.

"Maybe."

"Trust me Alexa, even if he has some evil plan in place, he will still need his rest, just like the rest of us." Zen smiled. "Plus, it's not like he would sneak in here with any success. Fiya would see to that."

"Okay, you have a point there."

"Come on, time to rest."

I prepared myself for bed and turned down the lantern as I pulled the blanket over my body. Fiya had settled into the blanket on the cupboard and fallen asleep. I lay awake in bed and heard Zen's steady breathing as he too gave in to rest.

I adjusted the pillow so I could see Zen. Did I really not trust Zen? Or did I not trust myself? Not trust that everything the elders had done was for our good anymore? So many voices telling me what to think. So many telling me was the truth. I wanted to find my own voice and listen to that, but where would I start if I did?

The oath I took echoed in my head. The dragons could wait. Ojerren had some connection to them, and I needed to know what before we continued.

I snuggled down into the warmth of the blanket as thoughts continued to plague my mind. I closed my eyes to the world and hoped that the darkness would clear them all, but inside when sleep came there were dragons. Not just any dragons, but a black one and white one. And they wouldn't leave my mind.

CHAPTER 24

My eyes opened to a dim light that filtered through the curtains. Beside me Fiya lay curled up on her little blanket with eyes wide open. I wondered what caused her to move during the night. Sometimes I had woken from a sleep still tired. Leila called it 'distressed sleep' and would often give me a powder to mix with some water before bed.

"You're ready to have something to eat, aren't you girl?" I whispered to her.

I propped myself up and glanced across the room to check on Zen. The covers still rested over his body. His head rested on the pillow with his hair spread out over the pillow and partially concealed his face in places. My heart beat faster. I shook my head and turned my attention back to Fiya.

Fiya pushed herself up onto her feet and did a little turnaround before she fluffed out her tail and turned around. She shifted from foot to foot while she chirped in low tones.

"I'll take that as a yes then."

I reached under the bed and felt the cold air attack my skin. I felt around for the bag I had placed under there yesterday after Zen had purchased grains, which I combined with the leaves I'd collected on my walk. I loosened the cord and took a handful of food. I tipped it into a round container on the floorboards. Fiya immediately approached the pot and pecked at the grains. I watched as her beak rhythmically beat the food. Such a simple action: Fiya, happy with what she had been given. I smiled at her before I averted my gaze back to Zen. His eyes looked back at me.

"How do you feel today?" he asked.

I had to admit that compared to the previous day, when I thought I was going to die, I felt pretty good. I only got up twice during the night to deal with it, which was a lot less than what I thought it would be. Now that he'd mentioned it, though, I felt the urge to go to the bathroom.

"Better thanks, but we've got things to do. We need to get ourselves ready quickly this morning." I threw back the covers and grabbed my usual outfit that had since been washed and laid at the end of the bed on a small cupboard ready for me to wear.

"Would you rather just rest, I mean..."

I shook my head. "I have to know what he's up to,

Zen. There seems to be more to it, there's more to him, there's more to everything we know. Somebody sent us up that mountain and I can't shake the feeling that it was Ojerren and I want to know why."

"Have you ever thought that maybe he didn't have another purpose, Alexa? He was a man we came across coming here. There's no proof he was the one that sent us up the mountain, it could have been anyone."

My hand rested on the door handle for a moment, and I turned to see he'd sat up in the bed. His hair framed his face and his shirt gaped to reveal more than it should. "Zen, all my life I've been told what I have to do and what I should think. The biggest rule of all was that I shouldn't trust any man. Why should I make an exception to that now?"

"But you've already made an exception with me, Alexa. That's why I don't understand why, if you can trust me, it's so hard to open your mind to the possibility of trusting someone else."

"That's completely different, there's no way you can compare the two things. I've known you my entire life and I think in that time you've earned my respect and trust. I met Ojerren a handful of days ago."

Before Zen could answer, I glanced away and entered the bathroom. I exhaled slowly as I leaned against the closed door. That was awkward. I had heard how my voice caught when I said the word 'trust'.

As I cleaned myself up, I tried to work out what to do about Ojerren. My plan so far had been just to find him… but then what?

"If he came to this village to get supplies like Zen, and I then there would be no reason to return so soon. Not unless something else brought him back. Something or someone," I murmured.

Zen would be just on the other side of the wall. Could Ojerren have returned for him? I shook my head and focused on myself. In a moment of forethought, I had placed two cloths in the bathroom where I hoped Zen wouldn't see but were convenient for me to grab.

When I emerged from the bathroom, I had dressed and was ready to go. Zen too had dressed and excused himself to use the bathroom, which allowed me to dispose of the evidence I had in my hand behind my back.

Fiya left no trace of her meal. She cooed before she flew up onto my shoulder. Fiya made so many unique sounds that I wondered which were her own and which were borrowed. She settled into her usual spot after her head scratch and I pulled the blankets up on the bed. I shouldn't have bothered.

The door to the bathroom remained closed, and I mixed my morning tea. It didn't taste as nice cold but as long as it did its job I could deal with it.

"Now Fiya, remember to be quiet today."

She wasn't the only one. I looked out the window at the rooftops and the forest beyond them.

"You sure it's wise to bring Fiya?"

My hand held my chest. I turned to see Zen beside me on the opposite side of Fiya.

"You did that on purpose."

He leaned forward and smiled. "Someone needs to check if you're paying attention."

We ate food downstairs before we ventured outside. The air hadn't warmed as much as I wanted, and while my outfit provided more warmth than the dress, I still shivered.

A few people mingled in the street as I looked up and down the road. My gaze fell on Maeja's house before I felt a warm hand rest on my arm.

"Yeah?"

"There are only a couple of places where he could've stayed overnight and the people here I don't think would welcome someone into their house even if he visited regularly," Zen said.

"So what are you saying?"

"I don't know. I guess, if Ojerren didn't stay in

the inn, then that narrows where he spent the night." Zen squeezed my arm. "People here are just as distrustful of others as you are."

"I'm not distrustful, I'm cautious."

"It's the same difference, Alexa."

Zen glanced up and down the road. I saw nothing unusual, but something piqued his interest as his hand released my arm. He stepped off the veranda and made his way down the road to where we had first arrived.

He kept a steady stride as we passed Maeja's house. I had to do a brief run several times just to keep up with him before he turned to the left and moved between two houses. He crouched down and passed his hand over the dirt. His frame blocked my view and I couldn't quite make out what it was, but I had a feeling he found a footprint of something. At least, that's what I hoped he'd found.

My feet crunched the dirt as I moved closer and looked over his shoulder.

"He's been this " Zen ran his finger around the edge of the shape. "These are definitely his footprints."

"How do you know those aren't mine, or yours, or some other random person in this village?"

A familiar smile appeared on his face. "Because Alexa, this is about the same sized shoe he was wearing the day we saw him in the forest. You are lighter than Ojerren, so your footprints aren't as deep. My feet are larger than his, so they're not mine either. And besides, I noticed he had a cut across the sole of his left shoe and if you look right there," he pointed to the raised mark across the footprint. "You can see it."

I crouched down and traced my finger along the line in the footprint. That detail I would have missed. I turned to look at the footprints I had left. They were different for sure. Only I had to check, whereas Zen just knew.

"You're fantastic, you know that, right?" I said.

"You can't just keep me around for my good looks. I have to be good at something else."

"Come on then show off. Lead me to where they go."

The tracks led behind a house and into the forest. The large trees had a thick canopy, which provided plenty of shadows for us to lurk in as we followed Ojerren. We had walked some distance when I noticed that a faint path had emerged from the thick undergrowth.

We stayed more in the thicker bushes, but it meant Ojerren created distance between us before he disappeared from view. I paused. Zen had crouched down some way ahead of me. I narrowed my gaze as I tried to make out what I could hear. The rustle of leaves in the breeze, the scratch of an animal in the undergrowth... the murmur of voices.

As I listened, Fiya landed on my shoulder without a sound. The direction of the voices was difficult to ascertain.

"Zen," I whispered.

His feet came to a standstill and he turned to look at me. I pointed to my ears. He stood there until I caught up with him and then together made our way through the thick bushes. The stems had small thorns that grabbed at my clothing and scratched my arms. I drew my sword and wished I could use it to cut the horrid things down.

The muffled voices continued. We were quiet, but I struggled to locate the source of the conversation. Zen reached out and touched my arm. I followed his gaze and saw two men appear. Branches obscured the other man's face, and I yearned to move to get a better view.

As we watched, at least three more men joined the conversation. Apart from hair, I couldn't make out anything distinct to identify who they might be. I couldn't even tell if they might have come from this village. The conversation they had continued. One man moved to the side and I saw a flash of orange material before the man moved back to where he had been.

I glanced to the side and looked for a way to move that didn't involve being torn to shreds by plants. The path Ojerren had walked was too open, though. My foot felt numb as I wiggled my toes in the shoes.

That's when the men took off their jackets. Two men loosened their hair that had been fastened high on their heads and it flowed down past their shoulders. Not quick enough though, as I had seen the black blur that curled around their necks. Each of them had the same black tattoo and I knew they were of a dragon.

Tattoo inkings weren't uncommon even in our village. I had one on my ankle when I reached the elite. I remembered the pain as the sharp needle went into my skin over and over. It wasn't something I was keen to repeat.

I tapped Zen on the shoulder and pointed to my neck. He nodded in acknowledgement. The men at the temple had a variety of hair lengths but high collars on the robes that showed very little of the neck. Zen had long hair, but when he was younger, it had been short. It had taken me a while to get used to him having hair as long as mine. My gaze drifted to his neck to reassure me he didn't have the tattoo as well. He didn't.

"Should we try to get closer?" I asked.

Zen shook his head. He didn't seem keen to move from our position. We waited a while longer until the men picked their jackets off the ground and put them on. Each took the time to turn the collar up and pull their hair out so it flowed down their back.

CHAPTER 25

My legs reached the point I could barely feel them. The other men walked away in the opposite direction while Ojerren stayed put. *Surely you've talked enough, gotten air. Move man!* My stomach growled and I winced. I should have had more to eat before we left this morning.

Ojerren walked in the village's direction again. Zen and I continued to follow him at a safe distance, but I felt compelled to check behind me more than once.

More people were about as we entered the village again. The sun was now high enough to be seen over the surrounding forests. I watched as Ojerren approached a man near the doorway of one house. A woman pushed past them to get outside without a second glance to Ojerren. Zen tugged on my sleeve and we stepped into the shadows of one house to watch Ojerren concealed from his view.

He met with yet another man and I focused on the neck. It was difficult to know for sure, but the upturned collar to me confirmed he had a tattoo, too. The tattoos and dragons were linked, but I felt like I was missing a piece of the puzzle. The conversation with this man ended, and they moved in their own directions.

We followed Ojerren for most of the morning as he wandered around the village. I counted five men he stopped to speak to. Some conversations were brief, longer than a mere greeting, but they looked like small talk being made. Other conversations went longer, one in particular for over an hour. Ojerren had stopped outside the shed where the woman had first pointed Zen and me towards the inn. The results of that night had left me distrustful of the woman who sat with a horse's hoof in her lap as she dug around the metal shoe with some kind of tool. Looking from the man to woman, I noticed the similarity in appearance. The man wasn't much older than us and nodded frequently during the conversation, causing his long blond hair that he'd plaited to swing as it hung down the centre of his back. A high-necked jumper concealed his neck but I knew what would be beneath it.

Ojerren shook hands with the man. I noticed he cast his gaze around his surroundings, just like I would have. Apparently satisfied, he smiled at the man. Zen and I followed him to the inn. I watched him through the window and saw the plate of food he ordered arrive. The steam rose from the meat, and my mouth salivated at the thought.

"Alexa, I don't think this is getting us anywhere," Zen said.

I lowered my feet until they were flat on the ground. My fingers still gripped the window's frame when I turned to face him.

"I think we've gotten a lot of information."

"I think you're trying to justify a wasted morning. He met a few men in the forest, chatted with some townspeople and now he is eating."

"There is something going on. He didn't just chat with townspeople Zen, he only spoke with men. In the entire morning he's barely looked twice at any female. It's almost like he's seeking the men for some greater purpose, though what I'm not sure."

"Why don't we ask him? Come on, he might surprise you and tell you everything you need to know to put that mind to rest. Besides, I'm hungry and bored, which is a dangerous combination."

I rolled my eyes. "I can't risk him knowing I think he's up to something, you know that, Zen. You might think of your hunger pains, but surely you're not claiming to be so naïve. The element of surprise might be the only advantage that we have in the situation and I will not give it up just because you're bored."

Zen sighed. He stepped back until I heard the clunk of his shoe on the wall of the building beside the inn as he propped his leg up. He crossed his arms over his chest and looked away towards the ground.

I shook my head and turned back to the wall. To see anything, I had to stand on my tippy-toes. Ojerren didn't mess about when it came to eating; he'd almost cleaned the entire plate. I felt a softness brush against my cheek as Fiya awoke. She purred before she stood and gave her wings a flap. I leaned my head to the side to avoid the feathers. After a final shake, she hopped off my shoulder and glided down to the ground. I watched as she stretched her legs before she busied herself with the dirt. She scratched and pecked at something I couldn't see, but it captured her full attention.

"See, even the bird thinks this is ridiculous."

"Oh, okay, we'll take a break then. Sheesh, one morning and you're ready to quit, or perhaps there's something upstairs that you'd rather be doing?"

Zen pushed off from the wall with his foot. I lowered myself to the ground and let go of my grip on the window sill. I brushed my hands against each other and then on my pants. When I checked them, dirt still covered the tips of my fingers.

"Come on, Alexa. Let's find you some water to wash those hands."

I let out a friendly growl directed at Zen before I turned to the preoccupied bird. "Fiya, you coming?"

The little bird paused long enough to look up at me and then busied herself back to her task.

"She'll find us when she's ready," Zen said.

He held my elbow as he walked past, probably to make sure I'd move as well.

We walked out from between the buildings and into the warm sun that now had passed overhead. Zen steered me towards one end of the main road to a well. I stood there and watched people who moved in and out of houses and while Zen turned the handle. A clunk indicated the water had arrived, and I looked towards him. He placed the half full bucket on the edge of the brick wall, and I rinsed my hands. They felt cleaner at least, and with a wipe on my pants they were dry as well.

"Alexa, Zen," Ojerren's voice cut through my thoughts.

Stones flew as I spun around. Ojerren leaned against the wall nearby with his arms crossed over his chest. I adjusted my feet as loose stones dug into the sole of my shoe. Beside me I saw Zen turn with ease, and the corners of his mouth rose.

"Ojerren, good to see you again," Zen responded.

Zen moved forward to greet Ojerren. A smile covered Ojerren's face as he opened his arms. The familiarity of the hug made me uncomfortable. *We've been following him all morning, Zen, what are you thinking?* Still, Zen moved to stand beside Ojerren with his arm draped over the older man's shoulders.

"Alexa, I see you've swapped your outfit."

"I can hardly wear the dress all the time," I replied.

"Perhaps you should." Ojerren turned to Zen. "I assume the dress was your idea?"

Zen nodded. "Change is a good thing sometimes."

"I would go a step further and say that change is inevitable," Ojerren replied, still watching me.

"Inevitable maybe, but not guaranteed to be positive," I said.

"True Alexa, very true. Consider though if no changes ever occurred, good or bad, what kind of world would we be living in?"

"A predictable one," I murmured, but I knew he heard when his lips curled up.

"Predictability has its place, I can't argue with that, but predictability also brings with it problems of its own."

"I don't believe that. Predictability means stability. You can plan and do without having to worry."

"No, it creates vulnerability. You might feel a

sense of safety, and draw comfort from it, but it limits you with what you see, feel, and experience. If you never move outside of what you know, how will you learn about new things, new ways, and find the person who you're destined to be with?"

"I prefer a quiet life, Ojerren, one where I wouldn't need to fight for survival."

"Really?"

Ojerren stepped towards me, and Zen's arm fell back to his side. When Ojerren paused in front of me, I stared back at his eyes, surprised to find he stood no taller than me.

"If you love predictability so much, then how come you're here in a place away from your home and with a man?"

"Because..." *Damn him,* I struggled to think of a counterargument. "Because I'm trying to protect the life that we have."

"Really? Or is that the lie you're telling yourself because of a sense of loyalty to your precious elders and the past?"

Before I could answer Ojerren, wings flapped as Fiya landed on my shoulder. She stood with her wings extended and tail feathers spread on full display.

"A teraca? Well, I am surprised to see one being so friendly. You know they have quite a reputation for being aggressive creatures," Ojerren said.

"She bit me when I tried to get close to her," Zen added.

"She's not aggressive; she's just selective with her choice of companion."

Fiya purred in response and wiggled her tail back and forth. I arched my neck to the side to avoid an eyeful of feathers.

"You see Alexa, if you were so fond of predictability, you wouldn't have brought a teraca here," Ojerren said.

Ojerren reached out his hand towards the bird. Fiya's beak darted towards his finger and snapped at air. His finger escaped injury, but Fiya growled and leaned forward. I doubted he'd dare do that again.

"Okay, birdy, I get the message." Ojerren distanced himself further.

Fiya's tail relaxed and she tucked her wings close to her body. I felt her snuggled against my neck as she found her spot on my shoulder. Her gaze remained focused on Ojerren.

"Zen, sometime soon I would like to have a private word with you."

"Sure, we're staying at the inn," Zen replied.

I narrowed my gaze on him and clenched my teeth. *No, no, no! You don't tell him where to find us!*

My hand balled up and I shook my head.

"Perhaps I shall find you there later on then. Until later. Zen, Alexa, little birdy." Ojerren nodded at us each in turn before he walked past me. I smiled as he stepped to the side to create extra distance between Fiya and himself.

"Come on, it doesn't sound like he's going anywhere at the moment."

"But we were heading south."

"Maybe we don't need to, Alexa."

CHAPTER 26

Zen had the books open again though I could hardly complain since one sat in my hands too. Fiya slept peacefully on her bed as we sat at the small table in our room. I turned the page and my gaze drifted over the pictures and words. To me there were many words that conveyed little useful information. That's how it felt, page after page of information. Leila said learning to read was a gift; to me it felt like its own burden that the unsuspecting had to deal with.

I looked over the top of my book at Zen. He sat there with his black hair tied back into a single bundle. His gaze focused on whatever was on the page. He hadn't turned a page in a while, so perhaps that book was more interesting. My finger found the corner of the page and flicked it. I focused back on the page and prepared to turn it. I paused. I moved the book closer to my face and studied the sketch of the man. The tattoo on his neck was clear and I'd seen it before. A dragon breathing fire that wrapped around the back of the neck from one ear to the other.

The information on the page told about a man named Haiak who had argued that dragons were not the enemy and should be welcomed into society. I rolled my eyes and wondered how long ago the book had been written. The pages had yellowed and dried, which made them awkward to turn. A musty smell emanated from it each time my finger brushed against it. Maybe a hundred years? The books had been well taken care of, so it could have been more.

Haiak claimed the dragons were an important key in the Dreaja Valley for the survival of dragons and people alike. He resolved that dragons should be protected and that communication should be re-established with them after the division caused by Roaia rejecting Tajea as a mate.

Names at last for the black and white dragons, which meant the book was written after that event. I tried to picture Uhandra and the other men, but all had their necks concealed. The chances were high that they had the same tattoo. Somehow it all connected with the dragons.

Haiak attempted to make peace between the valley village and the dragons, but was killed during the negotiations. A decision was made by the Draconia Alliance that no further attempts should be made to broach the subject with the elders.

The burden became more intense with each generation of dragons. It didn't matter how hard a dragon tried to resist the burden; it continued to take control of their true soul. Dragons were destroyed by their own actions, or those of humans who fought against them. The humans wrongly assuming the dragons could control their minds while infected.

More excuses. It seemed like the dragons took every opportunity to avoid the responsibility of what they did.

With the burden spreading throughout the valley's dragons, an agreement established by the neighbouring dragon clans. To stop the spread of the burden, it banned those in clans with a single known case from interacting with any untouched clan.

The Draconia Temple on Yalaan mountain will become the sanctuary for those identified but not yet turned in hopes we will find a way to rid the dragons of the burden. All members of the Dragon Burden Alliance shall work together, moving into the future.

The bottom of the page contained a sketch of the dragon tattoo I had seen many times now. Underneath it were the words *Dragon Burden Alliance*. I studied the picture, but it told me nothing more about any secrets it might have concealed within the ink.

"Something of interest?" Zen asked.

My body took a moment to settle after the rush of emotions that the text had swirled inside of me. I looked up at Zen and shrugged. He would have found that information interesting, he would have seen that as another reason for us to delay the journey. To delay revenge. I closed the book and rested my hand on top of the cover.

"Just dragon stuff. I'm hungry. Are you hungry?"

"Sure," Zen replied. He lowered the book he held in his hands. "I'll go see what I can get for us, unless you want to eat downstairs?"

"No, I need a break from there."

Zen nodded and stood. I watched as he retrieved the pouch with gold from under his pillow. A frown crept across my face; it didn't bulge like it had before. We had spent too much time here.

"Won't be long," he said.

"Zen?"

He paused at the door, and his hand rested on the handle. Zen turned his head in my direction.

"Yeah?"

"We're not going to run out, are we?"

Zen shook the bag, and I heard gold pieces rattle against each other.

"We'll be fine, Alexa. I won't be long."

Even after the door had closed, the thought lingered. We'd used more gold in a handful of days than we'd used in all the previous years I could remember.

A flutter of wings sounded, and Fiya landed on the table. She hopped onto the book that Zen had been reading and looked about. My fingers caressed the edge of the book. With nothing else to do, I opened the book back to the page I had been on.

The distinct tattoo left no doubt in me that Ojerren was involved with the Alliance, but the role of the temple still didn't fall completely into place. It gave no explanation to what 'turned' meant and since we only saw humans at the temple...

My finger tapped on the table. Fiya mimicked the noise with her own small feet and I smiled. A dance was part of the coupling ceremony. Most of the women looked forward to the dancing that took place. I liked to dance but preferred the privacy of the trees where no one could see and no feet would be injured.

The following pages were more about dragon behaviour and diet. I noted it had recorded nothing about dragons eating humans. Though... I couldn't actually remember a dragon ever eating a human; burning them, maiming them, and outright killing —most definitely.

"So if they're not attacking for food, why are they? Animals they'll take, but humans... Killing a human makes no sense by this man's theory," I said.

Fiya stopped her little dance and flew back to the floor, where she pecked at some feeds she had missed that morning.

I flipped back to the page and read over the information again. The book clarified that the only dragons affected were in this valley unless they came into contact with other dragons.

"Let's say this man is right, and I'm not saying he is, but let's amuse the book." Fiya made an excellent conversation partner and said nothing. "In order to create an alliance to ban infected dragons from interacting with other dragons, they would need to have societal rules of some kind. That's pretty smart if they did. I mean, if they were able to have a warning system in place and rules. But then how is it that any of this got written down? It's not like dragons talk with humans. So if he's a human writing this down, then what's he basing all this on? And then the men at the temple. If that's a sanctuary for dragons, then why is it now overrun with humans? This is exactly why I don't like books. You open them up and read them to answer a question and end up without an answer but fifty more questions."

I needed information that wasn't there to connect all the pieces together. I closed the book and sighed. My gaze glanced towards the window and then to the door. Zen had been gone awhile.

"Wanna go for a walk, Fiya?"

Fiya flew onto the table, hopped over to my outstretched hand, and climbed onto it. She fluffed her feathers and settled on my shoulder for the journey. I stood up and my body reminded me I needed to take a trip to the bathroom before I went.

Downstairs, only a handful of people sat at the tables. Most of them I didn't recognise, but it seemed many people passed through this town and only stopped for supplies or rest. It made me wonder at the ease the women travelled. Unencumbered by elder rules I had seen outside the valley, they had freedom and choice. I adjusted my harness that fit surprisingly well over the dress.

The man behind the counter tossed a cloth onto his shoulder before he leaned on the wooden surface. I tried to avoid eye contact with him as I looked around the room again, just in case.

"You looking for that man?"

His words grated against me more than they should have. I tried to shake off the feeling, but a smile wouldn't come to my face to hide my annoyance.

"Have you seen Zen?" I replied, putting extra emphasis on his name.

"He came down a little while back. Spent a while talking with someone out there on the veranda." He nodded towards the door.

I knew he wasn't there but glanced despite myself.

"Who was he talking to?"

He shrugged his shoulders and gave the counter a wipe like I would have. "Couldn't see. Just saw him standing there talking to someone out the front. I just went about my business, but when I looked back that way he was gone."

It wasn't exactly helpful but he had at least given me some information. I didn't doubt who he would have been talking to: Ojerren. Only Ojerren could have persuaded Zen to go off somewhere "for a moment". My stomach rumbled but with no gold I would have to try and find something editable on the way.

Outside of the inn, I stood on the veranda. The fabric of my dress moved in the breeze as I searched for Zen. No sign.

"When I find you, Zen, you are going to be in big trouble for making me leave that room and walk about," I grumbled.

I couldn't hurry as I walked down the main road. Maeja waved from the doorstep of one house, and I managed a smile. She had checked in on me that morning and assured me I would get used to the bleeding. Just another thing I wasn't convinced of.

There were many people out in the streets, but

none of them were Zen. After I exhausted the main street, I made my way strategically down each of the side streets. By the time I had walked down the one near Stevie's workshop, I had enough. The well provided me with something to rest against while my stomach reminded me I still hadn't eaten.

Fiya still slept on my shoulder and I gave her head a scratch. The trees of the forest were right behind the workshop which was closer than the inn. My hands pushed against the stone and I felt a pain dart across my abdomen. I bent over and held my hand against my dress until the pain subsided.

"There better be a berry or something there I can eat. And I will be so glad to be on that tea again," I said.

I turned to check on Fiya. Her eyes were open and her tail feathers were relaxed over my shoulder. She leaned her head to the side as I gave her a scratch. One more deep breath and I headed down the road until it no longer existed and the forest became my new surroundings.

With the village out of sight, I drew my sword. Loose strands of my hair swayed as I tried to familiarise myself with the sounds and smell of the forest. Faint, a faint smell I knew. With my eyes open, I gauged the best direction.

Parts of where I stood looked like the area Zen

and I had passed through the day we'd followed Ojerren. At the same time, it all looked like trees to me. There were no markers or flags to tell me to proceed or stop. The hunts seemed like silly games that hadn't prepared me to track now. I needed Zen's ability to track.

I headed west as my gut said to go that way. No rhyme or reason to it but I hoped it would produce some results — more than just standing around would do. The canopy thickened and I watched my steps. Fallen branches obscured the ground in places and reached out to trip me.

Ahead, the trees appeared to thin and I paused for a moment. It would take ages to get back and I wasn't sure I would be able to before sunset, if I could at all. I glanced over my shoulder at the way I had come. I should have left a trail I could follow back because my awkward footsteps would be difficult to see in the dark.

Annoyed, I turned and headed forward. My arms flailed as my foot got caught. Fiya's wings flapped. A nearby tree provided me with an anchor as my hand pressed against it. The other hand plunged the tip of the sword into the ground and only missed my toe by a heartbeat.

My breath steadied, and I turned to glare at the tree root that my foot had caught on. I hadn't done that since I was a child. My concentration wasn't where it should have been.

"Some elite warrior I am out here. At home I'm great, but out here it's like I haven't trained at all," I muttered.

Fiya flew down from a nearby tree and landed at my feet. Her feathers appeared ruffled, but otherwise okay. She hoped about and pecked at the ground. Even the bird had found something to eat.

I ached. My stomach hadn't been satisfied either. I debated the pros and cons if I were to betray my location. If Zen was with Ojerren, I wondered if he would be annoyed at me for interrupting their... whatever it was they were doing. My fingers tapped in turn on the tree in quick succession. I hated decisions I had to think about; being impulsive was easier.

"Ah, who cares anyway? I probably won't get back to the village without him anyway," I grumbled. "Zen! Zen!"

I pushed myself away from the tree but kept my sword at the ready. I walked with caution and listened for anything that could indicate3 I had company. Leaves rustled, something scratched at the ground, but no voices. I continued to head west and checked the sun's position frequently to know I headed in the intended direction.

A hill loomed in front of me. A hill that might

have well been a mountain. From the top, I would have an unobstructed view of what lay ahead, and it would give me the best chance to spot Zen. On the other hand, I didn't want to walk anymore. I needed to go to the bathroom. I wanted to rest.

"I was a fool to come out here. Zen? Zen, if you can hear me, can you please yell something back!" I waited, but there was no response. My feet took another step up the hill.

"Zen? Zen, if you can hear me, can you please yell something back!" It sounded like me, but it wasn't.

"Ah, Fiya, warn me if you're going to do that!"

Fiya purred as she landed on my shoulder and rubbed her head against my cheek. At least she could project her voice better than I could. I continued until I reached the top of the hill. All I could see before me were more trees as the forest extended out to the foot of the mountains in the distance.

I didn't need to look hard for the sun as my hand shielded my eyes.

"Alexa? What are you doing out here?"

I spun around to find Zen behind me. His black hair hung loosely around his face. There was a red tinge on his skin, and yet he wasn't out of breath. My gaze caught the scratches on his arms where the fabric of his shirt hung in tatters. I put my sword in the harness and stepped closer to him.

"What am I doing here? Zen, you left ages ago to get food and never came back!"

He ran his fingers through his hair and tucked some loose strands behind his ear. A crease appeared across his forehead as he looked at the ground and then back at me.

"Oh right, I must have forgotten, with everything that happened." He put his hands into the side pockets of his pants. "So why'd you come out into the forest?"

A growl made its way out of my lips. "Oh I don't know. Maybe because I was worried. Maybe because I was hungry. Maybe I just felt like going on a really long stroll when I feel like… What is wrong with you?"

"I'm fine, just a little tired. I'm sorry."

"Tired and what else? Look at you, Zen! Where have you been?"

He lowered his head. "I can't tell you that, Alexa. I learnt so much more today than I could have imagined. I need to figure things out. I need to work out what to do."

"Do? The first thing we're going to do is go back to the inn and get you tidied up and fed."

I reached out to grab his hand but he stepped away. He'd never recoiled from my touch before.

"What?"

He shook his head. "Nothing. Come on, I'll take us back there."

We walked in silence towards the village. I wanted to ask questions but I wasn't sure that I would get any straightforward answers.

"Zen, about the tattoos..."

"I know about them already, Alexa. I know all about them, what they mean..."

"Ah, I didn't think you'd read that book."

"Book?" He looked over at me.

"You didn't read the book?"

I watched his head confirm that he hadn't. Something had gone on. I turned and looked behind me in case someone followed us. Zen didn't even notice, and I had to hurry to catch up with him.

"You were with Ojerren, weren't you?"

"It's nothing to do with you, Alexa, let it go."

"Let it go?" I stopped.

Zen walked several more steps before he turned to look back at me. "Come on, it's getting dark."

"Why would you tell me to let it go?"

"I need to figure it out. Give me some time to think it through, please?"

I walked over to him and reached out again to

touch his hand. He stepped backwards, but I persisted and grabbed his arm.

"Please Zen, talk to me. Why won't you let me get close?"

His free hand moved to cover mine that held tightly onto his arm. "Things have changed, Alexa."

I watched as he went ahead. I bit my lip and felt the tears well in my eyes. Whatever Zen had learnt it didn't look like he was about to share with me anytime soon. It wasn't so much that he wouldn't tell me what he knew that hurt, it was that he didn't want me near him.

The secrets of each will always divide. The women were right; men couldn't be trusted.

CHAPTER 27

Zen had bathed, and I had looked over the clothes. They weren't in the best condition, and I wasn't handy enough with a needle and thread to make it any better.

We sat in the room and ate what the leftover food the innkeeper found in the kitchen. Zen barely said anything to me. Even as he lay on the bed with his eyes closed, I waited. I knew he wasn't asleep. The candle still burnt on my side of the room. Its steady flame cast shadows in places, but I could see enough.

I wondered what had happened in the time and he'd been gone. My mind raced with the possibilities of what Ojerren might have done to him. Physically, Zen seemed okay. The clothes he had worn were ruined by all the tears, but his skin seemed fine with only the barest of scratches. Still, he wouldn't talk about how he got it, or who inflicted them on him.

I lay down and hoped I'd either fall asleep or he'd talk. I felt helpless as my gaze remained fixated on him. Fiya lay asleep on the table next to the bed. I leaned forward and blew out the flame. The moonlight filtered through the windows and lit up the side of his face. Maybe the darkened room caught his attention, or maybe he just sensed me watching him. He opened his eyes and looked over at me. Any other time I would've seen a smile cross his face; something to reassure me we were alright.

I wondered if there had been any truth at all in what he'd said to me. Was it possible that he meant what he said? Or had that been all part of some plan I hadn't suspected? I hated the conflict I felt.

When we left, I knew what I wanted to do even if I didn't have a plan. Now I didn't even know what I believed. Would killing a few dragons make any difference? Would it spark more attacks until they wiped the entire village out?

"Alexa?" Zen murmured, and his eyes opened.

"I'm here."

Zen closed his eyes once again. I watched him until I saw his breathing steady.

At least sleep still came easily to him because it certainly didn't for me. I tossed and turned. Over and over and over again and I still couldn't get comfortable.

Sleep must have come. I opened my eyes to see the soft moonlight on the wall. I rolled to check on Zen. His blanket had been cast aside on the bed.

"What?"

I tossed my blanket off my body. My feet thumped on the floorboards as I ran to his bed. I felt the sheets and the pillow. All were cold to the touch. Whenever Zen had gone, he had a large head start on me.

"Damn you, Zen! What do you think you're doing?" I growled.

I pulled on my clothes and hoped I hadn't put on anything inside out. As I pulled on my shoe, I hopped past the window. The moon was still high in the sky.

"Why would you leave in the middle of the night? If you want to go, go during the day, leave a note. Ojerren is behind all this."

I fastened my harness and moved close enough to the window to look out. I let out a breath. There in the middle of the dirt road was Zen. I looked down at Fiya. If she had been asleep, I would have left her, but I must have caused enough noise to wake her. I held my hand out and grabbed some seeds from the pouch I had kicked when I retrieved my shoes. Her ability to mimic might come in handy.

My feet made a little sound as I exited the room. I went down the steps one at a time, aware of every creak the boards made. I stayed away from the light that came through the inn windows and walked to the door. He was right outside. I tried the handle, but it didn't move.

"These people who lock things," I muttered.

I turned around. The kitchen exit would do. I made my way across the inn but failed to see one chair. It scraped on the floor, but I caught it before it toppled over. I stood there and waited for someone to come downstairs or look through the window. When neither happened, I straightened the chair and hurried towards the back room.

The kitchen door had been locked but only with a metal latch, and someone had already unlocked it. I closed the door behind me and slowly made my way to the side of the building. There were enough shadows thanks to the moon's position that I walked with the wall at my back unseen.

When I reached the front corner of the building, I heard murmurs. I peered around the corner to see Ojerren shake Zen's hand and then pull him into a hug. The two of them began to walk down towards Stevie's shed. They were headed for the forest.

I struggled to keep up with them. My feet seemed to find every fallen branch, raised tree root, and rock. However, they negated the same path without tripping. At the distance I was behind them I couldn't hear the conversation but I saw the animated way Zen moved his hand. He did that when he was excited about something. I felt jealous seeing him have such a conversation with someone other than me.

They came to stop on a hill. A fire burned, and several other men greeted Ojerren and Zen. My heart grew a little colder. I watched in the dark and wished I had something thicker on. My arms were covered in goosebumps and my teeth chattered.

I shifted my feet, and Fiya peeped. Both Fiya and I remained still. Ojerren turned, and his gaze looked right at where we were in the bushes. My heart thumped as I waited for him to approach. I reached behind for my sword, but my hand slid off the hilt. A frown crossed Ojerren's face, but he didn't move away from the group.

He might have seen me, or perhaps the conversation had finished. Either way, the men abruptly parted ways. I stayed in the bush as Ojerren and Zen walked past. Their voices still low.

"Be careful, Zen. To trust someone completely can be a dangerous thing."

I kept them in sight as they headed back in the direction of the village. At least following behind that I wouldn't find myself lost out in the forest wishing for help. When I checked on Fiya her eyes were closed, she hadn't been much help this time; still I gave her a pat as I tried not to trip over my feet.

The lanterns of the village were a welcome sight. I diverted away from Zen and Ojerren and snuck down a dark lane between two houses. I peered up the main road and saw them a short distance away, their heads still bowed. *This might be my only chance.* I took it, and ran across the road. My teeth clenched as my feet sounded loud against the hardened dirt. Once across, I paused in the shadows of the inn and watched as they came to a stop.

"This might be our only chance," I whispered to Fiya.

I made my way to the back of the inn and snuck back up to the room. I put Fiya down on her blanket, and she adjusted her wings before she concealed her beak beneath her wing again. My heart thumped as I heard footsteps on the stairs outside of the room. The buckle slipped between my fingers as I tried to undo it. My fingers fumbled with the strap over and over until my sword finally slipped free. It clanged onto the floor and I froze. Outside, the footsteps ceased. That had not been my intention. I turned and cursed at the bed for not being closer to me.

Still no footsteps. I picked up the sword and placed it at the end of the bed. The footsteps resumed. I dropped onto the bed and tried to remove the shoes. *Damn thing! Undo! Undo!* But like the harness, they resisted my efforts.

The door opened, and I froze. I closed my eyes for a moment before I turned to look at Zen. He watched me as he closed the door behind him. Lines formed on his forehead.

"What are you doing?" he whispered.

The nerve! To ask me….

"Me? Are you serious? I wasn't the one who vanished for the afternoon. I wasn't the one who snuck out in the middle of the night!" I hissed back as one of the shoe straps finally yielded.

"You followed me?"

I shifted uncomfortably at the tone of his voice. "You snuck out first."

"Why can't you trust me anymore?"

My shoe fell to the floor and I attacked the other one. "Why can't you trust me? You're the one sneaking around, not me!"

The other shoe fell to the floor. *Sure, now they cooperated.*

"I don't see how any of this is your business. If I want to leave in the middle of the night, I should be able to do as I please."

I stood up. I didn't want to wake anyone else in the inn, but I would have my say. Besides, I hadn't seen many people outside going into the other rooms anyway.

"Because I care, Zen, I want to know that you're safe and okay."

"Then trust me, Alexa."

"How can I when you don't tell me anything? Ever since you met Ojerren, you've been thinking about dragons differently. I came out here to do one thing with my best friend and now I feel like I don't even know him anymore."

"You know what? Maybe you're right. You don't know me very well. Our friendship has always depended on you knowing what's going on. You don't get it, do you Alexa?"

"Get what?" My hand clamped over my mouth. We both turned to the door. I waited for footsteps to tell us to be quiet. I heard nothing other than the wave of emotions that seemed to affect the conversation.

Zen stepped closer to me and crouched down. We were almost eye-to-eye at that level.

"I don't want to fight with you, Alexa. Can we sleep first and talk in the morning?" he said.

"What don't I get?"

Zen shook his head. "If I have to tell you, then you're not ready to know it."

He moved to stand, and I reached out. I caught his arm and held tight. "Is it because... The other night Zen…"

"Just let it go for the moment, Alexa. Get some sleep."

He shook my hand free.

"Why won't you talk to me?"

"Sleep."

"I don't want to sleep! I want to know what's going on!"

"You don't get to know everything just because you want to know. I'm entitled to do what I want and there's stuff you don't know, and no, I'm not going to tell you because it has nothing at all to do with you!"

"Fine."

My arms folded across my chest, and I looked down at the wooden floorboards. I heard him sigh. I felt his hand touch my arm in the same way I had held onto him before.

"Alexa, please don't be mad."

I shook my arm until his grip loosened and his hand fell away. I laid down on the bed and rolled over so I faced the wall.

"Alexa…"

His fingers brushed the loose hairs away from my face. I squeezed my eyes shut and turned my head into the pillow. He sighed, and I felt the hair move back into place. I listened as he walked away.

CHAPTER 28

Two days. Two days passed, and I had said nothing to Zen. I'd made sure I woke before he did and left the room. I had spent a lot of time in the shadows as I watched him and where he went. He probably knew I would be. I suspected he even knew where I was as he looked over the area where I stood.

Still, this morning I should have been feeling great. I had drunk the tea for the first time in a while and thanked it for the power it had to make my life easier. I'd left my weapon back in the room, while Ojerren was definitely up to something, he didn't seem like he was an immediate threat to Zen.

Zen and Ojerren were in the inn eating. My stomach wanted to join them, but instead I sat across the road in the shadow of a house. I alternated my gaze between them and the book on my lap. Zen had brought four books down with him from the temple. A part of me wanted to find something in the book that would answer why Zen had suddenly changed so much.

Perhaps Uhandra gave him something at the temple, and it's only just now taking effect? Could Ojerren bewitch people with his words? I'd seen that once before, how some people talked when they came to the village. They were so convincing and you could believe that they were made of gold despite seeing they weren't. Ojerren seemed to like his words, but the way he spoke — close and privately — made me uncomfortable.

I had never had a disagreement like this before with Zen. Part of it could probably be attributed to my stubbornness, but I tried to remember that caution is how you learn what's going on. The day after the night-time adventure, I had gone to Maeja's, but the women had left. She told me she didn't know where they had gone. I didn't believe it was the truth. I couldn't trust Zen because I didn't trust Ojerren, but then I didn't trust Maeja either when she declared she didn't know where they had gone.

This book had been the one Zen had been reading when I had read about the tattoos. That book still sat up on the table in our room. Zen had touched none of the books since that night, or at least, he hadn't when we'd been in the same room together, which hadn't been much. He'd tried talking to me at night, waiting up, but I bit my tongue and said nothing. Fiya clearly understood my feelings as she growled in warning the previous night when he'd attempted to touch my hand as I sat at the table.

Leila had been right. Men were too much trouble. They messed with your head and priorities. Priorities. I hadn't forgotten why I left the village in the first place, but I couldn't just up and leave. The tattoos and their connection to the dragons meant I could finish this all here and now — if only I knew how.

Glancing at the window again, I saw them rise. My nose twitched as Ojerren walked out of sight. I waited to see him come out of the front door. Adjusting my back against the stone wall behind me, I glared at the door. *Where are you, Ojerren?*

I looked back to see Zen stand and move away from the window. He probably had headed upstairs to the room. The doors of the inn remained undisturbed.

"Alexa."

"Damn!"

I turned to see Ojerren crouched down beside me. *How could he move so quietly?*

"You need to let him go," he said.

Huh? Say what?

"Excuse me?"

Ojerren reached out his hand, and I moved away. His fingers balled into a fist, and he tapped it against his knee.

"Let him go, Alexa. Go back home to your village."

"I'm not leaving here without Zen."

"That's not your decision, that's his. You need to let him go."

"This is something to do with dragons, isn't it? You know a lot more than what you're saying." I wondered if I should say it as I studied his face for any reaction. "I know what that tattoo means."

Ojerren smiled and moved his hair away on one side to reveal the dragon's head with fire coming from its mouth. The entire tattoo was black, with lines of skin to define the dragon's features. It drew my gaze to it, despite knowing I should have focused on him.

"This one?" he asked.

"You know what it means, don't play with me," I said.

"Child, if you truly knew what this tattoo meant, then you would understand. And if you understood, then you would accept that you need to let Zen go. His path and yours are not the same."

He reached out again, but this time towards my face. I didn't move. I felt trapped by his gaze as a smile spread across his face.

"Who are you to say where Zen is going? His place is back in our village."

"No child, it's not. If you could trust him, then you would understand and maybe, just maybe, you could walk the path ahead together."

"Stop telling me I need to trust and understand when no one is telling me anything! Tell me, Ojerren, how can I understand what I don't know? How can I trust when something is kept from me?"

He shifted his position and glanced at the ground for a moment before his eyes once again met mine.

"It's not about knowing, it's about trusting Zen. You've known him for a long time, he says you have spent a lot of time together, even broken the rigid rules of the elders for him. Something inside of you knows the way things are isn't right, and yet at the same time you have closed your mind to the possibility of what life could be."

"You're right. I've known Zen a lifetime and he's only known you a handful of days. He won't stay with you if that's your plan. You won't trap Zen with your words into staying here. I'm telling you now, when I leave this place he will be by *my* side."

Ojerren's hand fell away, and he leaned back. His mouth turned up at the corners, as his attention never left my face.

"You care for him," he said with a curious lit to

his voice.

"He's my best friend."

Ojerren shook his head. "Are you sure? Perhaps before you can trust Zen, you need to trust yourself and what you are feeling."

I growled and slammed the book shut with a satisfying thud. "I don't have time for this."

Standing up, I clutched the book tightly to my body. Ojerren caught his balance with his hand outstretched behind him. He stood up beside me. I had no choice but to look up if I wanted to face him.

"If you can trust yourself, maybe there is hope still."

I watched as he turned and walked away. He didn't allow me a chance to respond, and I had no idea what to say. *Was he right? Did I not trust myself?* I shook my head. I knew that wasn't what he meant. His tone said it all. He had worked out what I hadn't said to Zen. My feelings were more than that of friends. I knew that. I didn't see him the same way as I did other men. That didn't mean I trusted him at that moment, but it was more that I didn't trust his judgement rather than him as a person.

Back inside the inn, I hesitated at the door. It hadn't been so bad coming in when it was later, I could assume he would be in bed and asleep, though he'd been neither so far, but he should have been. In the middle of the day, there was little chance I could avoid him.

My hand rested on the handle and I took a breath. I released the breath and turned the handle. Inside, I saw Zen seated at the table with an open book in his hand. I closed the door and walked over to the table. Time to talk. I placed the book down next to the other two... Two? There had been four.

"There's a book missing?"

"No, there's not," Zen said.

"Yes, there is. I can count. There were four and now there are three. Where has that one gone that I was reading the other day?"

"It will be here somewhere."

I couldn't make eye contact. Not after the conversation with Ojerren. *Coming back here was a bad idea. I should have gone elsewhere.*

"Alexa, would you sit down for a minute?"

I waved him off and walked over to Fiya. She flew down onto the floor and looked up at me with her enormous eyes. I reached into my pocket and pulled out some grains and seeds I had collected earlier in the morning. Her legs hopped back and forth as she flapped her wings.

"Here you go, girl."

The seeds spilled from my hand into a pile in

front of Fiya. Her beak pecked at the pile. I heard wood scrape against wood. Footsteps became louder, and I felt the vibrations on the floorboards. Fiya paused long enough to look up beyond me and then flew to the open window and outside onto a branch. I closed my eyes and made a wish before I turned around.

"You need to eat as well."

"I have," I whispered. My stomach betrayed me with a growl.

"I brought you some food. Come and sit, please, Alexa?"

Another growl from hunger. I had found a couple of berries beside the house that had smelt okay, but the bitter taste had prevented me from wanting anymore.

Zen stood in front of me. There was nowhere to move. I saw his hand move up towards my face. My lips trembled. He ran a finger down the side of my face. I bit my lip. Zen's finger paused on my chin. He lifted it up, and I closed my eyes. *Now is not the right time, Alexa. Keep your eyes closed.*

"I don't like the distance between us, even if we're going different ways... I can't stand having you angry at me."

I forced my eyes to close tighter. His body brushed up against my hands that I held awkwardly in front of my body. All I had to do was step backwards. Put the distance back. Keep the anger in place, the resolve in place.

"Alexa."

His warm breath tickled my ear. A tear escaped. I felt it run down my face and be wiped away.

"Alexa."

I opened my eyes. I could only see his hair as it flowed loosely around his neck. *Space, I need space.* I pressed my hand flat against his body. *Push. Push him away.* Yet my hand wouldn't move. His body moved closer until my hand had nowhere to go.

"Alexa," he whispered.

"I'm afraid," I whispered back.

"Of what?"

"Everything."

"Are you afraid of me?"

"I'm afraid I'm losing you." I closed my eyes.

"I'll always be with you, Alexa."

I shook my head. *No, that's not true. Different paths.* His face brushed against mine, and I opened my eyes again. He rested his forehead against mine, his eyes staring into mine.

"No matter what disagreements we have, I'll always be with you."

"Not like…" *Damn, I should have realised earlier. I should have taken the chance when he'd reached out for my hands days before.*

"Like what?" he asked. "Alexa? Like what?"

Tears welled up again in my eyes as I scrunched my face. I tried to keep them away. Tried to be the brave, elite warrior without emotion I had been told I needed to be.

"It's too late, isn't it?"

"Nothing is ever too late."

He closed his eyes. His nose brushed against mine. My heart raced. My hands shook. His warm lips rested on mine. *What am I meant to do? What should I do?* I swallowed. His lips pressed against mine. His hand circled my waist and he pulled me against his body. My hand reached up. I could feel his heart through his shirt. The gentleness of his lips on mine changed to more urgent and intense. His fingers pressed into my back. I parted my lips and fully tasted him. His scent enveloped me.

Zen pressed against me, and my foot lost its grip on the floor. His arm caught me before I could fall. My hand reached up and ran through his hair. It felt soft as my fingers became entangled. His hand moved from my face and to the back of my neck. *I need air. Don't I?*

But it's Zen whose lips paused. His heavy

breathing matched my own. I swallowed and tried to steady myself as I swayed in his arms. My fingers tightened on the strands of hair they held.

"I can stop," he said.

"Stop?" I whispered.

His cheek brushed against mine as his lips kissed my neck. A warm-chill spread through my body and I shivered. I turned my face and buried it in his hands, still holding onto his hair as his lips trailed along the edge of the neck of my shirt. *Skin, skin.* My hand moved across his shirt to where the cord had loosened. I felt impossibly warm as my fingers wiggled through the gap and finally touched his skin. The cord barred my hand from further entry.

My waist cooled as Zen's hand moved. The kisses stopped. He moved away. *I did the wrong thing.* I felt fabric brush against me. His hand rested on top of mine and pushed mine down. The fabric of his shirt passed under my hand until I felt the excess fabric. He moved my hand to the side and I felt warm, bare skin. His hand released mine. I guided it up under his shirt, across his hot skin until I found his chest.

"Oh, Alexa."

His lips found mine again. I tried to keep up with the quick succession of kisses as his arms wrapped around me. His weight pressed against me. I shuffled back. My legs found the bed frame. Zen lowered me onto the bed. Above me. His lips moved to the other side of my neck. I reached around the back of his neck and grabbed a handful of his hair.

With my eyes closed, I took in the touch of his skin. The touch of his lips. The way his body measured up against me. I only wanted to keep him like this.

"Zen."

His lips kissed mine once. I stared up at him. My body felt on fire; I didn't know I could react in such a way. His heart still beat against my hand.

"Yeah?"

Words. Where are my words? I followed the line of his jaw with my hand and pushed his dishevelled hair back from his face and...

My blood ran cold.

"Alexa."

I shoved him back and shuffled until I could sit.

"What? What's wrong? I thought you were..."

"Your neck. How could you Zen?"

His hand reached up and covered it from my view.

"Alexa, it's not whatever you're thinking..."

"You're with Ojerren. I've seen his tattoo, Zen. How could you?"

Zen reached out and I got off the bed. I ignored my shoes and left the room. The door slammed shut behind me as I hurried down the steps and outside.

I ran until I reached the cover of trees. Tears stained my face even after I had wiped my sleeve over it. My knees gave way and I fell to the ground. I covered my face with my hands as I leaned forward. *How could he?*

"Alexa! Alexa!"

I raised my head and wiped my face again. I hadn't even gotten to my feet when he crouched in front of me.

"Please, Alexa."

My body shook. "No, no, no. You hid that, Zen. You know I don't trust Ojerren, and yet you've joined his band of men determined to save dragons. Those dragons killed the elders, Zen! Have you forgotten that?"

"Let me explain." He reached out and cupped my head in his hand.

I jerked my head back from his touch. "There's nothing to say, Zen."

"Come on, we should go back to the inn at least. You can eat something and we can talk..."

"No."

I pushed away from him and looked at the

village. The women were right all along. I should have listened. How could I believe I knew better than all the generations of women before me?

"Alexa, you can't just walk away. What we feel is real. Are you going to throw that away?"

My feet stopped. I couldn't turn around and look at him. "I'm not the one throwing anything away."

CHAPTER 29

I hurried back to the inn, hearing no footsteps behind me as I did. In the room, I grabbed the new bag and shoved in any clothes I could see. My hand paused on the dress and the tears welled again. I didn't need the dress. With the sword slung over my shoulder, I turned to Fiya. She hopped up onto my shoulder and then flew out the window.

"Fiya! Fiya, where are you going?" She didn't return. "You left me as well. I have nothing, no one now."

My gaze fell on Zen's pillow. I walked over to his bed, slipped my hand beneath his pillow, and pulled out the money pouch. I loosened the cords and took less than half of what was in there. I scribbled a note and tucked it inside the pouch. Then the door closed behind me.

I made my way into the trees but where I could still see the houses. Once they were behind me, I emerged from the greenery and walked on the road. The repetitive nature of the walk took my mind off what happened. It was my fault. If I had listened to the elders, then none of it would have happened.

"There has to be another village around here somewhere. If Zen isn't going to help me, I'll do it my bloody self." I paused on the road. Trees surrounded me on all sides, and the mountains stood in the distance. "I am an elite. I have a duty. I will end this."

"Look who it is, ladies."

I turned with my sword drawn, ready for action. Kalana tapped her own weapon that hung from her belt. My shoulders relaxed and I put the sword away.

"Kalana, Tapaja, Janara." I nodded to each of them.

"I see you are both without your bird and without that burden," Kalana said.

I waited for her to fall into step beside me.

"We all parted ways. He no longer has a desire to complete my quest," I said.

"Perhaps there is hope for her," Tapaja said.

"We are headed to the next village," Kalana said.

"What about the girl?" I asked.

Kalana looked over at me. "Maeja will take care of her. We will return for the child when she is rested and healed."

"She will live, then?" I asked.

"She will but not without scars," Tapaja said. She spat on the ground.

"What will you do when you get there? To the next village?"

"Thinking of joining us, Alexa?" Kalana smiled.

I shrugged. "I don't know anymore. If you kill dragons and protect women, then why not? I left the valley to do just that."

"I'm sure we could learn from each other. When I first met Tapaja and Janara, they had the skills of a five-year-old. They've come a long way in a handful of years." Kalana sounded proud. It reminded me of how Leila would talk when she asked me to demonstrate to the younger warriors.

My thoughts turned to the girl. She had been injured, but the straightness of the cuts bothered me.

"Do all dragons use their claws the same way? When they attack?" I asked.

"Pretty much," Kalana said. "They prefer to grip a person and squeeze. That punctures the body. It can cause a lot of damage inside. Then, when they go to release, the tips of their claws are drawn over the body." Kalana demonstrated with her hand. That description was consistent with what I could remember of the attack.

"Why did the girl's wounds look cleaner? Not jagged?"

"What are you accusing us of?" Tapaja stood in front of me. I skidded on the stones to stop.

"I'm just asking. I noticed, that was all."

Kalana paused beside me. "She has a point, Tapaja. The cuts were straight. Maeja said so when she stitched them up. Perhaps just a freak accident."

Tapaja stared at me like I was prey. I shifted uncomfortably. Kalana seemed open to discussion, but Tapaja... I shifted my gaze to Janara, but her gaze was fixed on our destination.

I smiled. "Probably, things like that happen."

Tapaja continued to stand there for a few moments, and then she moved back next to Kalana. We continued to walk in silence. My shoes crunched the dirt in time with Kalana's. My feet ached from the impact with the hard road, but that was my punishment. I felt grateful the road was even, at least.

As the sun disappeared, I saw a glow of light ahead. I'd lost count of how many times I'd turn to look behind. Zen could find me anyway if he wanted, but I doubted Ojerren would let him leave now he was one of them.

The road curved towards the light, and my feet faltered. Some and flames filled the night sky. The houses were on fire. I heard the roar above as a large black dragon flew overhead and towards the fire.

"Ladies, we need to help," Kalana yelled.

The three of them ran ahead, and I lost sight of them amongst the people that ran back and forth. The dragon circled back and I tried to gauge where it would go.

"No you don't."

I weaved amongst the villagers. Several women had collected water from the well and passed it down a line to try and put out the fires. I didn't stop, but ran towards the roar that drowned out all other noises. Above, the black dragon circled. I reached back and drew my sword. It had been too long, I should have practised more.

"Tie it down! Tighter!" a woman barked. She strained against the rope in her hands that went over the back of a smaller dragon. "Wet its face before we all cook! Hurry up, man!"

A man with short dark hair hurried towards the dragon and threw a bucket of water in its mouth. The dragon squirmed, and I saw smoke rise from the ropes around its mouth.

"You need more water! He's going to burn through the ropes!" I yelled.

The man looked at me and then at the woman. "What are you waiting for? Do as you're bloody told! Help the girl over there."

I nodded and moved towards the girl on the end of one rope. She stood on her tippy toes as her body leaned back, trying to pull the rope as tight as she could. I drove the sword into the ground beside her and reached above her hands. Together we pulled.

Roar. The noise came from above as fire lit the sky.

"Steady everyone, we need this bugger," the woman yelled again.

"There's another one!" a voice called out.

I looked above to see a smaller black dragon circling. It descended towards us. The fire reflected off the scales on its belly as it approached.

"Pull hard on the count of three," I yelled to the girl beside me. Her blonde hair shook as she nodded. "One, two... three!"

We pulled. I took a step back. The rope pulled from my hand before the girl and I fell to the ground. My shoulder took the bulk of the fall as I rolled over on the stones and cursed at the pain.

"The rope's snapped!" I yelled.

Swoosh.

I grabbed my sword from the ground and raised it up as the dragon came in with its claws extended. The sword cut through the air and connected. Its growl echoed as the blade sliced through its front leg. Blood streamed down as his claws grabbed the other dragon.

"Let go! Let go!" the woman hollered.

The ropes dangled on either side of the dragon as it rose, but it failed to gain much height. I glowered at the dragon that had come to its aid. The surrounding people rubbed their hands and I knew mine hadn't escaped the wrath of the rope from before.

The third dragon came in close and flew above our heads. The two smaller dragons rose as the larger one pulled the captive one free.

A second chance. I swung the sword again. Missed. I turned. The smaller black dragon approached. I swung and caught it near the eye. It bellowed and flew out of range. My gaze remained fixed on the sky until they were out of sight.

When I turned, I saw Tapaja on the ground. I walked over to her and extended my arm, but she shook her head and got herself up. Tapaja brushed her hands over her clothes before she spat at the ground. She looked up at me before she picked up her sword and walked away.

"You there! Strangers," the woman said.

The man had returned to her with a bucket of water that sloshed over the rim and formed a puddle on the ground. She washed her hands in it before she wiped them on her clothes and approached me.

"You got a piece of one of them."

I glanced down to my top to see the blood soaked sleeve. *Bugger, now I have to wash the damn thing.*

"Sorry I didn't kill him," I replied.

She smiled. "I'm Aria. We have fires to put out. Who's your friend?"

"I'm Alexa. The others I arrived with are here somewhere."

Aria barked off orders as we used water and thick blankets to try to extinguish the fires. Janara came to help. I turned to grab the next bucket of water and saw Kalana slap Tapaja across the face. Tapaja pursed his lips and lowered her head. When Kalana turned towards us, I returned to the job at hand.

"Leave those, they're too far gone. The hall is saved but we need to concentrate on the medicine house."

I watched as the people abandoned the houses to focus on the one closest to the forest.

Aria wiped the back of her hand over her forehead. "Stay, we could use a few people that can use a weapon here," Aria said.

"We can stay a few days. The dragons sometimes attack days later, and it looks like you will need some help with the buildings," Kalana said.

Aria looked at me. Another time and place I would be tempted. I could start over and be around a new society that seemed to function like the village. If no one remained back home, I could have done that, but I had obligations to fulfil.

I shook my head. "I can't."

"Alexa, this is an opportunity. What happened to joining us?" Kalana asked.

"Too weak for us," Tapaja said. She reached for another glass and downed the liquid. "We only want believers. She questions too much. Second guesses too much. She thinks too much about men."

She laughed as she turned away. There was truth in all that.

"I don't know what's gotten into her," Kalana said.

"I'm sorry. If you ever go to the valley, I would welcome you, Kalana," I said.

I pushed the full glass away and stood. It was going to be a long night.

CHAPTER 30

I walked through the night. All feelings of tiredness had gone. When I arrived at the village again, I looked around. People stared at me, and I knew it was the blood that had their attention.

"Have you seen the man I was with?" Over and over I asked it only to have the same head shake.

I left the inn to last. Part of me hoped I would walk through the doors and there Zen would be, at the table with a book in his hand. But I was out of luck. The innkeeper allowed me into the vacant room, but his belongings, including the books were, gone.

My gaze fell on the forest through the window. If he wasn't here, then I knew who he would be with, but whether I could track them was about to be tested.

At the inn I found his belongings gone, including the books. Moving into the forest, I headed in the direction I felt I'd gone before to follow Ojerren.

Up ahead, I saw him. I couldn't see his face, but I

knew it was Zen. The way he stood, the way his black hair flowed past his shoulders. My heart raced.

"Zen."

He stood up straight, but didn't turn around.

"Zen, I need to talk to you. You need to see this on my sleeve. A dragon Zen. A dragon, a group of dragons, tried to attack a village. Most of the village has fire. You need to see this so you can see why Ojerren is a liar."

"I don't have to see anything," Zen replied.

I reached out and touched his arm, but he pulled it away. I walked to his side, but he turned his face away from me.

"Zen, I came back here for you. You need to see this."

"You left, Alexa. Without a word where you were going or if you would be back. I had no idea what happened. All I knew is you didn't want to talk to me and now you expect me to just listen to you?"

"Please Zen. The dragons…"

"Are none of your business, Alexa. Go home to the village. Go home where you belong."

His tone cut deep, and I bit back tears.

"Zen please, let's…"

"Forget it, Alexa, just go home."

Annoyed, I reached out and grabbed his arm. "Please Zen."

He walked away. I watched him walk away and leave me.

I plopped onto the ground and pulled my knees up. The thick canopy of trees hampered my use of the sun to navigate. Now, with the sun setting, I had no hope of finding the village before dark.

My eyelids were heavy, and my legs ached. I felt cold, but the thought of finding dry wood seemed impossible to consider. I had been trained better. When did I become so weak? I could hear Leila's voice as she rebuked me for the rest before I had completed the necessary preparation.

"Better do it," I grumbled.

I pushed myself off the ground with success on the second attempt. My legs objected to the movement as I hobbled around trying to find dry wood. The light continued to fade, so I moved into the cleared area a bit.

A collection of fallen branches lay just for me. I sighed with relief that I could rest soon. I bent down and a shadow appeared on the ground beside me. I tucked and rolled to the side as a dragon landed in front of me. Its nostrils flared. I drew my sword.

Swallowed hard. Watched it. It stepped to the right. So did I.

It moved towards me; I aimed behind its eye and stabbed with all my strength. Blood ran down the sword as the dragon fell beside me. I heaved the blade free, and the blood quickened its escape. Its tail pounded against the ground. A low growl. It seemed unable to get up.

"Seemed a little too easy," I said.

I took small steps as I moved towards its head. This dragon I had seen before, the one the villagers had captured. Rope marks were still raw across the scales. The grey mark on its face confirmed its identity.

"Met your match this time, didn't you?"

It stared back at me. Its red eyes faded to black and watered as the sunlight shone on them.

"Well, killing people isn't nice."

It watched me. Its eyes watched me. I couldn't look away. I wasn't sure what I expected to feel, triumph, accomplishment, something. Instead, I saw something familiar, almost human.

Footsteps behind me warned of people approaching. I turned in time to see a group of people; some were armed with weapons.

"She did it! She got it!" a woman yelled: Aria. "I

was worried when you left, but girl, you track like a dragon hunter expert."

I turned back to the dragon. It still stared at me. It blinked once, twice, three times. Its eyelids never rose again. A rush of warm air passed by my legs. Its body stilled. A cheer went up behind me.

"We shall celebrate here tonight! What a catch. A live dragon is better, but a dead one isn't useless. Hana, get the men to drag this bugger back to the village to Stevie. Come on Alexa, come celebrate with us."

I smiled and went with her in my blood-soaked clothes. Despite my smiles, I didn't feel that joyous. Every time I closed my eyes, I saw the dragon staring back at me. A familiar blue drink landed in front of me.

"You need it girl," the innkeeper said.

I picked it up. He was right. I needed to forget the last few days. I downed it in one gulp and set the glass down on the counter. Someone slapped me on the back and said I'd done a great job. My back felt sore from all the gratitude they showed.

I turned on the seat as the innkeeper refilled my glass. Across the room, a woman sat down at the piano and started to play. I hadn't heard music like that in a while. I'd missed it. I closed my eyes as I raised the glass to my lips. Down it went. When I opened my eyes again, everything looked a little less clear. I heard liquid slosh in the glass. *Good idea.*

I downed that one. My vision blurred further. My head felt light. Around me, people sang and danced. I slid off the chair. My elbow caught the counter and prevented me from collapsing on the floor. It felt so hot in there. I shook my head and headed for the door on the side of the room. My hands gripped the counter as I made my way there, one step at a time. My feet uncooperative as they failed to find the floor as my shoes slid about.

I pushed the door open and stumbled into the cool night air. It felt good, and my lips crept into a smile. Then my stomach twitched, lurched. I turned in time to see blue liquid splatter to the ground beside me.

"Serves you right."

I know that voice. I wiped my mouth on my sleeve before I cringed at the action. The blood had dried but probably looked bad. I scooped some water from the bucket that hung beside the door and wiped it over my face. Then turned to look at him.

"What happened to your face?"

Zen had a bandage stained with blood that covered most of his cheek.

"Don't worry about it, it's nothing. A scratch."

I walked towards him, but my feet still had

trouble finding flat ground. At least my head felt clearer. My hand felt along the wall of the inn until I stood next to him. My legs continued to wobble as I tried to straighten up.

"That's not nothing. Have you been to Maeja?"

"She put the bandage on it. It's fine." He sounded grumpy.

"I killed a dragon today."

He looked away from me.

"I heard, everyone heard." He nodded towards the inn. "Celebrating the death of a creature."

"Yeah, they are."

I leaned against the stones and appreciated the cool touch against my hot skin. My feet felt like they were on solid ground. Felt. My body moved of its own accord. Or was everything else moving?

"You didn't have to kill him."

"Him is it? Well, *he* attacked me, Zen. I didn't go looking for him. He found me. He moved towards me."

"Attacked you?"

"Yes, Zen, he attacked me, and I defended myself. Would you have rather I let him kill me instead?"

"No, no, I don't want that," he whispered.

"Zen, I think Ojerren has a way to..." Words were

difficult to find. "... control men with his words. Somehow he's tricking you all in to following him —"

"You're wrong about him."

"Like I was wrong about the dragon?"

Shit! Shouldn't have moved my hand. I felt myself fall forward, but muscular arms caught me around my waist.

"You need to sleep it off."

"Sleep what off?" My hand went to my forehead.

"Come on, let's find somewhere quieter where you can rest."

I tried to walk, but the ground wouldn't stay still. In the end, Zen lifted me up and carried me. If my mind had been clearer I would have objected, but as the noises faded behind us I relished the peacefulness.

In the forest, he knelt and lowered me to the ground.

"I'll watch over you while you rest."

I stared up at him. *Damn the tears.*

"Is that why you wouldn't look at me earlier?"

"I didn't want you to see it."

"Why?"

"Because, Alexa, being around you makes me feel torn. I want to be by your side, but I have something new in my life and I need to control it, I need to accept it."

"Who is she?" I murmured.

"It Alexa; it, not a person."

"Mmm."

He might have said more, but darkness came.

CHAPTER 31

The sun felt warm on my skin as I turned and reached out. Something warm and soft pressed against my back, and I snuggled down a bit more. My hand reached up and my fingers found strands to play with.

My eyes shot open and took a moment to focus. I could smell Zen's familiar scent on the clothes. My fingers in his loose hair. One arm beneath my head and the other wrapped around my waist. *Perhaps he's asleep. Should I move?*

"Don't," he whispered.

I relaxed back against him.

"We can't go on like this, Zen."

"I know. I want you to know everything. If you walk away from me today, then I won't see you again."

"Why so final?"

"You'll understand when you know."

I pushed myself up to look at him.

"Tell me now."

"You'll need to come with me; it will be easier that way, or at least it will make more sense."

He stood up and held out his hands to me. I took both and hoped my head wouldn't spin from the effects of the night before. We headed together into the forest. I recognised the bushes we passed by with the thorns. We headed to where we had seen Ojerren meet with the other men on the hill.

Zen didn't let go of my hand, even as Ojerren come into view. Ojerren raised his head and looked our way as we neared. He folded his arms across his chest and shook his head as he stepped forward.

"She can't be here," Ojerren said.

"You said I'd know when it's the right time. It's past due," Zen said.

"She's not ready."

I felt awkward being talked about and shifted from one foot to the other.

"You said she had to trust me, so do you." Zen turned to me and held both my hands in his. "Trust me."

He released my hands and walked past Ojerren. In the clearing a little way behind Ojerren, Zen joined a group of men. Ojerren turned to me.

"I don't think you're ready, but he's right. I only ask that you remain calm." Lines crossed Ojerren's forehead. "And assure all of their safety."

My gaze switched from Zen to Ojerren and then back. "Why?"

"You will see."

My gaze returned to Zen. He smiled my way, but it faded. My stomach twisted in knots, not knowing what was going on. I watched him get down on the ground and look up at the sky. His body grew and changed form. I reached for my sword, but Ojerren's hand caught my wrist.

"Trust him."

My fingers tightened around the hilt, but I didn't draw it further. Where Zen had been, a black dragon sat instead. He turned to me and walked over. I took a step back that caused Ojerren to stumble, and he released his hold on my wrist.

The dragon now stood in front of me. Green eyes looked at me. Familiar green eyes; they flickered between black and green. Then the dragon shrank, the scales receded, and the tail vanished completely. A human again Zen stood up in front of me.

"Alexa."

"No, no, no, no, no. No," I said. I wanted to grab my sword, but raised my hands and held them out towards him. "You're a dragon? You're a dragon."

"I didn't know until a few days ago. When I shifted the first time, that's when the tattoo appeared." He stepped towards me. "I never knew before then, Alexa, I never knew. I swear."

I stepped back. My gaze never left his face. "You're a dragon," I repeated.

"I'm still a man. I'm still Zen."

I looked at the scar on his face. My gaze narrowed on it. Below the eye.

My finger pointed at him. "That was you that night. You were the third dragon. I did that."

I turned to Ojerren. His shirtsleeve puffed out on one side.

"And you're the other black dragon, you've attacked me twice."

"I've never attacked you. I tried to save you the first time. It's why I kept circling when you climbed up the mountain. The burden affects dragons at different rates. I have been fortunate so far to have kept it at bay, but Rai, the dragon that did attack, it spread through him quicker than we expected."

Rai. A name. A name for a person. The word echoed in my mind. My thoughts turned to another dragon. The one I killed.

"I killed him. That other dragon. I killed a man," I whispered.

Ojerren took a step towards me and shook his head. "You weren't to know that."

I turned to Zen.

"All my life, dragons have been the enemy. Protect people from the dragons. Dragons kill. Dragons are horrible, stupid beasts. Those women were partially right, except dragons live amongst... people?" I directed the last part to Ojerren.

"It depends on the man, Alexa. Some men choose to isolate at the Dragon Temple. They look for a way to cure this burden. Others risk staying in the villages for one reason or another."

"What do you do?"

Ojerren smiled, and wrinkles appeared at the outer corners of his eyes. "I live amongst humans. A lady stole my heart and I couldn't leave."

"A human trait," I said.

My fingers ran through my hair.

"A dragon one too, Alexa," Ojerren said.

"If you want to go, you can," Zen said.

I bit my lip until it bled. "This is a lot to take in. I mean... What... How... Are all men dragons?"

"No, not all, but all current dragons are men as well. Female dragons have not been seen since the burden began, and that was long before my time," Ojerren replied.

"Alexa?" Zen stepped forward. He reached out for my hand. "Alexa?"

"Can we talk? Alone."

Zen nodded and released a breath. "Yes, yes, we can."

"Do I need to take your sword?" Ojerren asked.

I glanced at him before I shook my head. As Zen passed by Ojerren, he patted Zen on the arm. As we walked away, I turned to glance over my shoulder. Ojerren stood watching us with a warm smile on his face.

"This is what you couldn't tell me?" I asked.

"I wanted to, but I know how you feel about dragons. And I know why and I understand that, but I'm not them. I just kept thinking there would be a right time, and then that there wouldn't be. And I didn't know how you would react."

"I'm not sure how to react. You know this changes everything."

"You once said you would kill me. I might have been a little worried you would."

"If you have the burden, then I will. Probably. Somehow. Let's not complicate things at this moment. I'm having enough issues trying to deal with it."

"This is a part of me that's awakened, Alexa. It's selfish of me but I want to keep it. I don't want to lose you too, but I didn't think I could have both."

"You're a dragon and I'm not meant to kill you."

"Pretty much," Zen said.

I held my hand to my forehead. A predictable life was easier.

"Come on, I want to show you something," Zen said and reached for my hand.

"Something bigger than a dragon?"

Zen laughed and squeezed my hand. "Come on."

He led me through the trees, across a stream, and towards a mountain. I heard no one follow us and I sensed we were alone. At the base of the mountain, I saw a cave.

"Trust me," he said.

We walked inside and I saw the glow of the walls. I had seen that before when we had climbed the mountain. Inside, the cave was as light as outside. Vines covered the floor, making it soft beneath our feet. On the cave ceiling I saw paintings of dragons, white and black, flying.

"They've been here since the legend Ojerren says."

"Zen?"

"Yeah?" He stepped around, so he stood in front of me and I looked up at his face.

"If you're a dragon, then you could have the burden too."

"I could, but I'm okay at the moment. I came to help Ojerren get Rai. We knew he was infected, but he escaped the confines we had him in. We were only trying to help."

"But why did you attack me that night?"

Zen paused. "I didn't, Alexa. That woman with the black hair, she was behind you with her sword ready to run you through. I was only there to help Ojerren, but when she... I swooped. I just didn't expect you to swing, I guess."

"I argued with her but I didn't know..." I remembered how when I had turned she had been on the ground and refused my help.   I reached up and touched the scar. "And for that I..."

"It's okay Alexa, It's stopped bleeding and already healing."

My fingers shook as I touched his skin. His eyes closed.

"I'm so confused," I said.

"About what?"

I pulled my hand back and covered my mouth. Tears welled, and I tried to stop their escape.

"I can't kill you," I whispered.

"I'm happy to hear it," he said. He tucked some

strands of hair behind my ear.

"But what kind of elite does that make me, Zen? That's part of who I am and at the core of that is to kill dragons. Why didn't Leila tell me any of this?"

"She wasn't one of the council elders so maybe she didn't know."

"I'm not convinced by that. Our lives were lies. Your life and what you were… are… My life. Zen. My purpose. The reasons, they're all just lies. Dragons kill, but so do humans. This whole being able to change between being a dragon and human…"

"Change can be good, Alexa."

"Change gives me a headache." I paused. "So all the men who become dragons go somewhere. Is that why the men disappeared from the village? They were dragons?"

"Pretty much. The dragon temple members send out those who get a sense about others. A trade with the elders to keep dragons out of the village by having them taken away."

"I don't know what to do."

"I want you to stay. With me. I tried pushing you away. I thought it would be easier because you were so set on what you were going to do. I didn't want to, but… Alexa, I don't want to watch you walk away, but I love you enough to let you."

Tears rolled down the sides of my face. I felt him wrap his arms around me as he pulled me close. That's exactly where I wanted to be. That was the truth. Zen being a dragon should have changed that, but he was still Zen.

"I love you, too," I whispered into his shirt so he probably didn't hear it.

I felt his chest rise and fall. He had heard.

"So you'll stay?"

I looked up at his face. *How can I walk away now?* My heart beat faster. I just had to say it.

"I'll stay with you."

A smile spread across his face. He leaned in and I felt his lips on mine. A rush of warmth coursed through my body. I felt him pull the tie from my braid and my hair untwisted. I kissed him back as my hands travelled down to pull at his shirt. I wanted to be as close to him as I could. He pulled away, and I watched as he took off his shirt. His lips found mine again as I ran my hands down his chest, feeling every curve.

He knelt and brought me to my knees as well. He tugged at the bottom of my top to free it from my pants, and he lifted it up. We broke apart as he pulled it over my head and tossed it to the ground. He drew me close again. His lips pressed against mine as he moved me onto my back. Zen's body felt heavy on me, but I wanted to be nowhere else. I wanted no one else.

CHAPTER 32

Zen kissed the side of my face, and I tightened my arm across his waist.

"We're going to have to stop the burden, Zen. If it's something that can be stopped."

"I know. The books said the dragon put something, blood, into the mixture. Maybe we can reverse it somehow." His fingers combed through my hair. "There's something else too."

"I don't think anything would surprise me after today." I looked up at him.

"Do you know how happy I am at this moment? I really thought I would lose you from my life."

I looked at the tattoo on his neck. I brushed some strands of hair out of the way so I could see it closely on his skin for the first time. My finger traced along the edge of it until I reached where his neck rested on his arm, then went down along the bottom of the dragon until I ended up back where I had started.

"Do you hate it?"

Good question. I looked at it, a permanent mark on his skin. Difficult to conceal without high collars and long hair. I didn't hate it. I couldn't hate it if I wanted to be with him.

"No."

"I keep thinking I'm going to reach out and you'll be gone. That all of this is just my imagination. Ojerren thought you'd go."

"He doesn't know me like you do."

"I don't want anyone to know you like I do," Zen said. He rolled onto his side and pushed me back onto my back. He kissed me again. "We can't stay here forever, can we?"

I shook my head and traced over the healing cut.

"Sorry about that."

"You know, you look beautiful when you fight. You look beautiful all the time." He kissed the tip of my nose. "Except when you threw up, that wasn't a good look for you."

"Well nobody's perfect."

"True."

"And just so you know, I don't want to ever see that drink again for the rest of my life."

Zen smiled.

"You were going to tell me something before," I said.

"Yeah, the books tell of a village she retreated to. I think it's our village. When the dragons are affected by the burden, they seem drawn there. The elders were protecting something with the lies, so…"

"You're thinking there's something attracting them?"

Zen nodded.

"I think it's something in the Hidden. The one place that only a few are allowed."

"I already broke in there, remember? I left a little mess. Nothing seemed odd or out of place. Just a room."

"It would have been better if you'd waited for me," Zen said. "You were meant to wait."

"I had some things to work through."

"I know. I know."

The mess would either still be there or if an elder had found it, then it might be tidy again.

"But you weren't looking for anything like this," Zen said.

He brushed a few stray hairs away from my face.

"It's going to be difficult to convince those left. I mean, the elders hiding something might not be a big surprise, but once we get back there saying: Hey, we're going to work with the dragons to help them. That's probably going to take a lot more convincing."

"So we head back there?"

"We need to know as much as we can first. I assume you have those books somewhere safe?"

"Ojerren lives close to here, there's a little village of sorts deep in the forest, that's where I left them."

"Does he have food?"

"Yeah."

We left the cave and headed into the woods. Sunset hadn't yet arrived, but as we made our way through the forest, it slowly darkened. I saw the yellow glow of lanterns before Zen had a chance to announce we would arrive at the forest village.

I didn't need to look hard to know where to go. Ojerren leaned against a doorframe and watched as we approached. A smile played on his lips.

"Zen, as you are in one piece, I assume you have been accepted?"

"Accepted," Zen replied.

"I am both surprised and delighted. Now, Priya has some food that is almost ready to be served if you would care to join us?"

Zen looked at me. There was no chance of me saying no.

As we passed Ojerren, he reached out and touched my sleeve.

"I know you have had a lot to take in today, but I would like to have a word with you sometime soon."

"Should I bring my sword?" I asked.

"Alexa," Zen said.

But Ojerren smiled. "If it makes you feel safe, then you may, but I would prefer if wasn't needed."

"I guess considering you could just... transform anyway, you'd probably end up winning."

Ojerren held up his arm. "I doubt it would be so easy. But come, that is a discussion for another time."

Zen led me down the corridor of the wooden house. Wood seemed a dangerous choice for a fire-breathing dragon. The corridor opened into a larger room with a table in the middle set ready for four. Unless they had a couple of kids hidden away, it seemed they anticipated our arrival.

"Zen." A tall woman with brown hair braided to her waist pulled Zen into a hug. She stood taller than him, too. The woman turned to me. "You must be Alexa. I have heard much about you, but time for getting to know each other later as I have food that is waiting to be eaten."

"Priya, let them sit."

"I can't hug her too?" Priya asked Ojerren.

"It might be a risky move if you don't ask first," Ojerren remarked.

Was this the same man I followed a few days ago, full of suspicions? He seemed so normal.

"Oh don't be silly, look at her, she is a sweetheart." I felt myself pulled into a hug. "See, I lived to tell the tale."

I smiled as she released her hold and Zen tugged me towards the two chairs on one side of the table. Priya definitely had skills with food and cooking that could rival Zen, and my stomach was pleased for it. The conversation around the table was light. Priya chatted about being in the garden and visiting a friend in another house. Ojerren talked about the progress the newest men had made in shifting back and forth between forms. Zen and I stayed mostly quiet. I wasn't about to share what we had been up to with them.

After the meal, Zen and Ojerren stayed in the kitchen to tidy up, while Priya invited me to help prepare the room. I watched as she straightened a chair in the corner of the bedroom that was about the same size as mine back home. Then she folded a cloth she had taken from a drawer in a cupboard and gave the furniture a quick wipe.

I stood there doing nothing. When Priya turned to me after she had folded down the blanket on the large bed, I ventured a question.

"So you're human, right?" I asked.

She smiled and sat down on the bed. Her hand tapped on the blanket beside her, and I sat down.

"I am."

"How do you... I mean... you know obviously, but..."

"Dear, Ojerren is a dragon, and I knew that before our coupling."

"And you weren't afraid?"

Her hand reached out and rested on mine. "Alexa, I am afraid of many things. Of the burden affecting him, of him not coming home one day, but of being a dragon? No, I was never afraid."

"When Zen changed, I thought I should feel more fear than I did. All my life they taught me to fear them and yet at that moment... I don't know. Part of me..."

"You might have unknowingly sensed it. They say some have that ability more than others even in the men. It's why only selected men went searching for potential dragons."

"I doubt I sensed anything."

"I have heard so many stories about you, Alexa. Of your fearless nature, your willingness to protect another, of your desire to change but keep with what you were taught. Dear, do you not understand how much you have accomplished just by leaving your valley, by opening your mind and your heart to the possibilities? You have more power inside you than you know."

"I doubt that, Priya."

Priya laughed and shook her head. "Just like your father."

The word. My smile faded. "What did you say?"

Priya stood up and brushed down the skirt of her dress. "Dear me, look at the time. Oh... I meant... We must finish folding these..."

I stood up as well. "You knew my father?"

"I..."

"Priya."

I turned to see Ojerren at the door. He stepped back to allow a red-faced Priya to exit the room. I saw her mouth 'sorry' as went.

"I don't understand."

Ojerren nodded and stepped forward. "It wasn't quite how I planned to tell you."

"Wait, you're saying... You're my..."

"I've watched over you all this time. When you were little, I saw you befriend Zen. You would sneak off together when you should have been training, teaching him to use a sword. I was there to protect you even when I knew you were coming for us, the

358

dragons."

"Protect?" Today hadn't finished with surprises it seemed. "But… and Priya?"

He shook his head. "She's not your mother. Your mother went into the forest a few days after you were born. She never returned. I asked your grandmother, my mother, to take care of you while I searched. It was during that time I learnt of my dragon and knew I couldn't return."

"But why not come back for me and my sister? We had no family to care for us."

"Don't be too hard on Leila, she did her best."

"Hang on, are you saying she was… Is there anything else you want to just make me deal with today because I feel like I'm losing my mind with so many things?"

"Better than your mind than your temper."

"Not sure I agree with that."

"There will be plenty of time for us later, but Zen has told me of your suspicions about the Hidden in the village. I will send word for Uhandra to bring some additional books you and Zen may find something in that we did not."

"It will take days to get those books though."

Ojerren shook his head. "A human on foot would take days but a dragon can cross great distances in a much shorter time."

A knock at the door caused both Ojerren and I to turn towards it. Zen stood to the side.

"You both need your rest. Tomorrow we will work out a plan. Good night Alexa, Zen."

Ojerren left the room as Zen entered. He closed the door behind him.

"Sorry about… They only have two rooms in the house and I didn't want to… I can sleep on the floor if you'd prefer…"

I walked over to Zen and wrapped my arms around him. My head rested against his chest.

"I think we've reached a point where this is our new pathway, don't you think?"

Zen's arms tightened around me. Despite sharing a bed with Zen for the first time, I felt comfortable with the day. Somehow Zen being a dragon felt easier to accept than Ojerren being my father and Leila being more than a mentor.

I adjusted the pillow a bit and felt movement behind me.

"Are you okay?" Zen asked.

"I feel exhausted and yet… I don't know, alive?"

CHAPTER 33

"Ojerren should be back soon," I said.

Zen looked up from the book in his hand. The sun felt so warm on my skin.

"Depends on how long Uhandra keeps him there talking," Zen said.

"What's on your mind?"

"This all seems so impossible. How long ago was it we left the village so I could kill the dragons and life would return to normal? Now we are here trying to fix this illness that has been around for so long. There's nothing special about us. If all those men in the Dragon Temple couldn't find a cure, then what chance do we have? Seriously Zen, are we being too optimistic about all this?"

"Maybe we are." Zen placed his book on the table and leaned forward. "But leaving the valley seemed so impossible once. Right before the attack, you remember how badly I wanted to leave the valley. As determined as I was, I don't think I ever really believed that I would actually do it. Yet I did. We did."

"Leaving the valley is a far cry from solving an illness some woman may or may not have infected the dragons with."

"Doesn't mean we don't try."

"I know. It just seems overwhelming."

Zen moved his chair around to mine. "Remember the festival…"

"You're going to mention the dress, aren't you?"

"Don't interrupt."

"Remember the festival where you wore the dress. After the ceremony, we sneaked off with a tray of those desserts that Kaera made especially for the day."

The memory of those little cakes made my mouth water. Kaera had protected that recipe right to the end, and no one has made anything even close to it. It was probable she never shared the secret of the filling because it had come from outside the valley.

"We went to the rock we still go to. Ate the lot and then had to hide in the bushes when Leila came looking for us."

"Do you remember what you said that day?"

I leaned my head on Zen's shoulder. "Sure, I vowed I would never wear a dress again for the rest of my life. A vow you made me break."

"I swear they only had dresses to spare."

"You could have told them I was a man," I suggested. "Sure they would have found something suitable."

"Alexa, there wasn't a soul in that village I could have convinced that you were a man. Plus, you looked beautiful in it. You look beautiful all the time, but I did like you in the dress."

"Maybe I will wear it occasionally then. Just as long as I chose the footwear."

"Sounds perfect. Anyway, that's not what I meant. That day you said you wanted to be an elite warrior. The number of times you thought you weren't good enough, but look at you. You did it."

My hand reached out to the book. I traced the lines and crevices that gave the cover a picture of a dragon.

"And now I wonder what I accomplished. Taught skills to protect the village from an enemy that... What's in our village? Why our valley? Why are we the only village in that valley?"

"Hopefully, Ojerren will have more information than what we've found. I must have read these all three times by now."

"If the legends are true and she mixed her blood into the vial of whatever she gave him, then we have two things we need. First, we need to know what was in that initial concoction and second, we have to figure out how to add her blood to reverse whatever it is."

"Do you think we need to know what the original mixture was? A human created that mixture and intended at most to make him sick but not anything long term or final like death. I'm thinking it's her blood that's the key."

"But why?" I raised my head off his shoulder. "I mean, would my blood have the same effect or was there something about hers in particular?"

"Or did she add something else that's not in the legend? Think about it, she goes to the human and tells him she added the blood. He obviously didn't appreciate that because we know he was unhappy. To know that, he must have told someone who then recorded it," Zen said. "If she added something else and didn't record it, then that's going to be difficult to solve."

"Unless she was so angry at the dragon who rejected her, angry at the man who told her off..." I stood and turned around so I could lean against the table. Zen looked up at me from his seat. "What if the village was her sanctuary? I mean, outside the valley things are different, roles are different. In the valley the women are in charge and the men must know their place."

"So she created a village of women who thought the same and…"

"Went outside the valley to bring back men and made sure they wouldn't remember. She created a little world she could control."

"And to protect herself she ensured the women were in charge. She would have known the chances of men turning were high." Zen leaned back in the seat.

"So at some point they made a deal to remove those men."

"I hate to think what happened to them before the deal."

"I suspect there are bodies buried in the forest. It's what I would have done," I said and shrugged.

Zen's hair tumbled over his shoulder as he leaned his head to one side.

"Noted."

"What? Maybe my skills aren't entirely useless. We need to get back to the valley. I don't think any number of books or retellings are going to answer this. I think the answer is right back where we started."

"Do you want to wait for Ojerren?"

I shook my head. "We can tell Priya of our plans. Two is easier to sneak around, especially since we belong there. Who knows what would happen if

Ojerren was there too?"

"Things have probably changed since we left."

"Not that much it wouldn't have. If even one elder survived, you can guarantee they have everyone following the rules."

"You ready?" Zen asked as we stood within view of Ojerren's house.

"I need to get used to it so off you go," I replied. My hands waved in front of me, and Zen tilted his head to the side. "What?"

"It's serious, Alexa."

I tried to stifle the enthusiasm that built inside me. There had to be advantages to him being a dragon and me up in the clouds as I rode on his back — that possibility excited me. I watched as Zen crouched down and his body contorted and changed. It didn't take long until a black dragon lay on the ground in front of me.

"Okay, remember I am on your back, so no doing anything too out there. I don't want to find myself falling to the ground."

His nose twitched, and he winked at me. Even as a dragon, he was loveable. I stepped onto the elbow of his front leg, and he raised it up enough to allow me to climb on his back. Between the wings seemed the obvious choice, but I had nothing to hold on to. I adjusted the straps on the front of the harness to ensure the tip of the sword wasn't about to maim Zen.

"There's nothing here for me to hold on to."

Whether Zen didn't hear me or ignored my dilemma, I wasn't sure. But he crouched down before he extended out his wings. The trees soon faded below us as he flew in the clouds that were thin enough up close to see through, but seemed to conceal Zen's dragon form. I ventured to look down twice and saw wispy clouds around his lower body.

I recognised very little so high up, but Zen seemed to know where to go. My fear of falling off his back and plummeting to the sky appeared to have been unnecessary as I sat comfortably. When we reached the mountain, Zen lowered down to the platform.

"Not much further then," I said. My gaze checked over the plants and rocks nearby, just in case that spider lurked somewhere. As I did, Zen transformed back into human form.

"I think it's best if we wait until the sun sets. The last thing we want is to cause a panic because someone sees a dragon flying over. Besides, I need a rest. Carrying you exerted a lot more energy than I thought."

We both sat down. I could see fresh growth on some trees below. It hadn't taken them long to regrow after the fire. My gaze followed the scorched trees to a spot I knew was where I had lost my pack. The flames had been contained because of that stream, as none of the trees beyond that point blackened.

"So what is our exact plan?" Zen said.

"Land in the training grounds I think. Any closer, and even the cover of darkness might not be enough. From there we can head into the village on foot."

"Straight to the Hidden?"

"I think so. We don't want to be distracted by dealing with other people. I mean, we vanished without a word so the last thing we need is attention."

"It feels strange to be going back. It hasn't been that long since we left and yet so much has changed."

I couldn't argue with that. I thought I would return to the village with evidence of a few dead dragons, but I'm bringing home one that is very much alive instead.

The sun soon disappeared and we headed towards the field. When Zen landed, I climbed off his back and looked around. I had often been here at night, but tonight it felt cold and empty. My hands adjusted the straps of my harness until it sat snug against my chest and back.

"I'd feel better if you had your sword," I said.

Zen shrugged. "Nothing we can do about that. Besides, these are people we have known all our lives. I don't think walking around with a sword would be wise."

"Well, let's hope no one sees us. This is your lead now. We need to come in near the tree line and we can follow that to the end of the village where the Hidden is."

We walked down the hill towards the village. As we were in the tree line, I could see only a handful of lanterns on either side of the village. We both kept low as we hurried behind the houses in the warrior section and then crept towards the elders' section.

Zen paused ahead and pointed towards the Hidden. I cast my gaze over the houses I could see. Most were in darkness, but Sabine's house had a lantern that burned bright as she stood in the doorway. The elderly woman wiped her hands on the apron she wore before she turned and entered her house.

"We'll need to be quiet getting into the Hidden since she's left the door open," I said.

"She's probably still tending to the wounded by the looks of it."

As we watched a person moved by one window of the house; the silhouette was short and thin so it couldn't be Sabine. My thoughts turned to who it was that lay in there. I had been lucky, so lucky to survive.

Zen moved again, and I followed. We went wide around the edge of the village and emerged from the trees behind the Hidden. I moved ahead of Zen to the door and gave it a push. It swung open, and we entered. I closed after Zen entered, which limited the light.

The moonlight lit enough of the room to make out the mess I had left. I cringed at the tossed chairs and the table that sat skewed to the side of the room. No one had entered here since we left, otherwise they would have tidied it. At least, that's what I told myself.

"Okay, so my mess aside, what do you think we're looking for?"

Zen nudged a curtain that lay on the floor with his foot. He turned around on the spot before his gaze found me again.

"Something that doesn't belong. These curtains, why do they have curtains to hide the shelves?"

"To make it look tidy?" I said. My idea of tidying up was to find the nearest cupboard, shove everything in, and close its door.

"Books are everywhere here, but what kind of

books?"

Good question. I moved closer to one shelf and pushed the curtain aside. None had any writing on the spines, so I picked a book at random. The rectangular book had nothing on the cover either, so I opened it up. My gaze looked over the pages of writing and numbers.

"Seems like some kind of record book," I said.

"These over here are notes on the population. I checked and we're both in there, so are those who turned up without memory."

"Really? Does it say where they came from?" I asked.

"It does, but I can't read it. It's like they've written it in some sort of code. To me they look like random letters and numbers but I'm thinking they are days and places."

"Just a moment. What about the latest book?"

"Latest?" Zen sounded puzzled.

I turned around with the book still in my hands. "If the elders keep records of everyone here, then since the attack, the record should have been updated. Sabine is alive at least."

"Maybe she keeps it with her? In her house?" Zen suggested.

"Maybe, but I wouldn't count on it. All this

information is for elders only. Whatever this is," I shook the book, "it's something we're not meant to know but if this village is to survive, we will need to figure it out."

"Some names in here have black stars beside them."

Zen turned the book so I could see the page. From where I stood, the stars were clear.

"Your face says you know what they mean," I said.

"Those who disappeared before the coupling ceremony."

"Those they believed were dragons," I added.

"Okay, what about that wall?" Zen nodded to the wall on the east side.

"I've walked that side of the Hidden and there's nothing there." I put the book I held back in its place. "That corner over there. No windows and those curtains look worn compared to this one here."

"Because they get used."

I had the sword drawn as I turned. Sabine stood in the room with us. Elders, it seemed, possessed some skills of their own.

"Sabine," I said.

"Put the sword down, Alexa. If I wanted you two caught and punished, I would have turned you in to

Gerda already. Though, we don't have enough elders to form a council at this point." She turned to Zen. "We always suspected something would come of your friendship with Alexa. The two of you left the valley, didn't you?"

The question she directed at me. "I was angry and wanted revenge for the attacks. So yes, I left."

"I know you were angry since I found all this." She pointed to one of the broken chairs. "You both came back. Why?"

I wasn't sure Sabine was ready for the full truth just yet. "Because we saw what is like out there in the rest of the kingdom. How different everything is. We want this village to grow and change, to let go of the secrets that the Hidden keeps."

"Get me a chair, Zen," Sabine ordered, and Zen complied. She sat down on the seat and rubbed her knees. "I am not a council member, but my sister was. Kaera always struggled to keep secrets to herself. So I know more than I should. This building contains a secret, but I don't know what it is. When Kaera joined the council, whatever they revealed affected her deeply."

"Do you know what these records are?" I asked.

Sabine nodded. "The one Zen holds is part of the population records. Births, couplings, and deaths are all recorded in those. Part of my job when I became the head healer was to maintain them."

"You forgot disappearances and appearances," I said.

Sabine's mouth twitched. "I didn't maintain those records. You can see the handwriting is different."

"Do you know the reason behind them? The disappearances?" Zen asked and closed the book.

"Kaera once said they were tainted and needed to be out of the valley. I don't know more than that. I brought many of those who disappeared into the world and I saw nothing different about them." Sabine raised her finger towards me. "I suspect you know why, though. I can see it in your eyes."

I glanced at the floor for a moment. Now was not the time to confess. Not before we knew more.

"It's okay Alexa, I am used to secrets. Too many secrets for me. The book in your hand is what we traded with outside the valley. Food, fabric, anything we needed to bring in we had to give something in return."

"Like the baskets?" Zen asked.

Sabine nodded. "Yes, amongst other things. The council wouldn't allow certain skills to be brought into the valley so we had to trade what we could."

"What are those books, then?" I pointed towards

the wall near the corner.

"All written in a code that only the council members were privy to. Kaera said the corner of codes lead to secrets. No one will disturb you as you look for what you're after. When you're ready, you come and see me and let me know what this is all about. I never thought I'd live to know the secret, but change has come. Help me up, Zen."

Zen put out his arm and Sabine used it as support as she pulled her body off the chair. She left the Hidden saying nothing else. With the door closed again Zen, grabbed a chair and wedged it under the door handle.

"I thought you were good at sneaking up on me," I said.

"Yeah, I didn't hear a thing either."

I walked over to the worn curtain, where Zen joined me. He picked up the edge of the curtain and turned it over. The back of the curtain had marks on it. I put my hand over them. *Almost a perfect fit.*

"Sabine is right; someone moves this curtain more often than the others," I said.

"Grabbed and pulled by the looks of those marks, and see there, where the fabric is stretched?"

"So we do the same. Off you go."

"You want me to move it or pull the whole thing

down?"

It hadn't been that difficult to pull them down since I had managed it twice. I stepped back and pointed to the top.

"Might as well pull it down so we can see it all better."

"Count of three then." Zen moved the fabric to the centre and grasped it tight.

"One, two, three," I said.

The curtain pulled away on one side and Zen yanked on it again. Fabric tumbled to the ground in a heap and revealed more bookshelves.

I stepped closer. "Wait, that looks like shelves but..." my hand pressed against the books. "That's some fine painting. Those books looked real but they're just wood. Boxes of wood, painted."

"I guess if anyone saw them at a glance they would assume they were like every other shelf."

"So if this isn't a shelf I'm going to say it might be a door."

"Then all we need to do is find the way to open it."

CHAPTER 34

No latches or handles were in plain sight. We removed each set of fake books as well, but nothing behind them either except a few suspicious cobwebs.

"So nothing obvious, but if this is something they opened regularly, then surely it would make sense to be convenient," I said.

"Nothing on the wall, the curtain is down..." Zen went quiet.

I turned to see him move his foot over the stone floor. The moonlight didn't reach the corner we were in, unlike the other parts of the room. I crouched down. The stones felt cold as I passed my fingertips over them and were dirty. I rubbed my hands against my pants, hoping to rid myself of the grime.

"We need more light. Surely they have something in here we could use?" I said.

Zen moved off, and I heard his shoes as he walked back and forth around the room. He returned to me with empty hands.

"Nothing. Fire is not something they wanted in here."

"Do dragons get special eyesight at all?" I asked.

Zen crouched beside me. "Now that would be an impressive addition, but no. You start in the corner and I'll go from here. We need to find an uneven stone or something else that seems out of place."

I fell onto my knees and shuffled to the corner. The very corner of the room stood in total darkness. I didn't like the thought of a spider having an advantage. My body shivered at the thought, and I tried to focus on the stones.

They had grooves just like the rock Zen and I liked to go to. Nothing seemed out of the ordinary at that. My hands brushed over the join between two stones that had the filling to keep the stones together. Zen and I met in the middle when our knees met.

"What's that?" I said.

My hand tried to make out what I could feel as Zen moved beside me. I felt his hand find mine and sat back to let him feel the shape. The edges of it felt sharp and defined.

"What is it?" I asked.

"I have a feeling I know. I saw something..."

Zen got up and went over to the window at the other end. The moonlight lit his face as he ran his hand over the glass to the lower left corner. The curtain obscured my view, but I saw him pull something off the window. When he turned, I saw a piece of glass in his hand shaped like the dragon tattoo on his neck.

"I didn't see that," I said.

"I thought I imagined it. I saw something when I held up that book before but then Sabine came in and, you know." He crouched beside me again. "I think this goes in whatever you found."

"A glass key? Better not break it then," I said. "Huh, Matthias. That's what shone when he was at the gate."

"What?"

"Oh, I might have followed Matthias for a bit through the garden."

"I'm not surprised. I didn't think you'd find enough to interest you in a garden for the entire morning."

He lowered the dragon into the darkness. I heard the glass scrape on the stone.

"Okay now what?" Zen said.

"Press it? I don't know."

My hand reached out and found the smooth glass. Together we pressed on the glass. A scrape.

"Did we break it?" I asked.

"No, but I think we just found the way in."

I looked up to see the wall had moved from its place. Zen stood up. I swiped the glass dragon from the floor before it shattered. I pushed myself to my feet as Zen moved the section to the side.

A torch hung on the stone wall inside the opening, and I pulled it from the stand. An icy breeze came from the opening and while I couldn't see it, I suspected there were steps that led underground.

"We need light."

"Why are you looking at me?" Zen asked.

"Because you didn't think of it, plus, dragons can breathe fire." Both his eyebrows raised. "Come on, before someone crashes through the door."

Zen transformed into a dragon. He tried twice to direct fire at the torch I held — the first time his aim almost singed my hair. The second time I dropped it. I left it there as he blew a third flame and the naja lit up. He shifted back as I retrieved the torch and waved it in the opening to illuminate where we were about to go.

"If there are any spiders in there, it is your job to not tell me and just squish them," I said.

"They won't kill you. They don't even bite unless provoked."

"I don't care, they creep. Ready?"

I felt his elbow nudge my arm. With the torch raised, I stepped onto the first stone step. These stone steps differed from the floor of the Hidden. Each large stone wasn't smooth and precisely placed like above. The walls were rough in places and the stairs we descended varied in size and space.

Zen stayed close behind me as we walked further down. Ahead I could see light, familiar light, and I slowed my steps. Ahead, the walls glowed with the same blue crystals we saw in the cave.

"Someone thought they would be useful " I stopped long enough to run my finger over the crystals.

"The elders probably knew the way down well. Should we put the naja out?"

I shook my head. "We don't know what's down here. The space could be too small for you to change, best we just keep going."

That didn't take long as a wooden door came into view. Large metal hinges held it in place in the stone wall.

"Surprised they put a door down here," Zen said.

"Can you squeeze past and open it?"

I pressed my body against one wall, and Zen managed to get past. With the steady light from the naja, I watched as he pushed on the door. It opened with no resistance, and I moved forward. The light revealed a room with each step I took.

"Is that what I think it is?" I said.

I stepped inside the room. Shelves on one side held various bottles caked in dust and cobwebs. A small table was to one side of the room with an open book. At the back of the room, a skeleton filled an entire corner. A dragon skeleton.

"I didn't predict finding that," I said.

I hooked the torch into a holder near the table. Zen and I approached it together.

"Why do they have a dragon down here?" Zen said.

"We've only ever found a couple of dead dragons in the past. Kills before that day hadn't happened in my life."

I walked to the skull of the dragon and crouched down. Unlike most of the room, the skeleton only had a little dust on it. Someone had cared for it.

"This isn't one of the two we retrieved," I said.

"How do you know?"

I stood up. "It's smaller than the others."

"So the Hidden has a dragon that hasn't been destroyed but taken care of. Why?" Zen moved his attention off the bones and to the table. He crossed the room and blew dust from the pages. "If something was written on this, it has long since faded away. It looks old though. See how the book is sealed here?"

I couldn't see from where I was; I moved closer. My fingers ran down the stiff page and then to the spine. The spine didn't seem different to me. Underneath the open pages, I could see ink markings.

"I destroyed stuff above, so why not this book too?" I grabbed the page and tore it from the book before Zen responded. A cloud of dust sprang from the paper as I tossed it to the floor.

"You want to do the other page too?" Zen said. He turned away as he coughed.

"Of course."

The next page had nothing on it, so I turned the page over on the left side. I looked at the words. It was a poem: a love poem.

"Blessed be the ones at my side; Blessed be the ones that make the future; A love rejected and a burden to carry; May he suffer for the pain.

"Oh dear, definitely a one-sided love." I tapped the page and looked back at the skeleton. "You don't suppose... What did the books say happened to the woman, the one who cursed the dragon?"

"Tajea became human," Zen said.

"Until she confessed to adding the blood." My fingers tapped on the table. "We don't know what happened after that, but let's say our theory about this village is correct. That she started this village, could that be her?"

"The legend varied with her as a human and dragon. If they've always been able to transform then whatever she drank might have suppressed her dragon side."

"So what would do that? If males only find out they're a dragon when they're our age... I can't help but feel we are missing a piece." I glanced at the shelves. "She was last recorded as being human, but what if she got trapped in her human form then unlocked her dragon side again?"

"'A secret that would need to be kept'," Zen said.

"Exactly. If she convinced these women to start this village, everything they'd ever known. The elders hold a lot of power over us. What if they didn't want to let that go?"

"Why not destroy the bones?"

"Maybe they couldn't, or were fearful of something. Do you sense that?"

"What?" Zen asked.

I pointed to the dragon. "Her. You're a dragon; remember we thought the dragons might be drawn here? Maybe she's why?"

Zen shook his head. "I feel nothing. Just bones.

Then what's attracting the dragons here if it's not her?"

"Maybe it's something only those with the burden sense? Her blood in the mixture forms a connection of sorts, maybe," Zen said.

He leaned against the table.

"That makes sense. Upside, that would also mean you aren't infected as well."

"If the elders put her here to hide, do you think she might have written it down somewhere?"

Something about the bones held my attention. The shelves had long been forgotten, but the dragon hadn't. The book on the table hadn't been touched in a long time. *What else is in here?*

"Is that another door over there?" I said.

The table hit against the wall as Zen stood up. I had already walked around the skeleton and to an empty, low bookshelf. I stepped around it to better see the door. My hand grabbed the wooden handle and pushed. It didn't move. I gave it a pull in case. It remained sealed.

"You were right the first time," Zen said. He pointed to the edge of the door. "Count of three, and we both push. One, two, three..."

A painful creak echoed around the room. There was no need to retrieve the torch, since the walls were covered with the same blue crystals. A bed to one side and clothes hung from a hook on the wall.

"Someone lived here? Underground?" Surely not.

I went to the clothes and grabbed one. A dress in a style I hadn't seen before. A creature fond of fabric had eaten away parts of the fabric. I let the dress fall back into place.

"Alexa," Zen said.

When I turned, he stood next to a desk behind the door. He stepped to the side to reveal the wooden board on the wall. The name *Tajea* carved into it.

"Do you think she lived down here? Why would anyone want to do that?"

"Maybe it wasn't her choice." Zen picked up a book on the desk and opened it. He glanced up at me before he closed the book and held it out to me. "Read the first page."

I took the book and opened the cover. The writing hadn't faded and despite some words with strange spelling, I could read it.

I made a decision I thought I would not regret. For many years I didn't and after I trusted the human with what I had done, he turned on me the same as the Roaia had. This valley became my sanctuary and a place for me to belong. But in my old age, I yearned to connect with my dragon side again. I tried many things before I stumbled on a way to unlock her.

The problem was, I trusted women because they were women. I thought they would not turn on me the way men had. When I disclosed my dragon side to a few close friends, they turned on me. So here I am, locked away to spend the rest of my days.

One day I hope someone will fix what I started. This book is my gift to that person. The one who will make things right.

CHAPTER 35

"Why did you give it to me?" I asked.

I watched his shoulders rise and fall. "I don't know. She didn't write it for me," he replied.

"Well, let's see what else she has in here." I turned the page. A list of three ingredients that were to be combined. "A title would be helpful. I have no idea what this is even for."

The next page had another mixture on it and again had nothing to indicate what it would do. I flipped through the remaining pages to see sketches of dragons, the odd sentence or poem. The last page had an unfinished portrait of a young woman.

"You think that was her?"

"Maybe."

"Well, I suppose it can't hurt to try. If one of these unlocked her dragon, I'm assuming the other will reverse the burden, or cure it, prevent it? You know more of these words than I do, help me find what we need."

We moved back into the larger room and I placed the book on the table open to the first of the lists. Zen read through the list and rummaged around on the shelves. He brought two jars back to the table.

"That's the ground spice, and this is dried naja blossoms."

I picked up the jar of blossoms. They were brown and crumbling.

"Hope you're not meant to eat or drink this stuff. If she wanted to be so helpful, she had plenty of time to write out all the instructions."

"Maybe she feared they would destroy the book?"

"Anyone who read that first page would suspect," I said.

"Maybe someone made sure it survived. Sealed the room off."

"Maybe. Now that's two things, but it had three."

"There's no ground flowriya bark."

"What's that?"

"Are you telling me you drink that tea every day and you don't know what it is?"

I shrugged. "I did what I was told. Seriously though, we need some of that?"

Zen nodded. I reached into the bag on my waist and pulled out the last of the tea Maeja had given me.

"There had better be more of this stuff somewhere," I grumbled. "What do you think we do with them? How much?"

"Don't ask me."

I sighed. We had half what we needed to know.

"We know it's not complete," I muttered to myself. "She kind of made it sound like the person who had this would just know. Maybe I'm the wrong person."

"We could just try things?"

"Wouldn't take long to run out of all this, though. No, there has to be something in here that has the answer. Could she have scribbled clues on the walls or hidden them in bottles or something?"

Zen looked over the wall while I returned to the shelf. A small rock sat at one end, covered in dust.

"You'd think they'd clean everything in here instead of just the bones." I picked up the stone and it clattered to the floor. "Ow!"

"What happened?"

I shook my finger and saw blood drop fly towards the table. On the floor I saw that the rock wasn't a rock but some kind of tooth, a very sharp tooth whose point I hadn't seen.

"Cut my finger, oh that stings!"

Zen ripped a piece of fabric from his shirt and

wrapped it around my finger. It continued to throb, but at least it stopped blood going everywhere.

"I got some on the book too," I said.

"Alexa, look."

Zen stared at the open page. No longer half empty, there were further instructions. My blood had soaked into the paper near the top of the page.

"She seemed to be fond of blood," Zen said.

"Not funny."

"It wasn't that bad."

He moved out of the way so I could stand with the book in front of me on the table. His arms moved around my waist as I read what we needed to do. We needed equal parts of each and to crush them together. A small stone bowl sat on the table. This was the one time I would stick to doing what the instructions said. I poured in each and then used the stone handle to crush them together. That was all the instructions had.

"Okay, are you ready to try it?" I held the bowl out to him.

"Am I meant to swallow it?

"You can't, no liquid."

"Sprinkle it?"

"Sounds like a plan."

"Should I shift to a dragon? There is probably just enough room down here."

Good question. I nodded and waited for him to change. His black scales gleamed even in the limited light. I checked, no grey, but hopefully that wouldn't be an issue anyway.

He sat down and lowered his head to the ground. I sprinkled the powder over his head and stepped back. His nose twitched back and forth before I felt the combined mixture land on my skin with mucus.

Zen shifted back and looked up at me apologetically. "Sorry."

"Eww," I said.

I brushed the residue from my skin and clothes. Pressure built in my nose, and the room went out of focus. My eyes watered as I sneezed.

"Fine, you feel any different?" I asked him.

I rubbed my hand down my arm to stop the feeling that spread over my skin. The feeling continued to spread down my arm to my fingertips, from my shoulders to my waist, from my waist to my knees, from my knees to my feet. The room spun around me. "Zen, I feel a bit weird. My skin, it's all tingling."

"Alexa?"

I turned to where I thought Zen stood. The room

spun so fast that I couldn't define any objects or Zen. I saw the wooden beams above us that held up the stone ceiling. My hand reached up to my forehead and felt my legs give way.

"Alexa? Alexa?"

The pounding in my head subsided, and I opened one of my eyes a little. The naja still lit the room and a blurry Zen hovered in front of me. I forced the other eye to open and watched as the Zen came into focus again.

"You okay?"

"I think so. What happened?" I asked.

"Something unexpected."

"So you're not protected from the burden then?"

"I don't think that mixture was the one to solve the burden. It did, however, trigger something in you."

"Help me up as you explain." He pulled on my arms until I found my feet again. "Zen, are you going to tell me?"

His fingers moved to my hair and pushed it over my shoulders. I looked down at my clothes to see them torn in places.

"What? How did that happen?"

"You remember that day you found me in the forest when I looked a bit messed up?" Zen said.

"Sure, all your clothes were... What are you trying to tell me?"

"That was the day my dragon emerged, not a full transformation, more like a taste that something wanted to escape inside of me but couldn't quite work out how. My tattoo appeared that day."

"So what's...?" I reached my hand up to my neck. "Hold on, are you saying what I think you are?"

"You have a dragon tattoo."

"Yeah, I know what it is, but why is it on me?" I ran my hand over the inked dragon that covered my neck. My forehead creased. "You're saying I'm a dragon too?"

"Your father is, so maybe it is some kind of family thing? I don't know. That page must have been what she used to unlock her dragon. Think about being a dragon and see what happens."

I closed my eyes and focused on how Zen looked as a dragon. Of Ojerren as he flew overhead. Of flying in the sky amongst the clouds as they whipped around my body. I opened my eyes. Zen looked up at me.

"Oh, bugger!" At least that's what I wanted to say. Instead, a roar hiccupped out of my mouth. I closed my mouth, opened it again, then ran my large tongue over my new pointy teeth.

"It's okay, just think about your human self to

shift back."

I watched Zen as I pictured myself in my mind. Zen came closer and closer until I had to look up at him again. I ran my tongue over my teeth — not pointy.

"Female dragons haven't been seen since the burden. At least not around here."

"So we're all just in plain sight? How many of the women in the village do you think are dragons?"

"That's something we need to find out, I guess. At least it means we'll have help if this other page does as she promised."

"I wonder if it was my mixed blood that triggered the rest of the writing to appear? Had to be another female dragon?"

"Probably." Zen grinned.

"You are thrilled about this, aren't you?"

He held up his hand with his thumb and index finger parallel. "Just a little. But come on, we can dragon bond later, we have the other page to do."

I returned to the table and turned the page. My blood had soaked through to the new one and new ingredients appeared. Zen busied himself collecting those listed until he tapped his finger against the last on the list.

"I don't know what that is."

"I think I know. Those light crystals didn't just appear here, I think she collected some and brought them here to try."

"And being that we are in a cool, dark environment, the crystals thrived here long after she died."

"I'll grab some from the room. I suspect they are the older of the crystals and I'm hoping they pack more punch."

I walked towards the bedroom when Zen called out, "What about the blood? I can't see any of that stored in here."

"One thing at a time, dragon," I replied.

Inside the bedroom, I scraped some crystals into the bowl. They continued to cast out their pale blue light as I returned to the table.

"The bones."

"What about them?" Zen asked.

"That's all that's left of her. I say we crush the bones and hope it's enough."

"And then what?"

"I assume Ojerren knows where some dragons that have the burden are. If we make sure you've both had some of this, then I guess the only thing left is to try it on a sick dragon."

"Blood and bone. Do you think they'll work the

same?" Zen asked.

I shrugged. "It's all we have."

It felt strange to pull a bone away from the skeleton. I felt guilt rise inside at what we were about to do, but reminded myself that this was what she wanted. She had wanted everything put right.

We took turns to grind down the bone in the bowl and then added the other ingredients.

"We need water."

"Do you have any in your bag?" Zen asked.

"Yeah, we could use that."

Zen reached into the bag on my waist and withdrew the small container of water.

"How much?"

"It doesn't say, but enough for it to be drinkable. Remember in the original story she tricked him into a drink — we do the same. Except you know what's in it." Zen poured water into the bowl. "I guess I have to drink it too."

"There should be a cup around here somewhere. She lived down here, so there must be." Zen moved off and I watched him go into the bedroom. Something fell to the floor and I cringed. I hoped we were far enough underground to muffle any noises.

"Found one," Zen said.

He emerged from the room with a wooden cup in

his hand.

"You didn't break anything in there, did you?"

"The shelf broke as I leaned on it. She must have been tall to reach that high since I was on the tips of my toes."

"Needed Priya then?"

I laughed as he handed over the cup. The liquid flowed into the cup as I tipped the bowl, careful to not spill too much onto the table. I looked at the cloudy mixture as I sloshed it around.

"You going first?" Zen asked.

My face contorted at the thought, and I took a deep breath. I was about to drink part of a dragon. My body shuddered. I closed my eyes and tipped a mouthful of the mixture into my mouth and swallowed.

"Oh, that is just foul," I said. The taste lingered in my mouth and throat. "Okay, your turn."

I held the cup out to Zen. "Your eyes just glowed."

"They did what?"

"Glowed, just for a moment they glowed yellow."

"Well, better than another colour I can think of."

Zen took the cup from my hand and took a sip. His face screwed up as he closed his eyes tight when he swallowed. He opened his eyelids, and I saw his green eyes flash yellow for a moment.

"Huh, yours glowed too."

"Let's hope that's a good sign. We both lived."

"We need to try it on an infected dragon. You should fly back to Ojerren with the last of what we have. I'll put it in the water container."

Zen nodded. We collected what we needed, including the book, and started back up the stairs.

The Hidden looked the same when we entered it. I held the naja torch in my hand as Zen moved the door back into place. The glass dragon on the floor relocked the section into place.

"You going to be okay to fly back tonight?" I asked Zen.

We walked to the door and Zen kicked the leg of the chair. It fell to the floor and he dragged it away. He opened the door and stopped. The burning naja showed a figure clad in black sitting on the ground.

"You couldn't have waited?" Ojerren asked.

"We wanted to act, we had a theory and we think we were right," Zen said.

A breeze moved through the trees and I shivered as the flame swayed. A bucket of water stood near the door and I tossed it in. The smell of the naja smoke drifted away on the breeze.

"What's that?" Ojerren asked. He got to his feet

and walked towards me.

Zen leaned close and whispered. "Probably not the time or place to show you, but it seems this valley has at least one female dragon."

"Alexa?" Ojerren's eyebrows rose.

"Guess I took after you," I said.

"I did not see that coming in my future. That means there could be more." Ojerren pointed to the book in my hand. "Is this something I need to know?"

"It is." I unfastened the bag from my waist and held it out to Ojerren. He slung it over his shoulder before I handed him the book. "You want the second one for the burden. A mouthful seems to have some kind of effect but we need it tested on an infected dragon."

"You both tried it?"

"We didn't want to get hopes up if we were wrong. There is enough in the bag for a handful of dragons but if it works, you'll need to return here for the one ingredient that only exists in there." I nodded to the Hidden behind us.

"I'll fly back now to Priya and get started. I know a few dragons we can try it on. What am I looking for?"

"Eyes glow yellow. The change of eye colour can identify infected dragons. I'm hoping this will restore their regular colour and allow them to transform back into human form," I said.

"And you two?"

"Rest. Tomorrow is going to be a big day," I said.

"What's in there?" Ojerren pointed to the bowl that Zen held.

"That is going to reveal how many of us are in the village," I said.

"You have been busy. I'll return as soon as I have news. You take care though." Ojerren stepped forward and wrapped his arms around me. I allowed the hug; I could get used to the showing of affections.

We watched until Ojerren faded into the darkness. Zen reached out and took my hand. We walked around the Hidden and made our way down the street. Lanterns still burned at Sabine's house. I wasn't sure how long we had been underground, but I wanted to wash up and get some rest.

"We still have to decide on one more thing tonight," Zen said.

The stone elder houses were behind us as we followed the rocky path into the warrior house area.

"What's that?"

"Your house or mine?"

"Mine's closer, end of discussion."

Zen's shoulders shook as he chuckled.

"Fair enough."

CHAPTER 36

I hadn't felt so nervous since that festival with the dress. I felt comfortable in a clean set of clothes and had tied back my hair on the top but let the rest fall free around my shoulders. Even as I moved the strands of hair, I could still see the tattoo.

"Someone is bound to notice that," I said.

Zen had left his hair down, but being thicker than mine, it concealed the tattoo better.

"They're bound to notice when we transform as well."

My foot tapped against the wooden floorboard. "I'm half expecting someone to grab a sword and stab me with it."

Zen stood behind me, and I felt comforted by his closeness as he wrapped his arms around me.

"Only one of us at a time, and I think it needs to be you first," he said.

"I know, I'm the female... At this point, I wish I could lump it on you and run away."

"No, you don't, you're too stubborn to lose this one."

"I wish I could calm my nerves. I don't enjoy speaking in front of people, especially since we left. Who knows what's happened here since?"

"One step at a time, Alexa."

Outside, I could hear the chatter of people. From in the house it seemed like another day in the village, except I had Zen there with me. Leila had been wrong about being stronger without ties; even she could not abandon me. Now, I drew on Zen for courage and support. Today would be memorable in the village for one reason or another.

"Let's do this before I sneak out the back door and make a run for it," I said.

I let Zen lead the way out to the front door. He opened it, and the warmth from the sun hit my skin as I stood there. Zen tugged on my hand several times before my feet moved again. It didn't take long for the feeling of being watched to start.

It was a bold move, leaving the house together, holding hands. The message we sent was clear, but I saw the way the elite warriors we passed turned to each other and whispered. I would have done the same. Zen and I headed to Sabine's house.

I swear she anticipated us going there first. She stood in the doorway with her hands on her hips.

"I sent three elites to round up everyone. I sensed that whatever it is you're going to do, it will be today."

"Sabine, how many of the elders survive?" I asked.

"Nine including me. Council members, we still have two." Sabine sighed. "Old ways will be difficult to break. Be prepared that whatever happens today might not be what you hope for."

"We know, but we need to do this. If it means we leave after then so be it, but people here should have a chance." Zen had a way with words like Ojerren. I would not have been tactful.

A crowd of men and women gathered near Sabine's house. I saw the elders on the side as they sat on the chairs reserved for them alone.

"Alexa!" a voice called from the crowd, but I couldn't place which child said it.

Zen stood beside me as I stepped up onto the stone step that the elders used during the festival and ceremonies for announcements. That action silenced the chatter.

I stood there as my fingers played with the edge of my shirt. My feet shuffled across the rough stone's surface. Without my sword, I felt vulnerable.

"Many of you would have realised I left the village. I was angry at the dragons, at myself, and I thought I knew everything I needed to know to solve things. I know our village has been devastated and there is no going back to the life we had before. For generations we have lived in this village, guided by the rules of the elders and barred from the Hidden. The women have protected this village from the dragons all that time because we were told that was what we had to do. Many in the crowd have lost partners you loved dearly, an emotion that we were taught us to push aside and ignore.

"You all know who I am. I was born in this village, raised in this village, and I have fought for this village. When the attack occurred, I sought revenge. What I found were questions I never asked and answers I didn't want to accept. We have feared the dragons for so long, and I stand before you about to ask the unthinkable. To help the dragons."

A murmur rose from the crowd, and I shuffled forward.

"Please, the dragons are suffering from a burden. A disease of sorts that affects their mind and drives them mad. Zen and I have found something we think will cure them and prevent those unaffected from being infected."

"You talk nonsense, Alexa," Gerda said. She thumped her walking stick on the ground beside the chair.

"With all respect, Gerda, I do not. Tell them, tell them all what the Hidden hides. The secret that is underground and out of sight."

"You had no right to go into that building. You might be an elite but you are not a council member!" Gerda said. She shook as she raised her hand and pointed her finger towards me. "You have forgotten your place."

The murmurs intensified. I felt Zen's hand hold mine. Eyebrows raised on several faces in the crowd.

"No, I have finally started to find my place, to find myself." I turned to Zen. "Time to show them."

"We ask you to remain calm. You know both Alexa and I. Please trust us." He squeezed my hand and stepped away.

"The reason I know we have been lied to, made to believe in a truth that had been twisted for this village, is this."

I closed my eyes and concentrated on being a dragon, on flying. I hoped that I would have better success than the first time. My arms extended out. Everything fell silent for a moment. I opened my eyes to see many of the villagers step away from me. That had been enough. I returned to my human form.

"But females can't be dragons!" a voice called out.

"I know, that's what we were told, but they were

wrong. We have a cure. Zen and I have found a cure for the burden, but we need your help to cure the dragons. Many of you are dragons as well, the others we need as riders to deliver this. Please, who will step forward to find out the truth about themselves?"

"This is nonsense!" Gerda yelled. Hanna reached out and held her shoulder. She leaned closer to her and said something.

"There is a large kingdom out there none of us have seen. Some men have come here from beyond the valley. It's time we stopped doing what we always have and forge a new way, a new future together. One where men and women work together and respect each other."

"I'll try it," a woman said and moved to the front of the crowd. "What do I need to do?"

I turned to Zen, who handed me the bowl. I crouched down until I was level with her face. She wasn't an elite or even a warrior, yet she was the bravest of them all.

"Breath it in. If you feel dizzy, try to sit before you fall."

She ran her finger along the edge of the bowl and leaned over. Her nostrils flared as she breathed it in. She smiled.

"Nothing," she said.

She turned around and I saw her hand reach out.

"Somebody catch her!" I yelled.

I placed the bowl down, but a man rushed from the crowd to catch her before she hit the ground.

"Mallea?" The word was heavy with concern as he looked from her to me.

I watched her eyes. A flash of yellow. She shook her head and smiled.

"See, I feel fine," she said.

"Think about what it would be like to be a dragon," Zen said.

"Okay." Mallea closed her eyes again. Her body started to transform, and the man let her go. The crowd backed away from her as a black dragon stood where Mallea had been. She tilted her head to the side.

"She's an expert already," I said to Zen. This I would need to practise to make it look so easy. To Mallea I said, "Think about being a human."

If dragons can grin, then the show of pointy teeth was it. She shook her head before she crouched down. Her wings spread out and she flapped them twice. She launched into the sky and missed the tree; the roof of Sabine's house would need to be fixed.

She landed with a thud as her body skidded to a stop in the dirt. Mallea's body changed back to human, although one now covered in dirt.

"That was awesome. Come on love, see if you're one as well." She pushed the man who had caught her towards me.

The more who tried the powder, the more who became curious enough to try it. At least half the women were dragons and about a dozen of the men. Gerda even came over to try it herself, though when she transformed I felt nervous.

When Ojerren returned with Priya, I knew the mixture had worked. Plans needed to be put in place to make enough to spread to other places to treat the infected dragons and protect the others.

It was late in the afternoon before Zen and I managed to sneak away from what had become a celebration. We walked to our place at the rock.

"What a day," I said.

When I turned around, I found Zen right there. Just where I wanted and needed him to be. I took his offered hand in mine and smiled.

"A new beginning," he said.

Zen sat down and pulled me down. He caught me and lowered me onto the soft grass. I felt his fingers brush against my face as he attempted to tame my loose hair. His eyes focused on me as I stared up at him. A new beginning was long overdue for our village.

"For all, but a continuation for us," I replied.

A smile spread across his face. I didn't have time to see it long as he leaned down and his lips found mine. A future of possibilities lay before us, and I wanted no one else beside me other than Zen.

Jenni lives in Australia and
loves all things magical.

Reviews of her work are
welcome on any platform.

You can find information
about all her books
on her website

www.jenniwardauthor.com.au